LAST ORDERS

YOU NEVER KNOW WHEN YOUR TIME IS UP…

MARIA FRANKLAND

AUTONOMY
PRESS

First published by Autonomy Press 2023

First edition

For my fellow half-centurions

JOIN MY 'KEEP IN TOUCH' LIST

If you'd like to be kept in the loop about new books and special offers, join my 'keep in touch list' by visiting
www.mariafrankland.co.uk
You will receive a free novella as a thank you for joining!

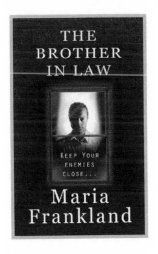

PROLOGUE

WE HAD some good times in this place. I can't believe they're going to demolish it. But apparently, what's left is merely a shell. I scan the fencing around the perimeter, my eyes falling on a sign. *Demolition Site KEEP OUT.*

I can't imagine who could possibly want to go in there after what happened. Kids and ghouls perhaps - that's about it. The inside has been totally gutted by all accounts.

It's eerie, standing here, staring at the boarded-up doors and windows, and the blackened brickwork. This pub was the centre of our world, our sanctuary, and for some of us, our second home.

Being out in the sticks, it was too far from where we lived to walk, so a taxi was the norm. We'd pull up outside, anticipating the evening ahead as the exterior invited us in. It was your typical semi-rural pub, though larger than most. Log fires, lamplit windows and everyone knowing each other's business. There'd be disco nights, quiz nights and lock-ins. Always a fund-raising event going on. The family who owned the place were great, we got really friendly with them - until everything turned sour. Really sour.

One minute the husband was letting me in on the plans for their silver wedding, the next there was venom flying. Absolute ructions. Apparently the landlady had cheated and was planning to leave him. Personally, I felt sorry for their two kids, stuck in the middle of it all. Although they were practically grown up, it still hurts when your parents' marriage is falling apart. Especially so publicly.

But what came next, you wouldn't wish on your worst enemy, let alone on two people starting out on their adult lives.

Rumour has it that what happened on New Year's Day wasn't an accident. I'll be attending the inquest to find out for sure. At first, there was speculation about whether a group of kids might have started it. Then gossip turned to whether it could have been an insurance job gone wrong, or something even more sinister. But surely what happened that day couldn't have been intended by the people who lived there? They didn't seem like those sorts of people.

Though when that charred body was dragged out, I couldn't help but recall the warning...

Watch this space. I'll give you all something to gossip about...

PART I

DEBRA

24 HOURS BEFORE
DEBRA 4PM

RELUCTANTLY I SLIDE my overnight bag from the seat beside me onto my lap. I've no choice really. The 16:03 from Leicester to Leeds is jam-packed. My bag's probably occupying the only available seat. This must be the last train today, with it being New Year's Eve. I'm so accustomed to driving everywhere that normally, I get really excited when travelling by train. But not today. It would probably be classier to get back home on a livestock transporter.

At least the woman wanting the seat next to me doesn't appear to be sozzled, unlike lots of other people in this carriage. Some of them have little chance of getting to midnight to see the New Year in, judging by the state of them.

The last thing I need is some drunk sitting beside me, regaling his or her sob story. Again. I must have one of those faces that says *emotional dumping ground*. This happened on the way down here. Two days ago. I ended up giving someone sat opposite us twenty quid after he told me someone had nicked his wallet.

A fool and their money... I could almost hear Bryn's voice. He never resists an opportunity to criticise me. It must improve his own self-esteem. Even the kids have commented on our constant bickering over Christmas, despite my best efforts to act normal. It's been a relief to get away from him.

But, I'd have worried about the young man on the train for the rest of day if I hadn't helped him out. Lance had nudged me as I'd handed the money over. He wasn't dissimilar to Lance; about the same age, with the same dark, floppy fringe. I'd like to think someone would look after my lad if he was worse for wear and had been parted from his wallet. This was also someone's lad and I couldn't have ignored him.

These seats are barely big enough to take something out of your handbag without rupturing the spleen of the person next to you. I give the woman a sidewards glance, offering a weak smile as she assembles herself beside me. She looks as frazzled as I feel. She smiles back. Though perhaps I should have looked the other way - she might take me smiling as a sign I want to make conversation. When really, I've got that much on my mind it's a wonder smoke isn't billowing from my ears. I need to think. I really, really need to think. Work out how I'm going to handle things when I get home. Two nights away from the place has made me certain that the time has come for action. No matter how guilty I feel about everything.

I glance up. I'm glad I got on here when I did. The train aisle has filled up with standing passengers and the stench of alcohol is palpable. As the train sets off, it's a wonder they all don't end up in the laps of us in the seats - a combination of the sudden lurch and their drunken-slowed reflexes. I would have been seriously upset if I'd had to stand for the journey.

I turn towards the window as though I'm watching the world go by, not that there's a great deal to see from it. Dusk has swallowed the last day of the year. Another year done. The thought is a weight in itself. Hopefully by turning away, I'm conveying the message to the woman next to me, *leave me alone please*. But within less than a minute, the darkening trees are making me dizzy as they speed past. It was the same when I tried to read after first boarding the train.

I've always been like this when travelling, I get nauseous if I try to focus, especially with the hot air pumping through the vent running alongside me. My tendency for feeling queasy whilst travelling used to irritate Bryn beyond belief. In our happier days when we'd go away on holiday as a family, he'd ask me to decipher directions and maps for him. But I'd go dizzy and my head would ache within minutes.

"Snap." The woman points at my discarded novel on the pull-down tray in front of me. Her sudden word jolts me from my thoughts.

"What do you mean - *snap*?" My eyes ache as I exchange staring into the twilight back to the strip lighting of the train. And I feel about as sociable as a teenager in a room full of great aunties.

She slides an e-reader from her bag. A couple of button presses later and I see we're reading the same book.

"What do you think of it so far?" She's around the same age as me, but looks to have allowed the grey hair in - something I'll never do. "Personally I thought it all happened a bit too fast." Like me, she speaks with a Yorkshire accent. "But it was a reasonable read."

"I agree with you there."

"There are a few brilliant twists though." She tucks the tablet back into her bag. "Anyway, what are the chances of this happening?" She gestures from herself to me, pointing with chipped nails.

I glance at mine. I must get them done when I get a moment. Another thing Bryn moans at me for - wasting time and money. "The chances of what?" She's totally lost me.

"Sitting next to a complete stranger on a train, then realising you're reading exactly the same book?"

"Pretty slim." I offer my hand, softening somewhat. "I'm Debra." Our literary allegiance can allow for a conversation, I suppose. It might even take my mind off things. Sometimes I get so sucked into my own thinking that I drive myself insane. Bryn often says I need to get my head out of my arse and talk more. Perhaps he means to him. But we never talk anymore, all we ever seem to do is argue, or give each other the silent treatment.

"Tina." She accepts my handshake. "It's good to meet someone like-minded. Do you always read thrillers?"

My life's just one long thriller, I resist the urge to reply. "Oh, erm, I just bought this at the station, but it's one of those things at the moment." I slap my hand onto the book. "I keep re-reading the same bit, and couldn't tell you what I've just read."

"That good, eh?"

"It's not that. It's just... I've got a lot going on. Life. You know. I'm struggling to concentrate on anything much." As if I'm telling all this to a complete stranger.

"Well, we can all get like that... although my life's pretty tedious, to be honest. I need a good book to liven things up!"

"If only mine was tedious." I laugh. "I suppose it takes a thriller novel for mine to feel normal by comparison!"

"How about a G&T? Will that help? If the trolley can get down the aisle, that is."

"There's not much a G&T can't fix." I could murder one if the truth be known. I'm relieved that people are making way for it. Even though it means that those sitting in the aisle seats, end up with someone's backside in their face as they allow the trolley through.

"What can I get you madam?" The steward pulls his trolley up beside us. I bet he can't wait to clock off.

I hate being called *madam*. It makes me feel a hundred years old. Especially by someone who looks as though he hasn't even started shaving yet.

"I'll have two G&T's please." Tina glances around the carriage. "If you can't beat them, join them."

"I'll pay for..."

Before I can stop her, the card machine beeps, signalling the completion of her purchase of both drinks.

"Well, thank you." I take the tin and the plastic cup filled with melting ice and a limp lemon slice. "I'll get the next round then. When he comes back up again." This was a good idea. A G&T or three might be just the thing right now. Suddenly I'm grateful for her company. And it's preferable to drinking on my own. I take a sip from the cup, the bitter tonic and sour lemon in keeping with how I feel about getting back home to Bryn. I should make my drink last, after all, we don't know how long it might take that trolley to reappear on its return journey along the aisle. But despite my best efforts, the drink is down in about three gulps. However, I'm more relaxed. The first drink is always the best, like nectar flowing through my veins. My drinking has been creeping up and up lately. A combination of trying to blot things out, and project an illusion that I'm having a good time, especially around the pub. Who wants a miserable landlady? Though when the regulars are pouring out their woes in chapter and verse, it's doubly hard to stay upbeat.

I was over the moon when I first got into the pub business back in my twenties, but I've outgrown it now. Like a lot of things.

23.5 HOURS BEFORE

DEBRA 4:30PM

"MY DAUGHTER'S NOT SO bad, but my son acts as though he's got the world's problems on his shoulders." Tina rolls her eyes under her spidery mascara. "He never talks about it though. It's woman trouble, I think. At least I hope it isn't anything more serious."

"Snap." I laugh. "My son's in the same boat. That's why I've been to Leicester. I've been spending a couple of days with him." I think of Lance and how I left him at his halls. It always breaks my heart to leave him. Especially with the way things are. "He's split with his girlfriend and needed a bit of TLC."

Even though his six-foot-two frame towered over me when he gave me a hug, he still reminded me of the little boy I once had to tear myself away from on his first day at school. At least he's got a clean bedsit and kitchen after my visit, as well as some food in his fridge. It doesn't matter how old and lanky he gets, I'll never stop worrying about him.

Lance's plan, now he's back there, is to spend New Year's Eve getting obliterated with some friends who are on their way back after Christmas. He reckons a wild night out with them will get Sophie out of his system. "He's at uni. Doing a psychology degree."

"Did he not want to spend the new year with you? Especially if you've got a pub?"

"His girlfriend broke up with him over Christmas. So he wanted to go back early. Get away from all reminders of her. He was more cut up than he let on, so I decided to travel back to Leicester with him."

"Ah right. Poor lad. It's hard when they're that age, even more so with her ending it at Christmas."

"I know. Heartless so-and-so." I laugh, but it's forced. I liked Sophie. We got on well and I'm going to really miss her. Which is more than can be said about the waste of space Hayley has been knocking around with. He never even seemed to change his clothes. Thank goodness she's seen the light with him. As far as I know. She had to find out for herself though. Whenever I went on about how unsuitable I thought he was, she just seemed to dig her heels in more.

"Have you just got the one son Debra?"

"Yes, and I've got a daughter. Hayley. She's just left home too. She's renting a place with a couple of her friends." It always makes me feel miserable to mention that they've both moved out.

"Ooh, how lucky you are. All that peace."

"I don't feel at all lucky." A vision of their sparse bedrooms fills my mind, rooms which Bryn wants to decorate and repurpose. He reckoned at one point that the kids moving out might go some way to improving our marriage. As if.

I try to chase these negative thoughts away as I remember that in less than three hours, I'll be back in the proximity of Jay, my bar manager. I've barely stopped thinking about him this past couple of days. Lance has even pulled me up a couple of times when he's been talking about Sophie. *Are you listening Mum?* For the last couple of months, I've been this way. Preoccupied. I can't wait to see him, and just hope we manage to find a few minutes alone over the course of tonight. When I'm with Jay, I feel half my age. I can't recall feeling a fraction of this intensity in the entire twenty-six years I've been with Bryn.

Jay never makes quips about how old I am, or how menopausal. Nor does he point out anything that's not just as firm or as tight as it once was, not that he'd know how it once was. I just wish I'd have appreciated what I had more when I had it.

"I can't wait until my two bugger off again." Tina swirls what's left of the ice around in her cup. It's a miracle it's still frozen.

Both our cups are smeared with lipstick. I never used to wear it but I need all the help I can get these days. I loosen my scarf, hoping for respite as more of this dreadful artificial heat belches out.

"I know I shouldn't say it, but them being back is a nightmare, especially my bad-tempered son." She looks sad as she continues. "At least I have a dog, so someone in the house is pleased to see me when I get home. It also gives me an excuse just to walk out of there when it all gets too much." She glances over her shoulder. "Now, this conversation's getting maudlin. Where's that trolley gone?"

I laugh, and I think of Sammy, our spaniel. She knows so many of my secrets whilst I've wittered away when out walking. It's a good job she can't talk.

I'm really struggling to ignore the dragging in the pit of my belly. It's hard to work out whether it's dread at the prospect of facing Bryn, or nerves at the possibility of getting the chance to rip Jay's clothes off again. Things have simmered for weeks between us. Ending up in bed was inevitable. It happened for the first time the night before Christmas Eve with a pub full of customers downstairs. That fear of being caught somehow added to the excitement.

Then again, in the early hours of Christmas Day when the pub was empty. And once more, the night before I left for Leicester. I've been replaying all three occasions in my mind ever since - I can't help it. Though I wasn't able to look Bryn in the eye on Christmas Day. I was certain he must have been able to tell that there was something different about me. The kids too. Despite how bad things have become between us, I do feel wretched. I never set out for any of this, it just happened, Blimey, how cliché this sounds. I turn to the window, wiping the steam from it. There's nothing to see now, apart from my own reflection. I try to shake my hair out; it looks to be clinging to the sides of my neck like seaweed.

Perhaps being so bored in my marriage is normal. The twenty-five-year itch. I turn back to Tina. "Do you have a good marriage?"

Her eyes widen. Maybe the question's too blunt, especially since we've only just met.

"Far from it." She crosses one trouser leg over the other. I never wear trousers. Far too frumpy. "But let's not go there for now." However, I'm intrigued. If I spill my dark secret, she might spill hers. I like to hear what life is like for other women my age. Then I can muse about how my own could have turned out differently.

"I've started an affair with one of my staff," I blurt, perhaps a bit too loudly as the man in front twists in his seat to look at me. I feel myself colour up. Thankfully, he turns back again.

"Did you say you own a pub?"

"That's right. He's my bar manager. Well, my temporary bar manager." My stomach twists as I say this. "He's leaving in a couple of months to go travelling and has invited me to begin the trip with him." This isn't strictly true. But the word *invite* sounds better than 'I've begged him to let me tag along.' He reckons I should have some 'alone time' too. To 'find' myself.

"*Begin the trip?* How does that work?"

"He recently broke up with someone. So he's now planning this *trip of a lifetime*. And he wants to 'set me free' but for myself as he puts it."

"I see. Is it serious between the two of you?" She sounds genuinely interested.

It actually feels good to talk about everything. "To me it is. Although with him, I get a sense that it's all a bit of fun." Saying this out loud makes me feel worse. I'd do anything to have a future with him. Especially now the kids are going their own way.

"Is that because of his recent breakup, or because you're married?" Tina slides her scarf off and unbuttons her jacket. "Gosh, is it warm on this train or is it me?"

"That's my go-to line with this menopause lark." I laugh. "I think it's because I'm old enough to be his mother." I look down at my hands - the biggest giveaway of my age. They tell the story of years of hard graft and bringing up my kids, often, so it felt, on my own.

"We've always been flirty, since the moment we met, but I think we were both pretty taken aback when things started to happen between us."

"Do your kids know what's going on?"

"Gosh, no, not a clue, at least I hope not. But I'll obviously have to tell them about Jay soon. I can't just disappear into the sunset."

"Jay, eh? How old is he?"

"Twenty-five." The man in front turns around again. I feel like telling him to butt out, but I don't. It's probably all bills and bins for him in his home life. Perhaps eavesdropping on our conversation is the most excitement he's had all year.

"Is staying with Jay for his entire trip a possibility?" The way Tina accentuates the word Jay amuses me. It really is a relief to be able to freely talk about him for the first time.

"I don't know. I'm hoping so. Now the kids have left home, there doesn't seem much reason to come back."

"What about your business? What will you do with that?"

"I'll get rid of it. Or if I don't, I could get a new manager to look after it. Fancy a job?"

She laughs. "I've got enough on my plate. Won't your husband want to manage it?"

"No chance. The place was mine well before Bryn and I ever met."

It dawns on me suddenly that Tina could be *anyone*. Bryn could have employed her for all I know as some kind of investigator to see what I'm up to. "I can't believe I've told you so much. We've only just met." I rub at the back of my neck. Phew, I wish the windows could be opened.

"Sometimes you just click with someone, don't you?" She fiddles with a loose stitch on her gloves.

"You won't have bargained on hearing my life story when you sat next to me."

"It's sometimes the best way, isn't it? Talking to a stranger. After all, the chances are that we'll never see each other again once we've left this train. Oooh look, the trolley's on its way back."

23 HOURS BEFORE

DEBRA 5PM

"WELL, we're certainly putting the world to rights today, aren't we?" Tina checks her phone. It's been refreshing, sitting with someone who's not totally phone-immersed. It's the first time she's looked at it since she sat next to me. "No messages. None of them would be bothered if I turned up tonight or not."

"Not even your husband? But it's New Year's Eve."

"Especially not my husband." A cloud crosses her face. "Maybe I should follow your example."

I pause for a moment in case she wants to elaborate. But she stays quiet. "It's been so good to talk to you Tina," I eventually say. Thanks so much for listening." It's true. I'm glad I got over myself and allowed for a conversation.

"Just don't forget what I said."

"Which part? We've talked about so much over the last couple of hours!" The journey from Leicester to Leeds seems to have gone on forever. Yet on the other hand it's gone too fast. A bit like life itself.

"About only getting one chance at all this." She gives me a knowing look as she slides her phone back into her bag. "Life's too short to be trapped with a man you don't want to be with. If you're really sure you don't, that is."

"I'm absolutely positive. Honestly, he makes my skin creep Tina. He swans around as though he owns the place and does nothing, absolutely nothing, apart from get drunk with the customers."

"I'm surprised they want to spend time with him, from what you've said."

"He's as thick as thieves with Hayley's ex, much to all our disgust. He treated her really badly, yet Bryn seems to be able to put all that to one side and sit, getting drunk with him."

"Can't you bar him?"

"Who? Bryn, or my daughter's ex?" I laugh. "I've told him he's not welcome but with Bryn giving him such a warm welcome..."

"It must drive you crazy."

"He's been coming in even more since she dumped him. No doubt to wind me up. He could probably sense from the get-go that I didn't approve of him."

"At least you've got your bar manager to distract you. You've said your kids don't know, but does your husband have any idea about your *thing*?"

"You could say that. It's all an absolute mess."

I do want to add that it's more than a *thing* between me and Jay, but what would be the point? I'm not sure what matters, or doesn't anymore.

"You sound like you're really going through it."

"I've just struggled since my kids left... Being around Jay, even before things went to another level, has been a welcome distraction. To be honest, if things don't work out the way I want with him, I'll be in absolute bits. In some ways it would be worse separating from him than it was from the kids."

"Really?" Tina's voice rises.

"Well, yes. At least I still get to see them. To talk to them whenever I want. I can't imagine a life without Jay in it."

"At least your kids talk to you." She sniffs.

I go to hug Tina as we part company on the train platform. Though she stiffens at my approach, she allows me briefly into her vicinity. She's shorter than she seemed when we were sitting on the train. I quickly stand back and study her face. It looks sallow in the station lighting, not to mention utterly miserable. I imagine she doesn't get many hugs and feel sorry for her.

"How are you getting home Tina?" It's on the tip of my tongue to invite her to the pub. She looks like she could do with a few drinks and a good night. But she's already mentioned needing to get back for her mum. And her dog.

"I've a taxi coming. A local firm."

"Ah right. It's a shame we can't share."

"It would cost a few quid, we're at opposite ends of the city."

I hesitate, wondering if she'll offer her number before she heads off. But she doesn't. So I don't offer mine either. It's just as well really. I've divulged far too much during our time together.

I feel an overwhelming sense of loneliness as she walks away. I sink to a bench at the side of the platform and the cold metal immediately chills through my skinny jeans. I shiver and button my coat. I keep meaning to buy a warmer one. Roll on spring. Roll on lighter nights and daffodils. That's if I'm still here. Jay's first destination is India - I've always wanted to go to Goa and visit the golden sandy beaches. Bryn laughed when I once suggested it, telling me I had ideas above my station.

Even if things don't work out with Jay, perhaps I'll go to India alone. It can't get to this time next year without me starting to see something of the world.

Leeds station would normally be heaving on a Friday evening. I glance up at the board. There are no more departures, only arrivals. Shouts of *have a good one* and *see you next year* echo all around me.

It's eerie, sitting here, with tannoy announcements few and far between. I'm the only person who isn't hurrying to get somewhere. I could be, but other than seeing Jay who'll be rushed off his feet anyway right now, I've no inclination to get home. Besides, I suddenly feel zapped. As though I could just curl up in a corner and fall asleep. Jay and the other pub staff can manage for a while longer without me - it's what I pay them for. I lick the lingering tang of the G&T from my lips, tempted to find somewhere that's not too busy to get another one. Out of a proper glass rather than a plastic cup. But I'll never get home if I do that.

No doubt my absence will have given Bryn the opportunity to order everyone around as though he owns the place. Him *not* owning the place has been at the root of so many rows over the years. It took sweat, blood and tears for me to buy my ex-fiancé, Kevin out of the pub when we broke up. As well as, loans, favours and credit cards. Whilst I accept that if we end up divorcing, I'll have to release some capital as a settlement for Bryn, he was never, ever going to be allowed to get his hands on it all - no chance. It's almost as if I could foresee things changing between us right from the start. He's not particularly business minded anyway and has always spent more time having days off than actually working.

"You alright love." A passing man looks at me. He's wearing a LNER uniform, so he's just doing his job by checking in with me rather than being kind.

"Yeah, fine thanks. Just having a moment."

"You look really miserable. Are you sure you're alright?"

"Yes. Honestly." My dad always used to tell me that when I'm deep in thought, I look as though I'm on the verge of tears. Other people have told me that too. It must be the reason for the man's concern. If that's what it is.

"It's a bit cold to be having a moment."

I smile at him. "Thanks for asking. I appreciate it. Have a good New Year."

He takes the hint. "A Happy New Year to you too."

I might be deep in thought, but spilling things to Tina on the train has helped me to feel clearer. It was perhaps self indulgent to offload, but she seemed happy enough to listen. One thing she was right about is that it's far easier to speak freely to a complete stranger than it would be to one of my regular friends. Plus, Tina told me what I needed to hear, but equally, what I probably didn't want to hear. And now, I can't get her advice out of my mind.

She thinks I should definitely leave. Not just Bryn but the pub as well. Take off with Jay for as long as it lasts. Leave life as I know it. She added that feeling trapped in her own situation, sandwiched between a mum who depends on her for everything, and grown up kids who sound like they should be long gone, she wishes she could just up and leave. And though she never spoke about it, her own marriage seems far from happy too.

This period of life has a lot to answer for. Hurtling towards the age of fifty when you realise there's probably more life behind you than in front of you, is pretty damn sobering. I must sigh really loudly. A couple walking past look at me curiously before they disappear in a cloud of heavy aftershave and perfume.

Leaving, a.k.a. running away, no matter how I do it, will be easier said than done, with the business and two kids who might think they're independent, but really, want to run back home when things go wrong. As they so often do. I've always tried to give them what I didn't have, and I've always been there for them.

I'll never forget my own mother leaving. She didn't say a word, she just upped and left. I'll never do that to my two - grown up, or not. It's looking more and more likely that Bryn and I are approaching our final curtain. But I'll always be there for Hayley and Lance, even if it's only at the end of a telephone for a while.

Dad did his best after Mum left but really, who wants to tell their dad when they've started their periods, or need to ask for boyfriend advice? Mum's departure left a gaping hole in my life. She was full of promises to keep in touch and see me regularly at first, but she moved so far away that all contact fizzled out. In less than a year. The irony isn't lost on me of how she ran off with a man half her age. He was more important than me. A thing for toy boys must be hereditary.

22.5 HOURS BEFORE

DEBRA 5:30PM

I'VE MADE sure Lance is alright, and now I must check on Hayley. Then I'll get moving. My bum's so numb with sitting here, I'm not sure if I'll even be able to walk.

"It's me." It sounds quiet wherever she is. "Where are you?" She can't be at the pub. It certainly won't be quiet there tonight. I check my watch. The mayhem will be just about kicking off.

"I'm at home, chilling. I'll be getting ready to go out shortly. Anyway, how's Lance doing? Is he feeling any better?"

She's a good lass, my daughter. I'm super proud of her. Even though she's gone through her own rubbish with Carl not leaving her alone, she still finds it in her to ask about her brother before anything else. "Ah, you know. Totally broken hearted but it's all part of growing up."

"I still think he should have waited before going back to Leicester. I don't like to think of him on his own."

"He's OK. His mates should be with him by now."

"He could've stopped with me if he didn't want to be around you old folks."

"Eh! Less of the old."

I'm not sure I'll ever get used to Lance not being around.

Hayley's always been independent but I'll never forget Lance's words to me when he was a little boy. *When I'm big and I've matched with someone, like you and Daddy match, I'll live in the house next door to you Mummy, so I can still see you every day.*

Relaying this to Sophie probably contributed to her getting cold feet with him. Lance looked daggers at me when I'd repeated what he'd once said when she came for dinner.

"I'll give him a bell tomorrow," Hayley says.

"I'm ringing to make sure you're OK as well love. Has there been any more hassle with *him*?"

"No. Thank God. He's actually gone silent over the last couple of days. Hopefully he's got the message. Like you said, I've stayed out of the bar so I don't bump into him."

"Have you heard from your father?" It's time to mention the unmentionable.

"Yep." She groans. "He was in a foul mood when I called round to take Sammy for a walk, so I didn't stay long."

"There's a surprise." Great. It's going to be such fun when I get back.

"What's rattled him this time Mum? He hasn't been right for the last couple of weeks if you ask me."

"Who knows? Perhaps it's the manopause!" I laugh at my own sad joke. I'm the only person who laughs at my jokes nowadays.

"You won't be laughing when you get home. Don't say I didn't warn you."

"I'll just keep out of his way." I've certainly gotten good at that over the last few months. I know every trick in the book for keeping out of my husband's way.

"You must have some idea what's up with him?" Hayley always needs to know the ins and outs of things. She's been the same since she was small. Thankfully, she doesn't know the half of it. "Has he said anything about what's up with him when you've spoken on the phone?"

"We haven't. Spoken, I mean."

"What, not at all?" Hayley's voice lifts a notch. "But you've been gone for days."

"No. Why would we?"

"Erm. Because you're married, that's why. What's going on Mum?" Hayley's voice rises another notch. "Me and Lance noticed you both over Christmas. There's something up, isn't there? Something big."

"It's nothing for you two to worry about love." Sooner or later, I'm going to have to tell her everything, but I won't be doing it over the phone. No way.

"You've been really off with each other. And we've heard you arguing when you think we're not around."

I can picture her brow, furrowed in concern. She's always had an old head on young shoulders.

"You're not going to get divorced, are you Mum?"

I can't say no to her. That would be lying and will only come back to haunt me.

"All marriages go through bad patches," I tell her. "We'll work it out one way or another."

"One way or another." Her voice rises even more. "Look Mum. I'm not going to lie." She falls quiet for a moment. "You need to know..."

"Need to know *what*?"

"Dad collared me as I was dropping Sammy back in earlier."

"What did he say?"

"He was asking if you'd said anything to me. About *him*."

"Was he indeed?" I'll kill Bryn, dragging Hayley into all this. Just when she's getting herself together after breaking up with Carl. "What do you mean, *him*?" I need to make sure what and who she's on about. She might just be fishing for information here.

"You know exactly who I mean Mum. Him. Jay. I could see as soon as you took him on why you had. And so could Dad."

I bet he could. He'll have been comparing himself, no doubt. Bryn's always enjoyed being the only man around the bar. Stephen, the chef, is usually in the kitchen. However, there's no comparison between Jay and Bryn. A patchy, mid-life crisis sort of goatee beard versus sexy stubble. A nearly bald head versus a head of hair I can run my fingers through. A beer keg, versus a six-pack. I could go on and on and on. But the main comparison is a sarcastic knuckle-dragger who makes me want to scream, versus an exciting younger man who I can't stop thinking about.

"You need to sort this out Mum. I can do without being stuck in the middle of whatever's going on between you and Dad."

"Look, you just focus on enjoying yourself tonight love." I look beyond the barriers of the station, still lit up with Christmas lights. "It's New Year's Eve. You should be out having fun, not worrying about me and your dad."

"I fully intend to. Oh, and *Jay* was asking if I'd heard from you too."

"He was?" I make my voice as nonchalant as I can. Her emphasis on how she said his name has made me sit up and take notice. Other than a few texts, I've not spoken to Jay either, since I left on Wednesday morning. Lance has been my focus over the last couple of days - he had to be. Sophie was his first proper girlfriend, so this is the first time he's ever gone through anything like this. You can put a plaster on scraped knees but a broken heart is something else.

Besides, when you're sleeping on an air bed in your son's halls of residence, there's not much opportunity to speak to any secret boyfriend. If I can call Jay such a thing. Perhaps I'm too old to have a boyfriend. He's not too old to be one though.

"Be careful Mum. Don't go making a fool of yourself. Or of me and Lance." Bloody hell. She does know about us. *Really* knows about us. She must do - perhaps after being around more over Christmas. I thought we were being discreet.

"Excuse me, young lady. Who's the parent around here? And what the hell has your dad been saying?"

"Nothing that everyone else isn't thinking. And noticing. Please Mum. Sort it out. For us."

"I don't know what you're talking about."

"Yes you do. Anyway, I'm off. Like you said, I should be out, having a laugh, not worrying if my parents' marriage is going up in smoke."

I watch as another train pulls into the station and just a handful of people step from it. The train crew chat to one another as they pass me, their heels clicking against the platform. I catch a snippet of their conversation as they revel in the fact that there's no work until Monday. Then they're gone. There's an increasing chance that I won't have any work after tomorrow - I'm just going to see how things play out. That somewhat trivialises what's coming, but so what. If I blow it up more than I already have, my brain might just explode.

The taxi rank queue is snaking right around the corner. I sigh as I join it - maybe I should have got an earlier train after all. But I wanted to wait with Lance until I knew his mates had definitely set off. I couldn't have risked him spending New Year's Eve on his own.

Couples and groups of friends wait ahead of me, their excited chatter juxtaposed with the subdued atmosphere clouding me. I'm the only person standing alone here. I don't know whether to be relieved, or sink into the cesspit of my loneliness at this realisation. One thing I know is that I've got to change things. There's more to life than what I've had with Bryn. I tug my phone from my bag again and slide my gloves off. Perhaps I won't look like such a loner if I'm busy on my phone.

On my way back. I hope you've missed me.

I add an emoji blowing a kiss, as I picture Jay's face in my mind.

I hope he's not left his phone on the bar where anyone might notice the message, especially Bryn. That's if Bryn's working, which I doubt very much.

> Of course. Hurry back - I'll be expecting you to pucker up for real at midnight.

> It's a date.

In the darkness, no one will see me smiling to myself like a madwoman. And I'll be puckering up for a lot more besides if I have my way. I sigh again. I'm so confused about it all. If only there was no such thing as Bryn. Life would be much simpler if he would just disappear into thin air.

22 HOURS BEFORE

DEBRA 6PM

FINALLY, I'm in the back of the warm taxi, even if it's moving literally at a crawl. The New Year revellers have started already. A man thumps against the car window, making me jump. He shouts *have a good one* through the glass.

Sinking back into the seat, I stare at the Christmas lights. It will be a relief when the council take them down. I used to feel dark and despondent after the twelfth night, but this year, I just want to be back to normal. Then I can make some decisions, depending on what happens next, that is.

"Been anywhere nice?" The driver's eyes crinkle in the corner as he speaks to me via his rear-view mirror. He turns his radio down to catch my reply. He needn't bother.

"Just with my son." Normally I'm really chatty with taxi drivers but my life is changing. Really changing. I have to focus on what I'm doing. This is no time for small talk, even if I do feel a bit mean.

"Doing anything exciting tonight love?"

"Just working." I pluck my phone from my handbag, hoping he'll get the message.

"You and me both."

He'll be after a tip and I want to tell him that he'll get a bigger one if he leaves me be. He'd get a bigger one still if he launched his disgusting-smelling air freshener out of the window. It's giving me a headache.

> I'll be there in twenty minutes.

It's my first attempt at contact with Bryn in over forty-eight hours. He's tried calling me once or twice, but I haven't picked up. Almost immediately three dots light up. It's as though he's been waiting.

> About bloody time.

Great. He's clearly still in the same mood Hayley was talking about. I'll just have to avoid him. After all, it's what I'm best at. It's not as if there won't be plenty of other people to speak to whilst I'm pulling pints all night. I don't normally work the bar, but tonight, it'll literally be all hands to the pumps. Hopefully, I'll be able to sneak off with Jay sometime after midnight if not before. I usually invite the customers to line up their drinks before then, so I can close the bar for at least half an hour. The staff deserve a break too.

Jay's face drifts into my mind. Those intense blue eyes which hold a glint reserved just for me. I hope it is anyway. Even if he is supposed to be enjoying his new-found freedom. Whether it was him, or her, that instigated their relationship break-up, I don't know. When I've asked him about it, he says that it's irrelevant - apparently, *he doesn't want to taint the present with the past.* He won't even tell me whether his ex was supposed to be accompanying him on his round the world trip. I've tried to find her on social media but there's no sign of anyone he could have been involved with on his profile.

Since the conversation with Tina on the train, I keep imagining the two of us - Jay and I, free to do whatever we want. I haven't had that freedom since my early twenties, before I went and got engaged to Kevin and saddled with the pub. Then, after we split, I jumped out of the fat and into the fire. Firstly into a brief rebound fling, and then Bryn came along. Before I knew it, I was embroiled in marriage, dogs and two babies. Dad told me to slow down, but I never listened. Looking back, I was probably trying to create my own 'proper' family, one that because of Mum's departure, I could barely remember.

If I end up travelling, I'm not sure what I'll do, but I'm sure I could make a difference somewhere. Doing voluntary work in other countries has got to be more fulfilling than having manicures, facials and going to the gym when I'm not working.

It's Jay's *trip of a lifetime*, he says. Backpacking for a year. He's going to teach English to help fund it all, and says he has loads saved already. However, he's adamant it's something he's planned, and wants to do most of it alone. So far, he's willing to let me accompany him to his first destination, but that's it. He reckons he'll be *soul searching* and what was the other thing? Oh yes, *character building*. But I'm working on him to keep me on board for the duration. And I usually get what I want. Somehow.

I really, really should have left Bryn years ago. I know I should. We're the classic case of staying together for the kids' sake. At least, from my point of view. I've mentioned the possibility of us separating when we've had arguments in recent years. His reply has been the same - *the only way he'd be leaving the pub is in a box.* I close my eyes against the vision of his face. Plus, the gin has made me sleepy.

"We're here love." The taxi driver pulls on the handbrake.

I wake with a jolt. I hope I wasn't drooling. My stomach somersaults at the sight of Jay's motorbike. Then sinks at Bryn's Toyota parked next to it. Even their vehicles are incomparable side by side.

No one's drawn the curtains yet. The pub's heaving. I'm glad I had the foresight to ask Stephen to stop serving food at five and help behind the bar instead. It's a good job I got Janice in as well. She's always happy to help. Last New Year, I was up early to help her with the cleaning. The place was a shambles. She's been our cleaner ever since we opened and knows nearly as much as the dog. But not quite. *The dog.* It's the first time I've considered leaving her. My gorgeous Sammy. Still, we won't be apart forever and I'm sure Hayley would look after her for me.

"Hang on a sec. I need to find my purse."

The driver turns his car around in the car park, and I stand for a minute, relishing this last moment of peace before the proverbial hits the fan. I can't see Bryn in there. He'll have his feet up somewhere whilst everyone else is rushing around. The pub looks inviting, with a welcoming lamplit glow emitting from each window. Appearances can be deceptive.

The air is so cold it hurts to breathe it in. I walk towards the door and swap it for a blast of hot air laced with hops. I used to love arriving back here, to my home, after being away. But it's become so unhappy that it doesn't feel like home anymore. I battle my way through the crowd behind the door. A Christmas song is blaring out. My first job when I get behind that bar will be to remove that wretched Christmas playlist. The decorations are jaded and spent after being up since the beginning of December. I can relate to them. They want binning. Much of the tinsel is threadbare and the streamers are older than the kids. I've been wheeling them out for years.

There's the familiar stomach flip as I spot Jay. I have known nothing like it since I first met Kevin. And I was a teenager then. This is ridiculous behaviour for a woman my age. Though I'm enjoying it, there's something disconcerting about having a man dominate your every waking thought and impulse. I've never been alone and do occasionally wonder if I should give it a go. The prospect really scares me though.

Jay hasn't noticed me come in - evidently too busy talking to a customer. Or, should I say, flirting with her. He's certainly an expert on that - it's how he manages to be the best tipped member of staff. I've always allowed bar staff to keep their own tips, but with the amount he gets, I should really make him share them out. Jennefer, who's worked here for ages, is always complaining.

I don't recognise the woman he's got his attention on. She shakes her mane of blonde hair as she throws her head back in laughter. From what she's wearing, she could be twenty years my junior. Probably with no ties either - no misogynist husband, or kids who seem to endure the same heartache in their own relationships as I always have. Something else which must be hereditary. Or learnt. I'm having a real wobble over everything tonight. I need to pull myself together.

The blonde woman Jay's engrossed in would probably look better on his arm whilst he backpacks around the world. That's probably why he's only allowing me to accompany him for the start of it. I'm OK for a bit of a flirt and an ego boost. But that's as far as it goes. What we've got is *fun, not heavy,* as he's told me several times since we got carried away before Christmas. I'm evidently not 'future material.' He's even told me that the way Bryn and I live is something he'd never want for himself. I wanted to tell him that the way he and I could live would be completely different. And I've got plans to persuade him.

I pause in the shadows around the corner from the bar, watching Jay and this woman. A horrid sensation creeps over me. Jealousy. For a split second I can imagine how Bryn might feel. I've never felt good about what I'm doing but I just can't help myself. Then I'm snapped out of my envy by a customer noticing I've got back. Then another. And another. They're all waving. All falling over each other to come and talk to me. At least *some people* are pleased to see me.

21.5 HOURS BEFORE

DEBRA 6:30PM

JAY'S EYES light up the moment he spots me emerging from the crowd. My doubt fades into obscurity as my entire soul lifts. That sort of look can't be faked. Immediately, he turns his attention from the woman and onto taking my coat. I resist the temptation to pull a face at her. Instead, I smile sweetly. She is a customer, after all. Sometimes the brewery send mystery shoppers in. We have to be on our best customer service behaviour at all times.

"Deb. You're back. Awesome!"

The woman gives him a strange look and then turns to speak to someone on her other side.

"You'll be wishing you stayed where you were when you see the mood your husband's in." Janice laughs as she pulls a tray from the dishwasher. I don't laugh back. Nor do I want him referred to as my *husband*. The word is laced with misery and guilt. But it's not Janice's fault. She doesn't know what's happening. Not yet. They all will soon enough. She's sweating as though she's just done a spin class. Being more than a little overweight, working behind the bar always takes it out of her - she's alright pootling around with the duster and mop at her own pace every morning. She certainly seems more comfortable wearing jeans and a hoody, instead of the dress she keeps yanking down each time it rides up. A night on her feet pulling pint after pint is something else entirely.

I should have been back earlier to help them. Bryn does have a point, even if there's no sign of him right now. There's a sea of expectant faces at the bar, all waiting for more drinks. I'd better roll my sleeves up. I'd wanted to get spruced up for the evening but it'll have to wait. Besides, if I go up to the flat to put some make-up on, Bryn will only accuse me of dolling myself up and accusing me of everything under the sun. Plus, if he corners me on my own, there's nowhere to hide. At least, down here, I'm busy and can keep myself out of his reach.

"I'll just hang my coat and dump my bag, then I'm all in." I've never looked forward to work as much as I do when Jay's around.

"How's your lad?" Jay swipes a customer's card and passes it back. "Did you manage to patch him up?"

"Yeah, he'll live. Although I wouldn't like his hangover tomorrow. He's got a night of de-Sophie-ing planned by the sounds of it."

Jay laughs. "I'd listen to Janice, you know - keep out of Bryn's way." He slides steaming glasses onto the overhead shelves. "He's got a face like a smacked arse."

"So I gather. I've spoken to Hayley." It must be bad. He's the third person to mention it now.

"What time do you bloody call this?" Right on cue, Bryn appears from the other side of the bar. The glass he's holding drops from his hand and shatters at my feet. "Whoops," he says, shrugging.

The whole pub falls quiet. It always does when someone drops a glass, but not usually to this extent. All eyes are on us. If it's me who smashes something, there's normally a cheer and a round of applause. The older I get, the clumsier I seem to be getting. I wonder if there's only me who saw Bryn do that on purpose. As if there isn't enough to do tonight.

To say it's New Year's Eve, and he's supposed to be behind the bar, he looks extremely unkempt. He desperately needs a shave and there's something horrid-looking spilt on his combat trousers. Then there's me, worrying about how I look... I actually feel embarrassed for him.

"I texted you, didn't I? You knew I was on my way back." I don't even know why I'm trying to appease him anymore. Habit, I suppose, after all, this has become our dynamic over many years. Anything to keep the peace. "Carry on everyone." I wave my arms in the air. "Nothing to see here." They really are nosy sods. Part of me is looking forward to the day when I no longer have to live my life in such a goldfish bowl.

"You shouldn't have gone off from here in the first place." Bryn's complexion's ruddy, as though he's spent the time since I left knocking back the drink even more than usual. He doesn't look to have sobered up since Christmas Eve. "Our busiest time of the year and you go buggering off down to Leicester to wipe Lance's sorry arse."

"Lance was in bits about Sophie, you know he was. I couldn't have just let him go back to his halls alone." I stare at him in disbelief as the hum of the pub picks up again, quickly rising to the same level as the dreadful music. "As his dad, you should give more of a shit about how he's feeling. Besides, I left the place fully staffed, didn't I?" I glance at Jay as I speak. Any excuse. "So don't give me this *busiest time of the year* crap."

Bryn's lip curls as he replies. "Lance is a big boy Debra. You're holding him back."

"My kids come first with me." I slide a glass from the shelf. "Your kids too. Not that anyone would know that with the way you carry on." I take a gin from the optics.

"I don't think so." Bryn reaches for my glass but he's not quick enough. "You need to be serving the drinks, not knocking them back."

"Whose name's above that door?" I point towards it. "Don't bloody tell me what to do."

"Now, now you two. This is no time for a domestic." Jennefer plucks the glass from my hand. "I'll stick you a tonic in that, shall I?"

"Get one yourself," I tell her, turning my back on Bryn. I'm not speaking to him tonight, not in the mood he's in. But I'll be forced to in the morning when he's sobered up. Time is fast running out. "And see what everyone else is having whilst you're at it." I nod towards Jay, then Janice and Stephen. "Where's it the busiest for you then Stephen - the kitchen or in here?" It's strange to see him in his 'civvies' and with his spiky hair on show, instead of him being head to foot in his whites.

"Definitely in here," he laughs. "I'll be glad to get my chef's hat back on tomorrow. Have a rest."

"I'm off for a break." Bryn spins on his heel. He'll be even more furious with me ignoring him. "Sweep that glass up will you?" He jerks his thumb towards Jay, then strides to the bottom of the stairs to our living quarters. For how much longer they'll be our living quarters is anybody's guess. I've already started squirrelling some of my more sentimental possessions in Dad's cupboard at the home.

"*A break.*" Jay's voice takes on a sudden edge. "He's hardly been down here."

"His mood's got worse as today's gone on." Stephen rolls his eyes as he takes the pint Jay's pulled him. "Cheers boss." He raises the glass in my direction. "Anyway, we're glad you're back."

"Never mind all day," Janice adds as she acknowledges a waiting customer. "He's been like that since you left with Lance."

"Look, I'm sorry guys. But Lance needed me."

"You don't have to explain. How is he, anyway?" Janice calls as she opens the fridge.

"Better now he's back in Leicester and seeing his friends. It was the best thing for him." I don't add that around here, and around us would be the worst place right now. Not just for him but for anyone.

"Any chance of a drink over here?" I stride over to Mal, one of the regulars, giving Jay's bum a squeeze as I go. If anyone saw me, I really don't give a toss anymore. But I'm nervous about what's coming. Really, really nervous. The time of action is getting closer and closer.

"And one here too, if you don't mind. I've been waiting for ages."

"I'll be with you next."

"Cheeky." Jay breathes into my ear as I reach up for pint glasses, nearly getting embroiled in a length of tinsel as I do. "I've really missed you, you know."

"See... I'm very miss-able once you get to know me." Smiling, I turn to face him, wanting to pursue this conversation.

"Maybe I'll have to keep you around Deb." He winks at me. I love it when he does that.

Him winking is what made me suspect the attraction I felt when I hired him, might be reciprocated. He'd done it on his way out of the interview, practically turning me to jelly. If anything, it should have been a good enough reason not to hire him, especially since Jennefer had shown an interest in the bar manager job. If she wasn't going through so much drama of her own right now at home, I wouldn't have even advertised the position. But I needed someone who would give their all, even if just in the short term, until Jennefer gets herself sorted out.

Jay was honest in the interview - he told me of his plans to travel - starting with India. Then he had ten other countries on his hit-list, he said. He added that he was looking for as many hours as possible, otherwise he'd have to work two jobs to inflate the savings pot he'd already amassed.

"Ooh, you'll have to sneak me along with you. I'll hide inside your suitcase." I wasn't entirely joking, as I've since proven.

As I showed him the ropes on his first day, there was an unmistakable chemistry between us. Once, we brushed hands and it felt like an electric shock. Jennefer gave me a look every time I went near her. She knew. And Bryn couldn't even bring himself to shake Jay's hand when I introduced them. No surprise there.

Hayley and Lance thought the whole thing was hilarious. They did to start with, anyway. According to Hayley, I kept giggling and shaking my hair over one shoulder whenever Jay was around. Clearly, they foresaw nothing coming of it. After all, I am completely old and past it.

We went on like this for a few months. Just... flirting with each other. But I knew I wanted more. Much more. Without even planning to, I was making more effort with my makeup each morning. Before Jay's arrival, it was a bit of slap if I had the time, and then out there. I've started wearing my hair, normally piled up in a bun, loose and curled around my shoulders. And I bought some new clothes. Pencil skirts and heels have replaced jeans and comfy pumps.

I look down at what I'm wearing now - somehow I'm going to have to find the time to get changed. As I am, I'm hardly dressed for New Year's Eve. I could do with Bryn clearing off somewhere so I can go upstairs to the flat.

As I wipe tables, I continue to allow my mind to drift. One day, when Jay and I were coming back from the wholesalers, he suddenly swung the car into a lay-by.

"What are you doing? What's up?" I'd thought something was wrong with the car and was pleased that we might have to spend ages waiting for a recovery vehicle.

He didn't speak, but just took his seatbelt off, leaned over and kissed me. No messing. That was it after that. And only a matter of time before it became more. But Bryn suspected it too.

I feel the smile fade from my face as I notice Bryn standing at the end of the bar, his thumbs threaded through his belt hooks, watching me, not taking his eyes off me, in fact. As I glance above his head, I'm unnerved to spot the camera pointing at right where I'm standing.

The focus of that camera moves around every five seconds from behind the bar, to the till, to the front of the bar, then the lounge, the tap-room and around the car park. And, like an idiot, I didn't wipe the footage from Christmas Eve.

The night when Bryn had gone to bed early after drinking too much. Whilst things got rather heated between Jay and I over the pool table. Damn. But at least I know now how Bryn found out.

I didn't want him to just *find out* about my affair. It threatens to take away any control I have over the situation. And I have to be in control of not only *when* Hayley and Lance find out, but *what* they find out. I have to be the one who sits down and tells them. Not Bryn. They need to hear it from me.

I'm only too aware that under normal circumstances, knowing what he knows, that Bryn would have turfed Jay out on his ear by now. But these are far from normal circumstances.

21 HOURS BEFORE

DEBRA 7PM

"Gosh, I'm so ready for this." I clink coffee cups with Jennefer. "Though our names will be mud when they discover we've sloped off." Even though I own the place, it still feels naughty to escape out here when I'm supposed to be working. Especially tonight.

The security light illuminates us as we lower ourselves onto crates in the delivery area. It smells permanently of steak from the extractor fan here - even when the kitchen is closed.

"Well I, for one, deserve a break - my feet are killing me. Have you still given up?" She waves her cigarette packet into my face.

"I wouldn't touch one now." The very thought makes me feel ill, plus I'd hate Jay to know I ever smoked. His mum died of lung cancer when he was thirteen. He helped to nurse her and had made her a promise that he'd travel and see all the places she'd never be able to. He told me about her on another trip to the wholesalers. How I looked forward to those trips. Just me and him in the car for half an hour each way. I had to take him there. He could hardly go to the wholesalers on his motorbike. But the time gave us a chance to really get to know each other. I could have listened to him for hours. Unlike Bryn. Every word he utters sets my teeth on edge.

"I sure wish I could give these up. But I'm too stressed right now." I noticed how pale Jennefer looked when I first got back. And she's lost weight. Her top is hanging from her. But she won't do anything about her situation at home. She just puts up with it. "He's been kicking off again."

"We've all got our vices." I point at her cigarette as I swallow a large gulp of coffee. It burns all the way to my stomach, reminding me that I need to find time to eat something more substantial than a packet of crisps. Jennefer's not the only one who's lost weight recently. Many of my old clothes are hanging off me too.

"Hmmm. Yes. And we've all noticed your greatest vice." She gives me a knowing look. "Can I ask you a question Debra?"

"Ask away. Though I can't guarantee I'll give you an answer." Uh-oh. What's this going to be about?

"Look, I'm just going to come out with it. You're not actually sleeping with Jay, are you?"

"Keep your voice down!" I wave my hand at her as I glance towards the door. "Bloody hell."

"Well, are you?" She cocks her head to the side, awaiting my answer. With her hair hanging loose around her shoulders, she doesn't look dissimilar to Sammy, when her head's cocked, with her spaniel ears dangling, awaiting a treat. Jennefer's hair is even the same sort of black as Sammy's fur.

I slurp at my coffee and look the other way, wishing I was back amongst the revelry and beat of the music echoing from inside. Where I'm not on the receiving end of an inquisition.

I obviously don't need to answer. "Oh Debra." My face must say it all. "But what about Bryn?"

Trust her to consider Bryn. "What about him?" My voice rises, so I quickly lower it again. Who knows who might be hanging around? "You've seen what a miserable sod he is. Surely I deserve to take my chance at some happiness for a change. It's not as if I'm getting any younger." I lean forward on the crate, perhaps partly to give myself a comforting hug, but more to warm my arms in the space between my legs and stomach.

"To be honest Deb." Jennefer pauses, as though choosing her words carefully. "Please don't take this the wrong way, but..."

"But, what?"

"Well, speaking as your friend, I think you should count your blessings."

"Blessings! Being married to him? You've seen what he's like!"

"I know he's got a face on at the moment but there's nothing wrong with your life as far as I can see."

"It happens to be pretty rough with him actually." I swing my leg back and forth as I speak, dangling my shoe from my foot. "And I know my life's good, in general. In so many ways, but not with him. Just because I don't talk about it doesn't mean things aren't falling apart."

Jennefer doesn't reply, but her face says it all.

"I'm just sooo bored as well," I continue. "Especially now Hayley and Lance are grown up. I keep thinking, is this it? *Is this really it?* I can't bear it. Even if Jay hadn't come along, I'd want out - I'm sure of it."

She's shaking her head. Out of all my friends, I might have suspected she'd be the least sympathetic. I suppose I can't blame her.

"I know I've said this before, but you ought to try being married to my husband."

She takes a deep drag of her cigarette and lets it back out in a long sigh. I do miss the ritual of smoking but it smells awful.

"At least your husband isn't violent."

"Am I supposed to be grateful? That Bryn isn't *violent*? He's plenty of other things."

"Such as?"

"Come on Jennefer. You know as well as I do that someone doesn't have to be black and blue to be classed as living in an abusive marriage." It's the first time I've really admitted it out loud. *I'm in an abusive marriage.* Speaking to Tina on the train has finally cracked me open like the Christmas nuts which no one ever eats.

"You can hardly call a few rows and the silent treatment an *abusive marriage.* You should try swapping places with me."

I wish she'd stop comparing us. It's like comparing a carrot with a handbag. "You know what I think about you staying with Chris." Here we go again. "I've offered to lend you money to get out. I've offered it so many times."

It's true. I've left it now for her just to come to me when she's ready. I can't do any more. It's soul destroying, watching someone you care about in that sort of situation, knowing you could help them if they'd only let you. When she's good and ready...

"It isn't that simple though, is it?" She sighs her smoke out again.

The security light goes off, plunging us into darkness. We must be sitting still enough, here on the crates. We're going to have to go back in soon. Before they send the search parties out.

"For either of us." We fall quiet for a few moments.

"Oh what am I going to do Jennefer?" I stare at her outline in the darkness which contrasts with the brick wall behind her. "I could go back in there. Paint on a smile. Talk him out of his bad mood. Play the dutiful wife - make out like I'm happy and content when all I want is..." The thought is as bitter as the taste the coffee has left. And I know I shouldn't be laying my woes on Jennefer, but if I don't talk about it, I'll go mad.

"All marriages go through lean spells, don't they? Come on, you've read the magazines. Sleeping with your bar manager really isn't the wisest thing to do." She takes another drag of her cigarette. "Listen to me Deb. Just let Jay go off travelling and sort your marriage out. You've only been having problems since you took him on."

This is not something I need to hear. I preferred the advice Tina was dishing out. I much preferred it. One thing she said which really struck me was, *shit's comfortable, shit's warm, but at the end of the day, it's still shit.*

It's probably the best piece of advice I've ever heard. But I don't think Jennefer's ready to hear it yet, no matter how applicable it is for her too. So for now, I'll keep the conversation on me, and what I should or shouldn't be doing.

"I know I must seem lucky to those looking on. Like you just said. But I'm so suffocated here." I stretch my arms towards the pub. "Look, I know you won't want to hear this Jen, but there's a huge world out there. And I want to see some of it. I want to live. Is that so wrong?"

"You mean you want to go backpacking with Jay." I can't see her in the darkness but I'm sure she'll be rolling her eyes. "I'm sorry." She takes a deep breath. "But I've got to say this. He'd be using you Deb. You'd be paying for *everything*. Like some sort of cougar."

"Thanks a bunch. It's actually not like that at all. Why do you think he's working here?"

She doesn't say anything, so I reply to my own question. "Because he's earning *his own* money."

"I understand it must be flattering, this fling with a younger man, but you're making a complete fool of yourself." I'm usually drawn to Jennefer's blunt way with words, but tonight I can do without it. Particularly when she's echoing what Hayley said on the phone earlier. The two of them have probably been conferring. It wouldn't be the first time...

"You're supposed to be my friend."

"I'm saying all this as your friend. And, if you won't listen to me, think of your kids. Someone's got to be straight with you." She flicks her ash into a plant pot. I'm glad it's dark - there's nothing worse than seeing tab ends floating about in yellowing rainwater. "Jay knows he's onto a good thing with you. Look at the tips you allow him to keep." There's a note of envy in her voice. I've heard her muttering about the situation with tips with Stephen, but it's the first time she's said anything directly to me.

"You all get to keep your own tips. that's always been the case."

"And I still can't believe you chose him over me for the bar manager job."

It's all coming out now. "You know why that was. The timing wasn't right. Not with what you've got going on."

Now's not the time to tell her that there could have been a home here for her and the kids. Maybe there will be if she ever finds the strength to leave Chris. And once Jay's gone, she could have had the bar manager job. But there's a lot to get through before we get anywhere near that stage. Many ifs and buts. Much depends on how things transpire with Bryn. There's a lot at stake.

"If you do go buggering off with Jay, what would you do anyway? You can hardly spend every day shopping and sightseeing." Jealousy's etched into her every word. Perhaps if her children were older though, she'd do exactly the same as me.

"I don't know. Some voluntary work, maybe? I've done my time here Jennefer. Well and truly." I glance at my watch. This has turned into a lengthy five minutes. I'm surprised no one's come looking for us yet. "We'd better get back in."

"Are you *really* going to leave Bryn?" She drops her cigarette into the plant pot where it lands with a sizzle. Yuk.

"I think I'm going to have to." I sigh. "This time of year forces us to take stock, doesn't it? As well as being nearly fifty. The thought of being in this predicament, next New Year's Eve, leaves me cold. And Jay will be long gone by then." The thought of it makes me feel desolate.

But I'd be lying if I didn't acknowledge my concern that Jennefer really has a point - Jay *might* see me as a meal ticket. Though if that's what it takes for me to leave here and have *my* time at last, then so be it.

"If you really think your marriage is over, perhaps you should just take some time in between. Be on your own for a while. I think it's a mistake to leave Bryn for Jay. What's that saying, *out of the frying pan...*"

She's probably giving me good advice but there's no chance I'll follow it. "That's something I've never done. Been on my own, I mean. I went straight from Kevin, to that other bloke, then to Bryn, now to Jay."

"Being alone sounds idyllic, if you ask me. At least your kids aren't little, like mine. You can still do what the hell you want. You don't have to run away." Jennefer gets to her feet and rubs at her backside, the security light flicking back on with her movement. "Blimey I'll probably have the imprint of that crate on my bum."

"You need to get some food down you Jennefer." I look at her legs. Clad in skinny jeans, they're sticking up like golf clubs from her boots. "You're losing far too much weight."

"Never mind all that." She turns to me. "What are *you* going to do?"

I glance at my watch. There's four and a half hours left of this year. I need to start the new year as I mean to go on. "I'm well aware that it could just be a fling with Jay. But I want to know for sure. And even if it doesn't work out, I... what the hell was that?"

We both stop dead at the sound of something clattering on the other side of the door back into the kitchen. The G&T I've drunk today has made me less conscious about lowering my voice. Which is partly why I'm out here, trying to clear my head with freezing air and strong coffee. I could have sworn I closed the door behind me. But it's ajar now.

A shadow moves from left to right at the foot of the door. Someone's been listening. Before I can make the move to investigate, footsteps die away along the kitchen floor, back towards the bar area. I wish I knew who it was. How much they've heard. Hopefully it was just Stephen, or Janice - but not Bryn. And definitely not Jay. I'd hate him to know I've been talking about him to Jennefer. I'm going to have to be more careful.

Though perhaps, deep down, I want to be overheard. Maybe I want to be caught out. Properly caught out. Things need to get moving, once and for all. After the Christmas we've all just endured, I'm serious about not wanting to spend another year like this. It's do or die.

20 HOURS BEFORE

DEBRA 8PM

"HAVE YOU HEARD FROM HAYLEY TODAY?" Gemma, Hayley's house mate leans onto the bar as I make up her cocktail order. She towers over it in the heels she's tottering about on. She's wearing what could be Hayley's red dress. The new one that she bought for Christmas Eve. I bite back the question of whether she knows she's borrowed it. It's nothing to do with me, and I wouldn't get any thanks from Hayley for interfering.

I love making cocktails, particularly the end bit with the sparklers. They're time-consuming but it gives Gemma and I a good excuse to catch up.

"We've been like two ships, as my gran would say." Gemma leans in closer as she shouts above the music. I'm sure someone has turned it up. Plus the dratted Christmas songs are back on. That'll be Jay's doing.

"I was out of the flat when Hayley came in," she continues. "And she'd left again before I came back."

"I spoke to her earlier. She was just about to get ready. Sorry," I say to a man, impatiently drumming his fingers against the bar next to Gemma. He can drum them all he wants. "I'm going to be a while. I'm just taking care of a large cocktail order."

"I was hoping she'd be in tonight. That's partly why we're all here. Have you not roped her in behind the bar? You normally do."

"No, she's out with her friends from Law School. I figured it would do Hayley more good to be in town, after all that's gone on." I gesture behind me. "Anyway, Janice and Stephen, my cleaner and my chef, are on triple pay so they're quite happy."

"Triple pay!" She laughs as she watches me snap the shaker shut. "I think I'll come and work here."

I shake the cocktail mixer around rhythmically, my next favourite part of the task. I look out over the bar. Everyone seems to be enjoying themselves. There's always a good atmosphere in here. Made even more homely with the log fire and the fairy lights. I'm really going to miss the place.

Or maybe not...

"Get your fucking hands off me." A scuffle has broken out at the other side of the bar.

"I said get out. Now!" Bryn's voice.

I might have guessed. *What the hell.* "Keep an eye on the cocktails," I say to Gemma.

I rush towards the commotion to find a lad squirming on the floor. He reminds me of an eel as Jay and Bryn struggle to keep hold of him.

"What's going on?"

Nobody answers me.

"You either leave now, or we get the police involved." Jay yanks him to his feet. Bryn steps back and watches on. I can tell by his face that he's peeved about Jay having taken charge. With youth, height and muscle on his side, he's got far more chance.

"We just caught this lowlife peddling his wares." Jay wrenches his arm up his back. He frogmarches him towards the door and calls back over his shoulder. "If it's one thing I can't stand, it's druggies."

"Don't you ever call me a lowlife." The lad continues to wriggle in his grasp. He can't be any older than Lance. I feel myself soften, until he says, "Or I'll show you exactly what a lowlife can do." A hush has descended over the pub again, just like it did when Bryn dropped the glass earlier. At least the audience is not for my benefit this time.

"I'll come back and burn the place down."

With one final push he's out of the door. Jay slides the bolt across. "I'll just leave it locked for a few minutes." He looks at me. "Is that OK?"

"You're the manager." I smile at him, resisting the urge to reach for his hand.

"What the..." Smoke billows across the room. "Leave that fire alone," I shout across the lounge. Two girls in tiny dresses are heaping coal onto it. I wouldn't mind but there's a big sign above it. *Only bar staff can stoke or add to the fire.* "Gemma will you have a word whilst I finish these." I return to the cocktails. "They are either not listening, or they can't hear me. I wouldn't mind but it's like a furnace in here as it is."

I watch as she teeters across to them. It amuses me how the young ones have fake tans for nights out. All sun-kissed bronze in the middle of winter.

"And now for one of your five a day." As she returns to the bar, I thread the fruit for each glass onto cocktail sticks.

"I'm glad to hear Hayley hasn't got back with that waste of space she was on with. She's seen sense this time." Gemma tosses her hair behind one shoulder. I remember mine being that thick and glossy once upon a time. But I never appreciated it. In fact, I felt inadequate every time I looked in the mirror. Looking back at old photos now, I don't know what my problem was. Whoever said youth is wasted on the young was absolutely right.

"She'll get back with Carl over my dead body." I finish assembling the glasses onto the tray.

"She's not sneaking off to see him anymore then?" She holds out her payment card, her charm bracelet jangling.

I shake my head as I reach for the machine. "I hope not. She'll struggle to pass her bar exams if she's hanging about with someone of his calibre." I realise how pious I must sound as soon as the words leave me. *Calibre.* But I don't care. The man was holding Hayley back. However, my disapproval seemed to prolong her seeing the light for herself. I was probably the same at her age.

"Personally," Gemma says, "I didn't like him from the moment I first saw him." She waves her card over the machine. "And I was right. I mean, what sort of bloke tries to stop his girlfriend from even hanging out with her friends? He was soooo jealous."

"He actually didn't seem that bad when she first brought him to meet us. Scruffy, maybe rough around the edges, but polite enough. He and Bryn got on like a house on fire. Mind you, that should have rung alarm bells in itself." I say the last bit more to myself than to Gemma. I shouldn't have said it - G&T speak again. I've certainly been knocking them back this evening.

"Meanwhile, he was eyeing up the family silver." She laughs. "I just hope he's leaving her alone now. He stalked her the last time she tried to break up with him."

"Well, let me know if you hear of anything like that happening again..." I'd like to add, *whether or not I'm here,* but until I've made everything official, I can't mention anything to *anyone.* "Hayley might not want me to know what's going on, but I'd be really grateful if you'd keep me posted."

It troubles me that Hayley has gone for someone exactly like her father. It's classic textbook stuff, and it's my fault after the example I've set all her life. Perhaps the best one I can show her now is, *pursue your heart, pursue your dreams, pursue your...*

"Isn't that Carl over there?" I follow Gemma's glittery red fingernail towards the lounge area. Sure enough, there he is, staring back at me from his place on one of the sofas. Thank goodness I agreed Hayley should go out, rather than help behind the bar.

With his brooding features and chiselled physique, it doesn't take a genius to work out what she saw in him initially. Though he always looks like he needs a good wash, a shave and a decent haircut. We lock eyes and he looks away.

I empty the remains of Moscow Mule from the cocktail shaker into a glass and down it in one. It's as sour as my facial expression must be after seeing him.

"Aren't you going to throw him out?" She says, wrapping her fingers around her tray of drinks. Her voice is a little too loud, even above the music. Gemma's voice is naturally high-pitched, and several people waiting at the bar look curiously at us both.

"On what grounds?" I speak in a lower voice, hoping she'll follow suit. "He hasn't actually done anything that I can throw him out for."

"Yet." She turns her attention back to me. "I just hope he doesn't recognise me. I don't fancy being grilled about where Hayley is, and who she might be with."

"Just send him over to me if that happens." I grit my teeth. "I'll deal with him."

Carl must sense my eyes still on him. He looks up again. We eyeball each other for what seems like an eternity this time. His face is unreadable. Him being around tonight is making me very uncomfortable indeed.

19 HOURS BEFORE

DEBRA 9PM

SAMMY NEEDS A WALK. And I desperately need a breath of fresh air. I'm not doing a very good job in here this evening. It's not really fair of me to be going out, given how manic it is, but my head's all over the place. I keep mixing orders up, or forgetting them completely.

Gemma's offered to help, which is a Godsend. She reckons to need the extra money, so has stepped in to collect and wash glasses. This will cover my absence for half an hour or so. I'm paying her triple time too. Until one in the morning, so she's happy with that. At first she offered to do it for quadruple time, but I laughed at her.

I grab Sammy's lead and call her down from the flat. She pelts down the stairs with the wild and grateful expression I love. If only everything was as straightforward as a dog. I know what Tina meant when she said she'd got herself a dog, so at least someone in the house is always pleased to see her. I slip Sammy's collar on and stroke her head. "Come on girl. Let's get out of this madness, shall we?"

I've told nobody I'm going out, only Gemma. Not even Jay. Before I left, I noticed Bryn, deep in conversation with none other than bloody Carl. I watched them for a while, hoping to get a clue of what they were talking about. Bryn was doing what he normally does, throwing his hands around as if they add weight to whatever way of thinking he's trying to force someone else into.

Carl's speech and movements were slower, more considered, to the point of having a sinister quality about them. The two of them could be hatching a plan to persuade Hayley to get back with Carl. He and Bryn are evidently cut from a similar piece of cloth; both mysogynists, both holding the belief that partners are a man's property. I'll be devastated if Hayley walks in my footsteps and ends up with a carbon copy of her father.

Anyway, he can hardly moan at me for going out when he's knee deep in a discussion with bloody Carl, of all people. He's probably only doing it to rile me. There's no point trying to rope him into working. It doesn't matter anymore.

Sammy and I leave by our flat's private entrance. It's such a relief to get some air, even just for a few minutes - away from the queues all around the bar, which are now four people deep.

As I turn the corner out of our lane, I let out a long breath. The quiet which replaces the boom of the music, the swarm of conversation and the shriek of laughter, is so welcome. The night is as still as a lake, as if Sammy and I are the only souls out here. I stare into the sky, noticing the plough and the bear formations. It's as clear as I've seen it for a long time. It reminds me of that wider world I want to explore, all hopefully with Jay. I wonder where I'll be this time next New Year's Eve?

"When everyone's preoccupied with the turn of the year, I'll collar him." I say the words out loud, my voice croaky at first. I check around to make sure there's no one in earshot, even though I know there isn't. "What do you think Sammy? Things are so simple for you dogs, aren't they?"

She twists her neck to look at me, her breath making clouds in the night air. "I'll hate to leave you though," I add. "When I leave."

The realisation washes over me again that I can't take Sammy. Not abroad. I'll have to leave her behind.

She sits at the edge of the kerb, giving me her sad Spaniel eyes. It's as though she understands what I'm thinking and saying. She probably does. I sit beside her for a minute, the sudden chill of the kerb through my jeans reminding me of the steel bench I sat on earlier at the train station. But sitting around and thinking isn't acting. And it's action that's needed right now. Big action. "You know I don't love Jay as much as you, girl?" I stroke her back as I talk to her. "It's a nightmare really. You've seen and heard it all, haven't you?" I pull her closer into me, enjoying her warmth. "I promise I won't be gone forever. I'll do my travelling, maybe for a year, and then I'll come right back for you. Hopefully, you can stay with Hayley whilst I'm gone. You'd like that wouldn't you?"

She gives me another look as if to say, *No I wouldn't.*

I get to my feet and pull her up with me. "We'd better do some walking," I say.

Pounding the streets, even just for twenty minutes, always helps my head to feel clearer. However, as the pub comes back into vision, my thinking clouds again. If it was as simple as just splitting up with and divorcing Bryn, there wouldn't be anything to weigh up.

"Its alright for you." Pausing, I pat Sammy's head. As long as you're fed, walked, and have your bed to curl up in, you're happy. And everyone loves you. I stand up straight again, the heat of tears pooling in my eyes. I'm surprised by how much the situation is getting to me. "Maybe there is a way I can take you with me. If there is, I'll find it. It's not as if I haven't got money available. Money that's nothing to do with *him.*"

Even in the faint streetlight, she gives me what I would call a knowing look. They say dogs are perceptive to their owners. Sammy certainly is.

"I miss who he used to be, you know, your dad." Hayley and Lance have always laughed at Bryn and I referring to each other as

Mum and Dad to our pets over the years. *Over the years.* We've been together for such a long time. Some might say I'm a bitch to be considering leaving my husband as we approach our silver wedding anniversary. However, I'd argue that I'd be more of a bitch for going through the motions and pretending to celebrate it with him. Surely it's kinder to let him go?

A vision of Bryn when we first met enters my head. He was always skint and always late, but I'd have forgiven him anything in those days. He was a completely different man, attentive and fun. Before the real Bryn emerged. "But he's horrible now," I continue, as though Sammy needs to understand my reasons. "He even shouts at you, doesn't he?" I reach down and stroke her back again. "We'll both be better off without him."

18 HOURS BEFORE

DEBRA 10PM

"YOU MISSED ALL THE COMMOTION, you know." Janice eases the dishwasher shelf towards her. Her face is crimson and her hair has escaped from the band she had it tied up with.

"You mean with that bloke and the drugs? I saw it. I haven't been out for that long."

"No, there was more." She fills a glass with water. "First there was a group of kids. Well, not kids exactly, but obviously underage."

"Were they asked to show ID?"

"Of course." She tears off a length of paper towel. "But they gave Jennefer a load of verbal when they realised they weren't going to get served again." Janice mops at her brow as she points at Jennefer.

"What do you mean *again*? Someone actually served them a first time?" I'm hoarse from an evening of raising my voice above the noise level.

"Yeah, they'd been tucked up in that far corner." She gestures again as she speaks. "And the oldest-looking one had bought a round in the first time. I don't know which of us served her."

"It's OK. There doesn't seem to be any harm done." I cast my mind back to when I was hollering at the group of girls earlier. "You mean the ones that were hanging around the fire, don't you?" I step towards her and start sliding glasses onto the shelves from the dishwasher tray. Janice can't work and talk at the same time. Which is why she makes a better cleaner than a member of the bar team.

"Yeah." She tugs the elastic from her hair and reassembles her ponytail as she continues speaking. "Anyway, they were making all kinds of threats when Jay and Stephen chucked them out."

"Chucked?"

"Well, there was some frogmarching of them out needed, then threats of calling the police."

"The police wouldn't have come out for something like that. They'll be busy enough tonight."

"They might have done with the threats they were all making."

"Such as?" Like seriously, what damage can a bunch of kids really do to a pub?

"You know, smashing the place up, putting windows through, that sort of thing. All because we wouldn't let them finish the drinks they'd already bought."

"Has it all been logged in the incident book?"

"I think Jay sorted it." She tilts her head in his direction. I follow the gesture but as my gaze falls on him, my thoughts are nothing to do with the incident book. He grins the grin that gets me going every time. *Get a bloody grip Debra.*

"So that was sorted. What else happened?"

"Jennefer's lovely husband rocked up." Janice shakes her head.

"Oh no." I glance over to her. She looks super-stressed. Now I know for sure that this is far more than to do with how busy it is in here tonight. She didn't really talk about it earlier. I suppose that I didn't give her the chance to. I was too busy warbling on about my own predicament. Things must be terrible between Jennefer and Chris for him to have turned up *here,* kicking off in front of the entire pub. Gosh, what sort of friend am I? I should have made more effort to make sure she's alright.

Instead, I've sat back, immersed in my own goings on, believing I've done enough for her by offering to throw money at the situation.

"He makes my hubby look like a superhero." Janice laughs as she folds a tea towel into quarters.

"You should have been here." Gemma appears at my side with more empties than I'd ever have thought it possible to carry at once. "Poor Jennefer."

"What actually happened?"

"He was absolutely hammered. But he didn't buy a drink here." Her gaze flits in Jennefer's direction. "To be honest, they'll be lucky not to be reported to social services. Or to the police, if he's driven here" She lowers her voice. I lean forward to catch it above the music. "He made no secret to everyone who listened that he'd left their kids in bed."

"Then he stormed out," Janice adds. "But before he slammed the door, he accused Jennefer of working here so she could, as he so nicely put it, s*hag her way around anyone in here drunk enough to have her.*"

"Bloody hell."

I look over at Jennefer. She's chatting to another woman and a bored-looking man at the end of the bar. I'll grab her when she's finished talking, whilst there's another lull in demand for drinks. Though any lull is only the calm before the next storm. But at least someone's turned those wretched Christmas songs off.

"Did *he* just leave then, or did he have to be escorted to the door as well?" Bloody hell. What a night. And to think I was feeling wistful as I looked around my comfy-cosy pub earlier. I've always had a tendency to view things through rose-tinted glasses. Until I'm forced to think otherwise, that is.

"It was awful." Gemma shakes her head. "He yelled out, *anyone who wants her is welcome to her. She's crap in bed anyway.* Before telling her he was going to change the locks. Then he buggered off."

I close my eyes momentarily. Even Bryn wouldn't stoop that low in public. "What an absolute..."

"Are you all having a good laugh at my expense?" Jennefer marches over.

"Of course not." I step away from Janice and Gemma. "Janice was just telling me what's happened with Chris, and we're certainly not laughing." I reach for her arm, hoping to catch her in mid-flight. She's understandably wired. "Are you OK?"

"Not really." Her eyes fill with tears as she turns away. "But hey-ho."

"My offer of help always stands," I say. "You don't have to go home to that pillock. Or do you need to go home *now*? For your kids, I mean?"

"No. I'm fine. I'd rather stay here. I've had a neighbour check things are OK." She brushes the tears with her sleeve. I try again to catch her arm but she tugs it back.

"Hey, you can stay the night here if you want to. Especially if you think he'll get handy with you."

"I've got my kids to think of, you know." She gives me a knowing look. Sometimes, I don't know why I bother. I'm here, offering to help, whilst she takes yet another cheap swipe at me, and lets me know her opinion of me as a mother.

"Well, the offer of help is always there."

"I might have known *you'd* be interfering." Bryn doesn't look up from the till as I walk past. I didn't even realise he was nearby. Even though he's got his back to me, he seems to sense me passing him. I'm surprised he's heard anything of our conversation above this din.

I ignore him, instead making my way over to a customer. Bryn appears at my side and hands a receipt over the bar.

"Where the hell have you been anyway?" He nudges me, making me nearly spill the wine as I pour it into the measure.

"Walking Sammy."

"*Walking Sammy!* Are you having a laugh?"

"I needed some air, if you must know. I've been getting one of my heads." He used to be sympathetic about my migraines. These days he just gets irritated.

"You go swanning off down to Leicester for two nights, leaving us..." he waves his hand loosely around the bar area, "here to cope with all the work, and then, you take off for dog walks on bloody New Year's Eve without a word to anyone. What are you playing at?"

"I don't need permission from you, or anyone else."

"I see you've even had time to get bloody changed."

"So what?"

"And are you sure you've got enough perfume on? We all know whose benefit that's for."

I start to walk past him but he blocks my way. This is all I need.

"Why do you have to be such a miserable bastard Bryn?"

"Probably because I'm married to such a miserable bitch," he snarls back.

"It's no wonder I want to get away from here. From you." The words trip off my tongue before I can stop them.

"What's that supposed to mean?"

"Can we have some service over here please?"

"Let me past. I've got a pub to run." I feel like slapping him. I've had enough of living like this.

He doesn't move. And Jay's watching.

Bryn glares at him. "Don't think I'm serving any more drinks in this place this evening." He grabs a glass from the shelf. "Only for myself."

"Do what you want Bryn. Like always." I march to the other side of the bar, away from watching eyes. It's bad enough that our marriage has fallen apart, but so publicly...

"What can I get you?" I stride towards a waiting customer, attempting to load my voice with joy and cheer. Hopefully he can't see my eyes shining with tears. A mixture of misery, anger and humiliation.

"I was worried about you, you know." Jay nudges me as I pour a pint of Guinness. "You shouldn't be going out on your own this late."

I'm warmed by his words. At least someone cares about me. "It's not exactly rough around here, is it. In any case, I was with Sammy."

He laughs. "If you were in any danger, her best offer of protection would be to lick them to death."

"I know." In an instant, just being in Jay's presence has helped me to feel calmer. "Anyway, *you're* going to need looking after too."

"How do you mean?" The glint I've come to know and love returns to his eyes.

"In all those foreign places, I mean. Never mind me just *starting off* on your trip with you." I flash him what I hope is a winning smile. "You could have a willing companion for *all of it* if you'd let me tag along."

"How willing?" He winks at me as I set a glass down and start filling another.

I glance around. Nobody seems to be listening. "I'll show you at midnight if you like." I stand on tiptoes and speak into his ear. We're so close I can smell his aftershave. "We're closing the bar for half an hour."

"It's a date. Where?"

"I'll let you know."

"Bryn's not taking his eyes off you, you know," Jennefer hisses as she swipes a bottle of champagne from the fridge. "Should you not be more discreet?" She sounds so fed up. Though it's no wonder with what she's got going on with Chris.

"What's the point?" I reply. "You said yourself that everyone knows."

"So how's your evening going?" I place beers in front of two of my favourite regulars.

"All the better now you're back where you belong," one of them replies. "This place isn't the same without you behind the bar."

"Ah, you sweet talker you." I reach forward and tap his arm. "You can have these on the house. Happy New Year."

As I head towards another customer, Bryn grabs me by the arm and tugs me backwards.

"Get the hell off me." Within a few steps, I've shaken myself from his grip. I don't have to put up with this. Not any more.

"What do you think you're playing at?"

"They're two of our best customers. If I want to give them…"

"You know what I'm talking about…." He spins me round to face him. Then moves so close I get a whiff of his sour breath. "You're the talk of this place. Thanks for making an absolute mockery of me."

Aware of eyes on us again, I shrink back. "Just leave me alone and let me get on with my work."

"I'm watching you Debra. And you'll be getting what's coming to you."

"Spoken like a true husband," I reply. But his words strike fear into me. I can tell he's seriously rattled. And he's already warned me that he'll do whatever it takes to prevent me from leaving him.

17 HOURS BEFORE

DEBRA 11PM

"I'M JUST NIPPING up to the flat. To make sure Sammy's OK," I tell Jennefer. "Bloody fireworks."

"You'd think they'd wait until midnight," she replies.

I ascend the stairs, taking in the photos of the kids as I go. Bryn berates me for the volume of pictures I have up. *Clutter,* he says. *Why do you need so many photos of the kids on the walls - are you scared you'll forget what they look like?*

Maybe I am. Life's flying by - I'd give anything to go back in time, even just for a day. I used to look forward to when they were older, more independent, easier to reason with. Now that they are, I want them to be little again. I miss how they were, how much they needed me. I've wished my life away. Now I'm wishing it back, but for something different. And this time, I'm going to get it.

I peer around the kitchen door. Sammy was terrified of fireworks as a pup. However, there's no sign of firework fear tonight as she opens one eye from her basket. She stretches, then joins me on the landing.

"Good girl." I close the door against the unwashed pots and

mess that's accumulated in my absence. Now the kids have left home, this flat should be tidy. However, Bryn, the man-child, thinks it's acceptable to leave the housework all to me. He recently suggested that I get Janice to clean the flat, as well as the pub, instead of moaning about it. The kitchen's even worse than usual - Bryn probably thinks there's no point anymore. This is one time I might agree with him. There really does seem little point any more.

I wander from room to room, taking everything in, and Sammy potters behind me. This has been my home for twenty-something years. It was strange at first, getting used to living in a flat. After Kevin and I finished sixth form, we rented a house together. Getting the pub was a huge decision which I'd agonised over. There were so many 'what if's.' Eventually I gave up my boring, but safe job with the council for this place. Then, when Kevin and I split a couple of years later, Dad and the bank helped me buy him out.

I stand in the centre of the lounge. I did this. It was me who worked for all this. And now I'm letting it go. Tears stab behind my eyes. I blink them away. This is no time for second thoughts.

My eyes flit to the wedding photo above the mantlepiece. As if I've given nearly twenty-five years of my life to that waste of space. I was so young, so naive, so afraid of being alone that I jumped at the first man who showed an interest in me.

Of course, Bryn wanted his name on things as soon as the wedding plans began. Which was impossible with his sketchy credit score and patchy work history. But to start with, he mucked in with the work, regardless. It was the only way we'd be able to spend time together. As the years have passed by, he's got comfy, and lately, only does the bare minimum, both here and in his so-called own business. He's earned himself a reputation for being a great sparky, but a no-show more often than not.

He parades around here like a catwalk model, but it's all for effect. When we first got together, we had plans to work hard, maybe set up a chain of pubs and become financially free. We said we'd travel and do as we pleased. He'd be the last person I'd want to do that with now. He's content with growing his middle-aged paunch in front of sport on the telly - drink in one hand, pork pie in the other. There's a Bryn-shaped dent in 'his' chair, and woe betide anyone who tries to sit in it when he moves. He doesn't travel much further than the kitchen for more food, or behind the bar for more drink. Tonight must be the longest stretch he's spent down there in months, and it's only so he can keep me under surveillance.

His conversation consists of criticising me - usually something to do with one or both of the kids. He often seems jealous of my giving them money, time or attention. At other times he'll go on about how much I've changed, and not for the better in his eyes. Being constantly put down about what I say, where I go, what I do or don't do, and being accused of what I'm thinking, or not thinking, has worn me down over the years. It really used to erode my self-esteem. But I won't let it anymore.

People might think Jay's breaking up my marriage but, whether or not I leave with him, I'm out of here anyway. There's no marriage to actually break up - it's already broken... I took my marriage vows so seriously once. *Till death do us part.* I look again at our photo. I feel like ripping it from the wall and stamping all over it.

I push the door into Lance's room. It's the tidiest it's *ever* been. Most of his stuff is with him in Leicester. How I miss going on at him to sort it out. At one time it was so bad, he wouldn't let Sophie in here. I called it the cesspit and paid Janice to fumigate it after Lance left in September. Still, I can almost taste the overpowering body spray he's used throughout his teens.

Dropping him off in Leicester was such an emotional day. After leaving him at his halls of residence, I spent most of the journey back in floods of tears. Friends promised I'd grow to love the peace, but I never have. Instead, I long for his appalling music, which isn't really music, and the days when he and Hayley bickered about anything and everything. If there wasn't anything to argue about, they'd find something. From leaving the bathroom in a state, to pinching each other's chocolate, or who'd got the biggest helping of pudding. They always had each others backs though. When one was upset, the other would be there like a shot. I don't think that will ever change.

As I sink to Lance's bed, I hope that wherever he is now, he's coping with his breakup, and hasn't got too drunk. I urged him to leave Sophie alone tonight. Bombarding her with drunken, pleading texts won't do any good. She's made it pretty clear they've outgrown each other. After four years together, Bryn reckons it's a good thing if it means he'll throw himself into his studies, and not feel compelled to come home every weekend. He keeps telling me that it's time to let Lance go. He would say that, would't he? Just because he's jealous. But soon I'm going to be forced to let Lance go even more.

And Hayley. In some ways, it's even harder with her. She's so much like me, and I desperately don't want to see her making all the mistakes I made - ending up trapped with some deadbeat like Carl.

I close Lance's door and walk across the landing to Hayley's room. The wall is patchy where the light has faded the walls where her posters once were. It's completely stripped of her stuff. The only things remaining are some of her soft toys and a few clothes that she no longer wears. All of it should go to the charity shop, though I don't think I could bear to drop it off. It would be like admitting that a chapter of my life is definitely over.

I stride to the wardrobe, burying my face in one of the dresses still hanging there. Yes, it smells like her - a combination of perfume, soap and hair spray. I reach for the face cream she's left behind on the dresser. *For young skin.* If only...

I sit in the semi-darkness for a few moments, listening to the hum of conversation from the pub below, the continual thud of music and the occasional screech of laughter. I should get back down there but I'm not feeling it tonight. Not in the slightest. My get up and go has got up and gone.

I slide my phone from my pocket.

> I'll be busy at midnight. So just wishing you a happy new year before the network gets jammed. Hope you're having a good night. I love you.

First I send it to Hayley, then copy and paste the words into a text to Lance. I only ever tell them I love them by text. I always find it difficult to say it out loud. It's the legacy I've been left with after being motherless from the age of eleven.

16 HOURS BEFORE

DEBRA - JUST BEFORE MIDNIGHT

"I'll be glad to see the back of this year."

"Next year's going to be different."

"Only twenty minutes to go."

"Have you made any resolutions?"

I wander around the pub collecting empties, listening to snippets of conversation, whilst trying to avoid being drawn into them. What's being said amongst everyone is much the same as this time last year. And every year. I do love this place, but after all these years, I am ready for change. Somewhere different. *Someone* different.

This might, after I've spoken to Bryn in the morning, be my last night here. I'm trying to get my head around it all. I keep checking in with myself that I'm doing the right thing. In terms of life changing, it's monumental. And risky.

"Thanks for the present Deb." One of the regulars swings me round by the arm. "You always give such thoughtful gifts."

"You're welcome. I'm glad you like it." This year, I put more effort into my presents. Though if I'm honest, I was probably trying to assuage my conscience somehow.

"We must meet up for a coffee in the new year," she says.

"Yeah." I pull away, part of me wishing I could make definite plans into the new year. I've pretty much made up my mind now though, I'm unlikely to be here. Though I really am at Jay's beck and call in terms of where I'll be going, and when. Hayley and Lance's faces emerge in my mind. They are going to be devastated when I break it to them. I'm dreading it.

I wander aimlessly around the periphery of the pub. I'd normally get more involved with the customers. But tonight I avoid eye contact with everyone as I gather as many glasses as I can stack against my arm. Most of the regulars will sense the need to leave me be, having witnessed a couple of the altercations over the evening. Gossip spreads like the flu in this place. Others will be too drunk to care.

I sigh. If I don't get some more of these glasses in that dishwasher, everyone will be moaning. We can't seem to wash and refill them fast enough tonight.

I look around for Bryn - it's best to keep an eye on where he is. In doing so, I catch my reflection in one of the darkened windows, always a flattering place to look when checking oneself, especially at my age. Much better than the full-length mirror in the natural light of my ensuite. Saying that, I'm not in bad shape for nearly fifty. Nothing's really headed south yet. I remember my grandma when she was my age - she really looked like an old lady. I've no idea about my mother. She was still in her thirties when she cleared off. I've tried looking for her once or twice on social media, to no avail. She could have remarried, and changed her name. For all I know, she might even be dead.

"Last orders folks." Jay rings the bell. My stomach lurches with a combination of excitement and nervousness.

"You've got to be kidding." Someone says as I pass by. "It's not even midnight."

"We're just closing for half an hour or so," I reply. "We minions want to celebrate the new year as well." A shiver reverberates through me as I contemplate what I've got in mind as a celebration.

I'm suddenly lifted. Enough wallowing, enough thinking. It's time for action.

I point the remote control towards the big screen. New Year is gearing up in London. The BBC camera keeps panning between the crowd and Big Ben. It always looks really exciting down there. This will be the twenty-eighth new year I've spent in these four walls. *Twenty-eighth.* I've always loved when the old year becomes the new, that sense of a new beginning. I don't know why - it's not as if anything really changes. But this year, everything changes.

No one's taking any notice of Big Ben. In fact, one of the bar staff seems to have turned the music up. I head back to the bar. It's nearly time. "Right get yourselves a drink." I sweep my arms around the staff. "On the house, of course." I glance around again for Bryn. He's sitting across the table from Carl, again, waving his arms about as he speaks. Carl's nodding as though his life depends on whatever Bryn's saying. Bryn's either drunk or has a point to make. Or both. He's got his back to me. I watch for a few moments. I'd love to know what they're talking about, but I'm staying well away from Carl. And Bryn for that matter. Anyway, at least I know where he is.

I raise my glass towards Jay who's leaning against the back of the bar, his once crisp white t-shirt bearing traces of the manic evening. There are few men who could look as good in jeans and a white t-shirt as he does. I do like this younger man thing. OK, so it might be more time consuming for me to ensure I too, look the part, and can keep up with him, but he's more than worth it. "To you," I say. "Thank you."

"For what?" He wipes froth from the stubble on his upper lip. I like his stubble. Bryn's facial hair looks unkempt, but Jay on the other hand...

"Where do I start?"

"Ten minutes to go." He glances towards the TV whilst taking another gulp from his pint. "Blimey I'm ready for this. Cheers Deb."

"What else are you ready for?" I sidle up beside him and cup his butt cheek with my hand. "Are you still up for it? Taking advantage of the bar being closed?"

"As long as you know Bryn's just over there?"

I follow his gesture. "Never mind *him*. He's too busy talking to that lowlife anyway." I glance over at them. "And everyone else will be otherwise engaged - seeing the new year in."

A smile spreads across Jay's face. "I'm game. Besides the thrill of being caught is always a turn on."

"You make it sound like it's happened a lot."

I want him to assure me it hasn't, that I'm the only one he's ever risked being *caught* with, but he doesn't. "You go first. I'll follow. Where are you thinking by the way?"

"The utility room. No one will dream of looking in there for us." Perhaps I've replied too quickly, but this is what I've had in mind all evening. It's not the most romantic setting but no one will look for us there.

"Does it lock?"

"Nah. It all adds to the fun though, doesn't it?"

"I can't think of a better way to see the new year in."

"Be warned. It's freezing in there."

"I'll soon have you warmed up."

I glance around again. No one seems to have cottoned on to what we're planning. No one would be interested. Four minutes to go. A crowd has finally gathered around the TV. It's obscuring my view of Bryn and Carl.

Hopefully he'll stay exactly where he is - after all, our days of wishing each other a Happy New Year with a hug and a kiss are long gone.

16 HOURS BEFORE

DEBRA - JUST AFTER MIDNIGHT

"You bastards."

I hear Bryn before I see him, silhouetted in the doorway. Who knows how long he's been standing there.

"Shit." Jay pulls away as Bryn snaps the light on. I don't know if he means *shit* because we've been caught, or because we've been interrupted.

"How could you fucking do this to me?"

There's more anguish than anger in Bryn's voice as he lurches towards us, which strangely evokes a twist of guilt in my gut. I'm unprepared for this, it's the first time I've felt anything other than a sense of entitlement that I'm putting *me* first for once. Guilt is not part of the plan.

"People like you..." Bryn stops mid-sentence, his lip curling as he moves forward and squares up to Jay, "who think it's OK to fuck other men's wives. You're going to get it, you are."

"I was getting it until I was so rudely interrupted."

When Bryn takes aim, it's obvious that he's had more than a few drinks. Jay doesn't have to do much to dodge the punch. Besides, Bryn's never been a fighter, at least, not with his fists. His words are another matter, and probably cause just as much damage. I drop from the counter to the floor and swipe at my discarded knickers. This really isn't my finest hour.

"Is that the best you've got?" Jay laughs as he pushes him back with one hand, and zips himself up with the other.

"I'm not going to let you do this to me, either of you." He points from Jay to me. "You just wait. You won't get away with this."

I stand beside Jay. "I've had years of your threats Bryn. There's nothing you can say that worries me anymore."

"I think you'll find there is. How could you do this to me? To us?" Bryn lunges at me now. "You're nothing but a slag."

Jay catches him mid-flight as I jump back. "I don't think so."

"You let me go, or I..."

In one move Jay has Bryn's arm up his back. He walls him up next to the dryer.

"Get the fuck off me. You're breaking my arm."

"You go near her again like that and that's exactly what I'll do." He must twist it some more as Bryn yells out.

"Do you hear me?" Anger twists in Jay's jaw. I've never seen it before and I don't like it.

"So you shag my wife and then you attack *me* - is that it? What have I ever done to you?"

The pub's gone deathly quiet. Why did they have to turn the music off? Everyone's probably listening. Shit. How can I go back out there? This will get back to my kids. What was I thinking of? Tonight of all nights? That we could get away with sneaking back here? What an idiot. I wanted Jay so badly that all common sense eluded me. And I thought Bryn was otherwise engaged.

"I said get your hands off me." Bryn must find his fight again as he thrashes around in Jay's grasp, kicking his legs out and squirming like a scorched moth. But his strength is no match for Jay's. It never could be. He's still holding Bryn back with just one arm.

"I'm not letting you go until you calm down." Jay's bicep ripples beneath the sleeve of his t-shirt. This goes on for a few moments, me just standing here, not really knowing what to do, until Jennefer puts her head around the door.

"What the hell's going on?"

Janice is right behind her, peering around her arm.

"Leave us, will you," I say, trying to keep my voice steady. "This isn't anything for you to be involved in."

I don't know if it's because another person has entered the room, but the fight seems to suddenly drain from Bryn. Jay must sense this, for he lets go of one of his arms.

"I want to speak to my wife," he says. "Leave us alone. All of you." He moves his gaze from Jay to the doorway, his voice calmer than I ever could have predicted.

"Will you be alright with him?" Jay looks over Bryn's shoulder at me.

I nod. I was going to wait until the morning to have this conversation. Though it's probably best to be got over and done with now.

Bryn glares at Jay. "Of course she'll be alright. I'm not some monster, you know. Whatever she might have told you."

Jay lets go of his other arm. "I'll be out there if you need me Debs. Just shout."

"I will."

"*Debs.*" Bryn spits the word out as though it's stale chewing gum.

Jennefer holds the door wider, shaking her head as Jay walks towards her. It falls closed behind them all. Here we go. He's either going to rant at me, or beg. Judging by his expression, it'll be the latter. Much of his constant putting me down and name-calling takes place behind closed doors, so out there, it will be me who'll be cast as the villain.

He doesn't speak straight away, which makes me nervous. At least I won't be having to spend my time pre-empting and tiptoeing around his unpredictable moods any more.

"Why, Debra?"

"Why, what?"

"Why now? Are things really so bad between us?" What he's walked in on certainly appears to have sobered him up.

What am I supposed to say to that? "For me they are. They have been for a long time."

"I've seen how you look at him. I knew you'd end up sleeping together as soon as you offered him the job."

"If it hadn't been with him, it would have been someone else. I'm sorry Bryn. Really I am."

"Am I that dreadful?" Pain is etched all over his face but it doesn't soften me. Not any more.

"Yes, since you ask."

"Why?" He raises his voice again and the single word reverberates around the stone walls. He sounds like a wounded animal. I can't look at him. I feel cruel right now but I don't love him anymore. He needs to accept this.

"I want a divorce."

"You've got to be joking. Just like that."

"I'm sorry Bryn. I don't know what else to say."

He's quiet for a few moments as he stares at the tiled floor. Perhaps he's just going to accept the situation. After all, you can't force someone to stay with you. Then his expression hardens and his hands bunch into fists. "Not as sorry as you're going to be."

"What?" I look at him now. "Is that supposed to be a threat?"

"Look. It's not too late Debra. You can stop all this. Only *you* can stop this." He clasps his hands together as if he's praying for a miracle. I'm more repulsed than ever. He's walked in on me having sex with another man, I've told him I want a divorce, but here he is, thinking that I don't mean it.

"For me it *is* too late. All the rows, all the silent treatment, all the insults. I've had enough Bryn." I really have. No matter what he threatens me with. Perhaps he won't go through with any of it. Maybe he'll find someone who'll give him something back. Sure, he's lost most of his hair but he's still reasonably good-looking.

There must still be a decent person in there, deep down. Like when we married. But we've got to where we bring the worst out in each other. The very worst. But it's not too late for us just to walk away from each other without inflicting even worse damage.

"How about we go for counselling or something?" He steps closer to me and his knees buckle as he speaks. For one awful moment, I worry that he's going to fall to his knees as a way of 'begging' me but it's probably just the volume of whiskey he's consumed.

"Debra. I'll do anything. Please don't let this go too far."

"How can you say that, after what you've just walked in on? Have some self-respect Bryn. *Counselling.* Maybe if you'd listened to me when I first suggested that, we might have stood a chance." I step back from him, leaning into a button on the washing machine which beeps beneath my weight. I spring forward again.

"Bit jumpy, aren't you?

"I think we've said all that needs to be said here, don't you?" It's happening. It's really happening. This will be my last night under the same roof as Bryn. Life is moving on.

"Debra please. Please. Listen to me. It's alright for you. You've got this place. The business. Somewhere to live. You've always had the upper hand. What's going to happen to me?"

"Maybe you'll have to do some proper work at last." I resist the urge to call him *man-child* to his face, the name I call him within the confines of my mind. But this is how it's become, like having a third child. Someone else I've got to provide for, clear up after and put up with a load of crap from. He's given me more work and aggro then both kids put together.

"So you're expecting *me* to leave then?" His jaw tightens. "Whoever said it's a woman's world wasn't wrong."

"Oh, don't start with the chauvinism. It's nothing to do with it being a *woman's world*. It's my graft that's paid for us to live here all these years." In fact, with his jealousy and constant put-downs, he's been more of a hindrance than a help.

"How dare you say I haven't pulled my weight? You've spent our entire marriage putting me down."

"Because you haven't. You dish out a few orders to the staff, pull the odd pint when you can be bothered, and sit on your arse the rest of the time. You haven't even looked at that dishwasher wiring like I asked you to." This is all trivia in the scheme of things. I should probably challenge his comment about *putting him down* as he calls it, especially after how he's been bullying me lately. But what would be the point? We've gone around and around in circles quite enough.

"It's been Christmas. It's been busy."

"So you're saying I should pay to get someone out? When you could probably fix it in five minutes. It's a bloody fire risk and you know it."

"You do this to me Debra, and I'll..."

"You'll what, exactly." I fold my arms across my chest and narrow my eyes.

"I'll make sure you regret it." His shoulders go back as he squares up to me.

Yeah. I know you will. Which is why I've got to protect myself. "More threats eh?" I lean against the dryer. "You don't scare me anymore. Pack your stuff Bryn. It's over." I stare at the ceiling. I can't look at him anymore.

I used to spend hours in this room when the kids were little. With my wretched twin tub for company. Each inch of this place is etched with memories. But I've changed, and I don't need bricks and mortar to keep the memories with me.

"What? So you're going to throw me out now?"

"No, but I think it's for the best if you stay somewhere else tonight."

"You'd really throw me out into the night at the start of the new year? You're joking. I have rights - you can't do that."

"Go stay at Carl's or something. You've been cuddled up all night." A delicious thought occurs to me then. If I can get Bryn out tonight, Jay can stay. We can finish what we began. But I don't think for one minute Bryn will go anywhere. Not without a huge battle. Maybe I can get the police to remove him? Maybe not. It's not as if I can prove any intention he could have to cause me harm.

"Please Debra, I'm begging you. What do I have to do, get on my knees?"

I watch in horror as he promptly falls to his knees in the same spot where my knickers lay a few minutes ago. "Get up Bryn, for God's sake."

"End it with him." He's crying his eyes out. "We can get back what we used to have. I know we can. We were happy once. We can be happy again."

"No, we can't. I've had enough of it all. So get up, you idiot."

"I'm begging you. Please. Please! Don't leave me." It's the drink, not me, that's making him cry. He's never been able to handle a skinful.

"I'm not leaving you. You're the one who's leaving." This is the best way forward. Everything's out in the open now, and I feel better for it. And I'd feel safer without him around. He's too unstable right now.

"Just tell me what I have to do. I'll do anything." He lunges forward and to my disgust, wraps his arms around my calves. "Don't let things go any further. You can stop it all. You can stop it now."

"Get off me." It takes a few goes to kick him off me but he's that drunk, he quickly falls away. I step back.

Only a couple of weeks ago before things really got going between me and Jay, I was part of the fixtures and fittings. Bryn's meal ticket, the mother of his children, his emotional punch bag, his servant.

"Are you OK?" Jay reappears in the doorway.

"Bryn's just leaving," I say.

"Like hell I am. If anyone's leaving it's *him*." Bryn gets to his feet now he's got an audience again. "One way or another."

For a moment, his stance suggests he might fly at Jay again. Instead, he pushes past him and lurches towards the door into the bar.

"We'd better go after him." I smooth a hand over my hair and down my skirt. "He's capable of anything in the state he's in."

"I'd fasten your buttons first." Jay points at my blouse. "And don't worry. I've got you."

"Hopefully you can unfasten them again later."

Now I've got to persuade Bryn to go quietly. That way, my greatest problem will just be getting the pub managed after I set off with Jay. The alternative could get very ugly.

15.5 HOURS BEFORE
DEBRA 12:30AM

THE PUB'S shrouded in a hush as I throw the door open. No one would ever believe that we're thirty minutes into a new year. Normally, I'd have set our new year playlist going, starting with Auld Lang Syne just after midnight. But the position I'm in right now is far from normal. I've no idea how much the customers know about what's going on, or what I've been up to. What I do know is that things can't be put off any longer.

Everyone's eyes seem to bore into me. My face is on fire, yet in the semi-darkness, that shouldn't be seen. Nobody's taking too much notice of Jay, so maybe they're none the wiser about what's happening right now. They probably wouldn't suspect the two of us as being in a relationship, if it can be called that yet. People might think he's out of my league... but then they'd be wrong.

I watch Bryn to see what his next move will be. We're like opponents on a chess board. And there can be only one winner. He's got his back to me as he pushes his glass up on the whiskey optic. Again and again and again. I step forward. How many shots is he getting? Though maybe I should let him get on with it. If he falls down drunk tonight he'll be out of my hair at least. I glance around for Carl - I could do with knowing exactly where he is too. *Keep your enemies close*, as they say.

"Carry on with your evening everyone," I call out. "Don't mind us." I step towards Bryn. I really want to get him out of here tonight if I can. And then he's not getting back in. Ever. A conversational hum rises which I'm grateful for.

"Don't you come anywhere near me." Bryn spins around to face me, then sweeps his gaze from one end of the bar to the other. "I have an announcement to make." He clears his throat.

"No, you have not."

A fresh quiet descends over everyone and there's a collective clink of glasses on tables as everyone looks towards Bryn.

"No, Bryn. Stop it. Not now." There was a good reason for calling him *man-child*. I could be speaking to Hayley or Lance when they were toddlers or teenagers. Trying to reason with them. Bribing always used to work. *If you do this, you'll get that...*

"Bryn, if you stop this now, we'll talk, I promise."

Jay shoots me a look.

"I'd like to make an announcement." Bryn staggers around to the other side of the bar and bangs his glass on it. Then he draws one knee onto a bar stool.

"Easy mate." A male voice cuts through the crowd. Perhaps if Bryn falls and cracks his head on the concrete floor, that will be the answer to my problems. It will be a lot less hassle than trying to force him out of here tonight.

Everyone's watching as he brings his other knee onto the stool next to it.

"What the hell are you doing?"

He slides his glass to the left, and then hoists himself onto the bar in the same way he just got up onto the stools.

"Get down Bryn," I shout. "You're making a right show of us." Gemma appears at my side. I'm grateful to her. I'll have to get her to keep quiet with Hayley. At least until things are absolutely definite.

"Oh believe me darling, you've done a good enough job of

making a show of us on your own. Or should I say, with *him*?" Bryn ascends to his full height, his head nearly touching one of the ceiling beams as he balances his triple or quadruple whiskey in one hand. With his other hand, he points squarely at Jay, leaving everyone in no doubt who I'm making a show of myself with.

A gasp rises as he stumbles. I don't know if the gasp is in response to him stumbling, or to who he's just pointed at. Jay, after all, could have his pick of women. Someone near the pool table sniggers. I watch Bryn's face. That will be like a red rag to a bull, whether they're sniggering at Jay's choice of woman, or the action Bryn's taking to deal with it.

"So a Happy New Year to one and all." He holds his glass aloft as the words slur from him. If I go over, I'll only make more of a spectacle of it all. I still hope he'll fall from there and knock himself out. Or break his neck. It will save me a job.

The watching crowd remains silent. If I were to look closer at them, I'd probably be able to see them holding their breath to see what he's going to do next.

"So at least one of you in here thinks this situation's laughable," Bryn continues. "That's what you're all doing, isn't it? Having a right good laugh behind my back, whilst she," he swings around to point at me. He's very close to losing his footing. Very close. If there wasn't a pub full of people watching...

"Come on Bryn. You've made your point." Gareth, one of the regulars, steps forward and holds out his hand. "I'll help you down, then we'll have a drink, shall we?"

I look around. Where's Carl? Has he gone? That can only mean one of two things.

"I haven't even got started yet. So leave me alone," he shouts and someone laughs again, a woman this time. A titter of conversation echoes around the room. "I'm going to say what I've got up here to say." His knees buckle again but he recovers himself.

"Look at you all with your boring, sad little lives, getting off on watching our boring, sad little lives." Bryn takes a gulp of his whiskey.

"It's hardly boring Bryn. Far from it, in fact."

More titters erupt amongst everybody watching. They'll be talking about this for days, weeks even. Though who knows where I'll be a few weeks from now.

"If it's more drama and action you're wanting." Bryn raises his glass again and moves it in the air from left to right, "make sure you watch this space." Bryn's eyes bulge as he sweeps them over his captive audience. "Watch it very carefully."

"Give over Bryn." A different voice this time.

"You'll see. You'll all see."

"Get down before you hurt yourself."

"Nothing could hurt me as much as she's, she's..." he waves his finger around, seemingly searching everyone's faces as he tries to locate me.

There's a hum of reaction. One voice takes over the others. "Gosh, who needs the TV when you've got *The Dales Inn*?"

More laughter.

"You think it's all so funny, do you? My wife, in there, having it away with *him*?" Once again, he scans around, possibly trying to locate Jay. I'd be surprised if Bryn can recognise anyone, the state he's in. What I've been up to is a hundred percent out now. Hayley and Lance might hate me to start with, but in time, I'll be able to repair things. When it comes to me and their father, their allegiance has always been with me.

"Well let me tell you all, you nosy, two-faced bastards." Bryn starts up again. "If it's drama you want..." He nods as he rants. "Some more action? Yeah? Well, you just stay tuned, alright?" He nods again, grinning manically. "You watch this space. I'll sure as hell be giving you something to gossip about."

PART II

BRYN

6 HOURS BEFORE

BRYN 10AM

I CAN BARELY OPEN my eyes, let alone lift my head from the pillow. Tapping my watch, I squint as I attempt to read the time. My tongue roams across my furred teeth - it tastes as though something's died in my mouth.

Out of habit, or maybe hope, I stretch my arm across to Debra's side of the bed. I don't know why. Of course, she's not there. Why am I even checking? She hasn't slept in our bed for weeks, preferring to sleep in Hayley's room than beside me. Once, we would pride ourselves that the only time we'd ever slept apart was when she was in hospital, having the kids. What I'd give to have those days back.

I pick crusts from the corners of my eyes. I don't know what's up with them. They're literally welded together. Hoisting myself onto my elbows, I catch sight of my swollen face in the mirrored wardrobes. My eyes look like piss holes in the snow.

Shit. It's all coming back. I was all over the shop last night. Laid on the floor at one point, sobbing like a girl. Not that females particularly sob these days. Hard as nails, most of them. They're too busy trampling all over us. Well, not this time - I will not end up like most other men. Out on my ear with absolutely nothing but black bags. No way. Shit. I was *really* crying last night. The full works. I haven't cried like that since they chucked me out of home. The bastard my mother took up with was always more important than I was. And that's, what, bloody hell, thirty-seven years ago. But the rejection from my wife is hitting me harder than the rejection did from my mother. Back then, I was second best to my half-brother and now I'm second best to that prick.

More events from last night steamroll over me. Feeling as sick as a dog, I lean back against the pillows. My nausea isn't just down to the whiskey I put away last night. Walking in on Debra at it like that was a right kick in the bollocks. Seeing her with her legs wrapped around another man. I know our life together has become stale and boring, but I've hung in there. Until I clocked her, at it with him, on the CCTV. It was the day before Christmas. Merry Christmas Bryn. Until then, I'd thought it was just a flirting thing that would burn itself out.

Whilst Debra was away with Lance, I even tried getting through to Jay. Yes, it might have been through clenched teeth, and really, I might have wanted to wrap my hands around his smug neck and throttle him. He bare-faced lied to me by denying everything. I realised then that I'd have to be more strategic than they would have given me credit for, so I swallowed the urge to confront him with my evidence.

If they think they can sell this place from under me or they can get someone else managing it, they can think again. Debra would do that to me, I know she would. Go swanning off around the world without giving me a second thought. Leaving me homeless and penniless.

Without Jay sniffing around, we might have been able to fix our marriage. Despite things not being good, I haven't gone running off with the first woman that showed an interest in me. Not that they do. Not even the woman who helped me down from the bar and tried to talk to me. I took her being nice to me last night as a sign she wanted to get into my pants. Far from it. What an idiot I was.

She just felt sorry for me. I was well pissed off. I wanted to prove to Debra, Look, *I've still got it, I can attract and have sex with other women too.* Maybe then, she'd think twice about leaving me.

It's not just what she's doing, it's how blatant she is about it. Clearly, she doesn't give a rat's arse about me, to have been carrying on right under my nose. I wanted to kill them both last night, and I *mean,* kill them. Twenty-five years of marriage in the end, has counted for absolutely nothing. In the utility room too - she probably wanted me to catch them. Why do it right under my nose otherwise?

She'll have been laughing her head off when I asked her on Christmas Eve what we should do for our wedding anniversary. No one's ever looked at me like she did, as though I was diseased. She replied, *it isn't as if we've got much to celebrate anymore, is it?* She'd carried on with the ironing as if that was far more interesting than any sort of conversation with me. And that's how it's been every time I've tried talking to her lately. Belittlement. Hostility. And I've reached my limit. Desperate times call for drastic measures.

I haven't told her what the video camera caught yet. But today, I'm going to lay my cards on the table. Tell her I already knew about them carrying on, well before last night. This is one reason I didn't kick up too much of a stink when she disappeared with Lance. I needed the space to work out how to deal with it. Plus, at least I knew where she and Jay were - not together.

So it's last chance saloon. The outcome of my trying to talk her round will decide whether Plan B needs to go ahead. But even after all she's put me through, I'd give anything for it to be Plan A.

I know more than anyone that our marriage has become boring. What was the word she used? *Stale.* All of this has been a real wake up call though. The bottom line is that I still want my wife. I'm going to fight for her. I'll do whatever it takes to stop her leaving me.

Then more of last night comes back with a bang. I reach for Debra's pillow and bury my face beneath it with a groan. Me, staggering about on top of the bar, giving it chapter and verse in front of the whole pub. What was it I ended up saying? *I'll give you all something to talk about.* Well done Bryn. If Plan B ends up being instigated today, that's my cover well and truly blown. Everyone was there, everyone heard and no one seemed nearly as drunk as I was. They'll remember.

Only one person asked if I was OK last night. And she'll probably keep her distance from now on after me making a move on her. And literally no one else gave a shit - they just carried on. The only other person who spoke to me last night was Carl. And that's merely because of what he stands to gain out of me. He benefits hugely if Plan B wins out.

Beyond that, after today, I'll probably never see him again. Or any of them. Life, as we all know it, could be about to change beyond all recognition. It's all up to Debra now. She doesn't seem to grasp how much damage she's done to our family, not to mention how much she's about to do. And doesn't appear to have a remorseful bone in her body.

The hoover is being pushed around downstairs but I can't hear any voices. I stare at the wallpapered ceiling. All these years I've woken up in this very spot with my wife breathing softly beside me. It smells of her face cream in here, my body spray, our lives together. It smells like home.

The first proper home since Vince chucked me out. I've been thinking about that a lot this week. Mum stood by and let it happen, evidently only bothered about Tomas, the weasley half-brother who'd replaced me as her son. It was as though she could only love one son at a time. Whether the row was my fault, I was only sixteen years old, with nowhere else to go. And now, it seems I'm in the same position again. Women are all bitches. I hate the lot of them.

I need to shift myself from this bed. Get some water and

paracetamol down my neck. Get my arse moving. I get back up onto my elbows and swing my legs around until my feet are resting on the carpet. My head swoons with the movement and I'm shaking like a shitting dog. Spirit hangovers are the worst. I sit still and listen. The hoover's gone off and the place is in silence now. Normally Sammy would be straight in here at the first sound of squeaking bedsprings or floorboards. Debra must be out with her. Unless she's already left me. Whatever happens she's not keeping the dog. Sammy's my dog and I'll fight for her as well.

Though this isn't over, not yet. I've got to give it one more try. One more try in the cold light of day. I'll get Debra to listen. Twenty-five years together has got to count for something.

My tongue feels like a dead slug. I'd love to be one of those people who wakes with a clear head on New Year's Day and goes for a run. I'd like to be someone like Jay. Energetic and confident, with my whole life ahead of me. Instead, I've become a nobody. Washed up, bald and boring. And I don't know what to do about it.

5 HOURS BEFORE

BRYN 11AM

I FEEL SLIGHTLY MORE alive after a shower. Slightly. Though really, I don't know why I'm bothering. What's the point anymore? I might as well go around stinking like a tramp. My wife wants me out of here.

I tug on comfy joggers and a hoodie, whilst trying to ignore the sickness in the pit of my belly. It's a combination of hangover and what needs to be faced today. One thing's for certain, it's going to be a day to remember. After my final try at dealing with this mess rationally, if it doesn't work, there'll be no other way to go.

I'd make a coffee but I can't face digging through congealed plates to find a cup. I head into the lounge. There's no sign of Debra up here. She's either out, or in the pub, maybe helping Janice, whilst avoiding me. Part of me is desperate to speak to her, the other part is terrified of facing her, and facing reality. Every time I allow my mind to wander, all I can see is her straddling the dryer with that bastard between her legs. It's an image I don't think I'll ever be able to erase, whatever happens from now on.

My eyes fall on our wedding photo, blown up into a canvas above the mantlepiece. *Forsaking all others.* Yeah, right. We went off on our honeymoon to the Lake District, straight after our reception.

We couldn't have been happier. I had no family to invite, but in that instant, Debra became my family. After years of not being part of anything, I finally belonged somewhere. She gave me so much, and now she's snatching it all away.

I had the picture blown up for our twentieth wedding anniversary, and gave it to her whilst we were out for a meal. She loved it when she unwrapped it. Things were so different then. The kids were still living with us, and Debra and I still made an effort for one another. Nights out were regular. So were civil conversations. We even had sex. And what have we got now? Nothing.

I finally pluck up the courage to venture downstairs. Jay's hunched over the bar with the order book and a steaming coffee beside him. The fact that he doesn't even look at me sends my irritation level sky-high. It shoots up so fast; it feels as though my head might explode with rage. If I threw that coffee into his face, would it scar him?

I half expected him not to turn up today, not since I *physically* caught them in the act last night, especially with the entire pub knowing. He seemed to disappear when I went off on one in front of everyone.

"You've got some bloody nerve, being here. I thought you'd have stayed away after what you've done."

"My employment contract is with Debra, not *you*." He grins then. This cocksure weasel who's shagging my wife right under my nose is actually standing here, grinning at me. If I wasn't feeling so nauseous, if there wasn't a bar dividing us...

"Where is Debra?" As if I'm having to ask him for the whereabouts of my own wife.

"Out." He runs his pen down a page. Does the man have no conscience at all? Though looking at him, he's probably never gone through anything anywhere near like what I'm going through right now. He's that far up his own arse, he'll be the one doing the choosing, the deciding, the dumping. Women probably throw themselves at him. Women like my wife.

"I can see that. Where?"

"Get in touch with her yourself if you want to know where she is."

My world is falling apart and the woman doesn't give a toss. She's probably with a friend having a nice, cosy coffee. When I need her here. We have to talk, before it's too late.

I pull up a bar stool and sit astride it. Let's have one final attempt to reason with him. However much I'd prefer to rip his head off. Perhaps this can work. I really would prefer it to. But that's up to them now. To him. And to Debra. They're in charge of their own fate more than they know. And the stakes are greater than they realise.

"What is it you want here *Jay?*" I spit his name out as though it's a lump of phlegm.

"To get on with putting this order together." He tugs a box of crisps from beneath the bar and writes something on his notepad.

My fists clench at my sides. I should *make* him stop. *Make* him look at me. But I have to stay calm. I can't blow. If I'm forced to go to Plan B, he has to be here.

"Do you actually see a future with my wife?"

I glance around the bar to make sure no one else is listening. I know what they're like around here. Anything and everything is gossip fodder. There's really only Janice the cleaner, and perhaps Jennefer that I'd expect to see around at this time though. However, Janice seems to have been and gone. She's left the stench of furniture polish and what could be toilet fresheners in the men's. My stomach turns as I glance toward the propped-open door to the toilets. At least I haven't got far to run.

Jay laughs. "A future?"

"Don't you think I have a right to know?"

"We're just having fun."

"You mean *you* are, is that what you're saying?"

And that, to me, is the main problem. The way Debra feels about *him*. I've been able to see it in the way she's been behaving for weeks, no months. New knickers. More attention to how she looks. Changing the password on her phone. Avoiding me. There was already a distance between us but now it's as wide as the Gulf of Mexico.

"So you break up someone's marriage, just for a bit of *fun*? Tell me, how do you live with yourself?"

"I'm not the one who's married." He puts his pen down. "Therefore, I'm not doing anything wrong."

I wish so much that I'd insisted on taking over the bar manager duties now. Instead, I've handed my wife to this man on a plate.

"You could have any woman you want. Why go after someone who's married? Why Debra?"

"Why not Debra?" He runs his fingers through his fringe, a stark reminder of the hair I lost many, many moons ago. The kids used to laugh at my hair loss, not realising how touchy I was about it.

"Perhaps if you'd appreciated her, and treated her like the woman she deserves..."

"Like you do, you mean?"

He shrugs again. He's so damn sure of himself. I suppose I would be, if I still had his youth and good looks on my side. But I've got neither any more, and everything that's ever mattered seems to be slipping away. I've got to make him listen. If he'd just leave us alone.

"Look Jay, I'm going to level with you here."

"I'm listening." Yet he carries on writing. In a minute I'm going to rip that damn book from his grasp and launch it across the room.

"You've admitted that this thing with my wife is, in your words, *a bit of fun*. Therefore, I'm asking you, man to man, to end it with her."

He stops writing but still won't look at me.

"To give me and her a chance at sorting it out. We've been married a long time, like I said." I can hardly believe I'm doing this. Asking this man to leave Debra alone, almost pleading with him. I couldn't hate myself any more than I do right now. When he tells her about this, she'll probably laugh. That's all I am - a laughing stock.

"She doesn't want you any more Bryn." He meets my gaze directly, and I swear there's the hint of a smirk playing on his mouth. "If I hadn't come along, there'd have been someone else." He's repeating exactly what she said earlier. They've had all this planned, I'm absolutely sure of it.

Still, I'm not giving up. "No, there wouldn't be *someone else*. We've been happy together for years."

"That's what you think."

What the hell has she been saying about me? Of course, Jay could be making things up. "We've got two kids together, for God's sake."

"They're not exactly kids anymore, are they?"

"Look, what is it you want from her?" Not for the first time I realise he must see one hell of a meal ticket in her. Money. That's how I'll solve things. It will be a damn sight less messy than Plan B.

"Nothing. Nothing at all. And that's why she's fallen for me." He shuts his book.

"*Fallen for you!* You're deluding yourself."

"Whilst you... you depend on her for everything, don't you?"

"I'm asking you, no, I'm *telling* you, to stay away from Debra. Leave my bloody wife alone."

"We'll both be out of your hair soon enough." He laughs again as his gaze roams to the top of my head, where there's more hair on a cue ball. What hasn't left of its own accord, I've shaved away.

"What do you mean?"

"Well, I'm off, aren't I? I always said this job's short term. I'm going to go sooner rather than later. In fact, I'll be looking at flights after my shift."

"That's something at least." And it is. If he's really going, I'll talk to Debra. If she's sorry, really sorry, I'd try to forgive her. Couples get over affairs. Plan B has always been my last resort. And there's still time to put it on hold. If only I can get through to her. The fact that he said *I'll* be looking at flights, rather than *we'll* might mean he's planning to go first and for her to join him.

"Well, since you're in such a calm, conversational mood, you might as well know that Debra's coming with me." Jay steps back, almost defensively. It's as though he suspects I might jump over the bar and go for him. If only I had the energy.

"Coming with you, coming with you *where* exactly?" As I stare at him, my stomach lurches and for a second, I think the puke I've been holding down is going to erupt. I dart around the bar towards the sink and stand for a moment, swallowing and trying to get some breaths in. I fill a glass with water to drown the bile-tasting saliva that's filled my mouth.

"You OK mate?"

"You're no fucking mate of mine." My voice is a snarl. I gulp at the water. If liquid's going down, at least nothing can come up. "I had a shitload to drink last night, after what I walked in on." And I'm suffering on all counts this morning.

"Debra thought you were busy. You walking in wasn't part of the plan."

"So that makes it alright then?"

I'm too miserable to be angry and too angry to be miserable. She'd moaned about feeling useless when the kids moved out, calling it *empty nest syndrome,* or some other load of crap. And she was constantly complaining about nearing her 'half century' of years. I'd laughed and told her there was nothing to it, whilst making some wisecrack about her cellulite and saggy boobs. Jay probably compliments her from dawn to dusk. That'll be why this is happening. However, I can't lose her. It'll finish me. If it's compliments she wants...

"Do you know which friend she's gone to see?" I'm getting

nowhere here. My *last* resort is to get through to her. Now that I'm sober and can string a few coherent words together. By knowing exactly what's going on now, maybe I can save things. She won't leave me when it comes to it, and she certainly won't throw me out. I might not do a lot around here but she won't see me homeless.

"I didn't ask. I don't know her friends."

"That's just it. You know bugger all about her." I bang the glass down on the bar and he jumps. I'm glad. "Why can't you just leave us Jay? Let us work our marriage out."

"She doesn't want to work things out. She wants to come away with me. Within the next few days."

"When was this decided?"

"Earlier this morning." He glances up at the clock. "It's for the best."

It's nearly opening time. The regulars will pour through these doors soon, happy with their lives, their wives and their lot. Meanwhile, for me.... I've got to sort this.

"So you and her. It's for real, is it?"

"Nope, not at all. The last thing I want is to be tied down. Debra's setting off with me and that's it. We'll part company within a month. I need to find myself, and so does she?"

"Does she heck. Her place is here, with me, Hayley and Lance."

There's a banging at the front doors. "Is anyone in there?"

"Debra and I have agreed the way forward." Jay unhooks a keyring from his belt and starts towards the door.

"Agreed? Agreed what?" I go after him. "Look if it's money you want."

"Bloody hell. You *are* desperate, aren't you?" He swings around and faces me. "If you want my advice, you'll let Debra go Bryn. Let her live a little. If you think anything of her..."

"I think *everything* of her. Which is why I'm asking you to back off now. Look, just tell her you've changed your mind. Her life is here, with us, not gallivanting around the world."

"She's a grown woman. She makes up her own mind."

"What about this place?"

More banging.

"She's putting things in place. That's probably what she's doing now. I'm telling you Bryn. She wants out. You're going to have to accept it."

"But what am I supposed to do?"

"You're asking *me* that?" He laughs again as he turns the key in the lock.

"About bloody time." Two of the regulars push past me, looking as rough as I feel.

I should tear Jay apart for what he's done, but I doubt I'd have the strength to tear a paper bag apart right now. At least things are nearly in place for what I've got planned. Everything's just about good to go. If Debra thinks she's leaving with him, she can think again.

4 HOURS BEFORE

BRYN - MIDDAY

"Where have you been?"

"Out."

Anger prickles at me as she gives me the same answer Jay did. "Out? Where?"

"Just having a cuppa with a friend. Not that it's any of your business. Not any more."

Debra's sitting at the mirror in our bedroom caking her face in make-up. Dolling herself up for him no doubt. She's probably wearing matching knickers and the business. I've seen her bank statement. I've seen the cream, lacy things, barely big enough to cover her arse, poking their way out of the laundry pile. Two hundred quid in some fancy department store. She's never spent money like that on knickers to wear for me. She never even bothered to hide the statement, there it was, just sticking out of the letter rack when I was getting a drink earlier. I hate her, yet want her all at the same time.

"You don't normally get so done up at this time of day."

"Leave me alone, will you? The last thing I want is another bloody argument." She's got all the emotion of a brick wall. She wouldn't care if I dropped dead on the floor in front of her.

"So when were you going to tell me?"

"Tell you what?"

"That you're leaving me. With him."

"I have told you. I've told you until I'm blue in the face. Perhaps you don't remember that I asked you last night for a divorce. After the amount you'd had to drink."

She dabs a tissue over her face. Anger pulses in my temples. Exactly like it was with Jay, I'm not even worth stopping what she's doing for. I might as well be something she stepped in.

"You never told me you were actually leaving."

"Whether I'm leaving or staying, we're still getting divorced."

"Well, I've got to consent to that, and I'm not going to. Do you hear me?"

She smiles a strange smile. I don't know what she's up to, which makes me hate her even more. One thing about Debra is she's always got something up her sleeve. And I'm always the last to know.

"I need to get down there anyway. I've told Jennefer she can come in late with all she's got going on."

Our marriage is falling apart and she's wittering on about staffing levels.

"Loverboy can manage on his own. Me and you need to talk."

I sit on the bed, watching her face via her reflection. Her eyes won't meet mine. I search her face for guilt but I only see defiance, with a trace of amusement. I want to wipe that smirk from her face. How dare she treat me like this?

"You and Carl seemed to have a lot to say to each other last night."

I'm not sure whether it's a statement or a question. "I'm not on about Carl. We need to discuss me and you."

"What did he say? Carl, I mean?"

As usual, she completely ignores me.

"About what?"

"About anything?"

"Nothing."

"You were sitting with him for ages. You must have been on about something."

"Hayley mainly."

"What about Hayley? I've got a right to know if he's planning anything. So I can warn her."

"We haven't finished talking about us yet."

"There's nothing left to say."

"Well, I've got plenty to say."

"I'm going with Jay, I'm going to rent this place out, and you're moving on."

Debra's got it all worked out, at least, she thinks she has. "I don't think so. This is my home. You can't just turf me onto the street."

"You're a grown man for God's sake Bryn. Now the kids have gone, you'll have to find somewhere else. It's over between us. Besides, I can hardly get this place up for rent with you still living here."

"You can't do that." I used to love watching Debra put her makeup on. There was something really sexy about it. Now I just want to throw it on the floor and stamp all over it.

"I think you'll find I can. Have you forgotten it's all in my name? And it's not as if you can't sort out your own income."

"When did you get so hard-faced? I really don't know you anymore."

"When you thought it was OK to constantly poke fun at me, put me down and basically treat me like shit. I think I'm being reasonable; you'll get a generous divorce settlement."

"Surely what you're doing to our marriage is bad enough, without kicking me out of my home as well. In fact, you're doing exactly what my mother did to me. Do you really hate me so much?"

I probably sound even more pathetic, bringing my mother into things, but Debra knows full well what all that did to me. Especially since she never even came looking for me afterwards. And she died, ten years later, without us ever having the chance to talk about why she allowed my stepfather to attack me and throw me out into the night.

"I've spent most of my adult life looking after you... as well as the kids." She zips up her make-up bag and rises from her stool. "And now it's my time. I'm sorry Bryn. You'll have to work something out." There's an air of finality about her that says *subject closed.*

"But I want to work it out with you. Please love. Let's talk about this. I don't want this to go any further."

I threw my guts up after trying to reason with Jay before, but I feel strangely better. This is my strategy today. Talk. Be reasonable. Stay calm. Then if I have to go to the next stage and implement what I've arranged, my conscience will be clear, knowing I tried everything I could beforehand. The bottom line is that Debra is my wife and there's no way I'm going to lose her to him. Not just her, but *everything.* Including the respect of my kids if I don't put up a fight here. What they'll never know, and can't know, is just how much of a fight I'm prepared to put up if it comes to it.

"Bryn, look, you can beg and plead all you want, but I've made my mind up. We're getting divorced, and that's all that's left to say."

"Over my dead body. I've got to agree to it. And I never will."

"I've already taken advice Bryn. I can divorce you for unreasonable behaviour. And there are certainly enough examples to apply for an exclusion order to get you out of here."

"Anyone would think I was beating you black and blue, the way you're carrying on."

"You have done. Emotionally."

"Oh, give over. You're being ridiculous woman."

"There you go. A prime example. I'm going travelling with Jay, and nothing you do or say will stop me."

I snort. "He only wants you for what he can get out of you."

"Well, you would say that, wouldn't you? Judging everyone by your own standards." She sits back down again and sprays on some perfume. For him.

"You're just a bit of fun, that's what he told me."

She slams the bottle down. "Just leave me alone, will you?"

"He also told me that you'll be parting company after a month. He wants to go off on his own. Probably so he can find another married woman to leech from."

"I mean it Bryn."

"Can't you see he's using you, you stupid cow?"

"I wondered when we'd be back to the name calling again." She slams the dressing-table drawer. "You can act all innocent in this, but you're the one who's driven me away. With your chauvinistic, nasty ways. I've had enough. I'd had enough years ago."

"Oh, come on Debra." If that bastard hears me shouting, and tries coming up these stairs to interfere, I'll be pushing him back down them. "Whilst you're sitting in front of that mirror, you should take a long, hard look in it."

"Piss off, will you?"

I stare at her through the glass, seeing the woman I thought I knew inside out, but yet I don't know at all anymore. "I'll tell you what you should see in that mirror, shall I? A middle-aged, hormonal, and self-centred bitch who's making a total fool of herself. Just because you're bored. And you're making a fool of me. Can't you see he'll dump you when he's got what he wants from you, whereas I..."

"You'll abuse me and take from me for as long as I let you."

Debra swivels around on her stool and looks at me directly for the first time since I came in here, her blonde hair flying out behind her as she does. It's gone grey really, but she spends a fortune making sure no grey can be seen.

"The kids have grown up and gone, I've built up this business almost single-handedly, and it's my time now. We only have one life Bryn."

"Your life is with me. Our life should be together. We're

married, for God's sake. Surely that counts for something?" I stand from the bed and pace the floor. I really don't know what to do with myself.

"Once upon a time, yes. But this happens all the time. What is it - one in three marriages?"

"Surely we're better than that?" I catch sight of myself in the mirrored wardrobes again. I'm alright going on at Debra about how she looks. With my unshaven and lined face, hoodie and joggers, I look like an elderly chav.

"It's over Bryn. I'll keep telling you until I run out of breath."

"But I still love you."

"I tell you what." She takes a long breath in, then sighs it out like she has the weight of the world on her shoulders. "I'm going to give you some money up front, before the divorce, so you can get sorted somewhere else. We both know you can't afford to live here on your own. The only way is for me to rent the place out. Which I'd have to do anyway because of the business."

"Ooh, you're going to give me some money. And I'm supposed to be grateful, am I?" It's happening. All of it. She's leaving me. And as far as she knows, there's nothing I can do about it.

"And, like I said, there'll be something in the divorce settlement. Not that it'll last you very long, the way you are with money."

"Another dig. Carry on Debra. Dig. Dig. Dig. Dig. Dig." I sit on the edge of the bed. I feel dizzy.

"I need you to move out as soon as you can. Don't make me have to force you through the courts."

"You reckon you've got it all sewn up, don't you?"

"You can't force me to stay with you. I've had enough."

"I've got rights. You can't just turf me out of here." I dig my fingers into the edge of the mattress. I'll keep pushing her. See how far she'll go.

"If you make this any more difficult, you'll have even less. I've got witnesses, diaries. So we can do this the easy way or the hard way."

Too right. Though she has no idea about my easy and hard ways.

"So are you going to accept my decision, or what? Accept it and move on, I mean?"

I stare at the carpet. The carpet we chose together. I let her have cream even though I wanted grey. "How can you treat me like this? In all these years, I've never so much as raised a hand to you. OK, so we've argued, or I've been sarcastic, but..."

"There's more than one way to beat someone up." She rises again and walks toward the wardrobe. I notice the heels she's wearing. And the skirt. She's all dressed up for him. I would never have thought she could be this cruel.

"None of this would be happening if he hadn't come to work here."

"I agree that my meeting him made this happen faster, but I'm sorry. I like him and we're making a go of it."

My fists curl inside the pockets of my joggers. The anger is bubbling again. I've tried to be reasonable. With both of them. But they still reckon they're leaving together. It's time to make sure they're stopped.

3 HOURS BEFORE

BRYN 1PM

SAMMY WAGS her tail as I reach the bottom of the stairs. At least someone's pleased to see me. "Come on girl, let's get out of here, shall we?"

She rises in her basket, arches her back and then trots towards the spot where her lead hangs. I slide my arms into my leather jacket. A gift from Debra a few years ago. I was over the moon with it - when things were different. When we actually enjoyed each other's company. Everything I own tells the story of Debra. Of the marriage she's tossing away like a worn out bra. As I'm tying my trainers, she appears at the top of the stairs.

"Where are you going?"

"Like you care. Out with the dog. Or are you going to try to control that too?"

"We need to make some decisions before you go anywhere." She descends a couple of steps then sits herself down on the top one. "Starting with you staying somewhere else tonight?"

"No chance."

"We need some space from each other." Debra wraps her arms around her knees. She's got some fucking nerve. And she really doesn't give a shit about me.

"You mean *you* need some space from me?" I yank the lead from the hook. "Well, you know what you can do!"

What am I supposed to sort out for myself on New Year's fucking Day. I'm absolutely fuming.

One in. One out. I can't believe it's come to this. The selfish bitch. The switch inside my head has definitely flipped. Plan B it is - I just need to send a text.

"I just think... the longer we prolong the agony, the longer..."

"You don't seem to be in any agony. No. It's all alright for you, isn't it? You just wait until the kids find out about all this." I shield my eyes against the sun which is belting through the landing window as I look at her.

"Leave the kids out of it this time. You've used them as pawns far too often."

"Don't ever tell me what I can and can't say to my kids. You might control some things Debra. But you can't control everything. As you're going to find out."

"What's that supposed to mean?"

Jay pokes his head around the door bringing the hum of the taproom with him. "We can hear every word in there you know."

"Fuck off."

It's as though Sammy can sense the hostility. Her ears are flat to the back of her head as I tug her through the door, slamming it behind me, making her jump. "I'm so sorry girl."

I sink to the wall of the porch to our private entrance. Tears are pouring down my cheeks. I don't really want to do what I've got to do. I'm not sure I'll be able to live with myself afterwards. There's no telling whether it will even work. But if I don't try, she's just going to leave me. So I've got to go through with it.

Even the dog doesn't want to be around me. I have to almost drag her along our lane which makes me angrier. She keeps trying to pull back to the pub. At one point I have to carry her. But by the time we reach the end of the lane, she must realise we're heading to the park, as she settles down.

"Everything OK Bryn?" Gareth, our most drunken punter is heading back for more. His wife trails after him. If she didn't join him in the pub once in a while, they'd probably never see each other. At least she's not leaving him to run off with some man half her age in full public glare.

"What do you think?" I call back, wiping at my face with the back of my hand. "You heard it all last night."

"What I remember of it." He laughs. "You'll sort it out. You always do."

Too right. I damn well will sort it out. Once and for all.

I trudge along, the breeze chilling my damp cheeks, but easing my hangover at the same time. Debra and I would normally go for a walk together on New Year's Day. Especially on a day like this. It's as though the weather's taunting me. The way I'm feeling, it should be thunderstorms, not bright and sunny. We should be walking along, hand in hand, sharing our resolutions, even if they are always the usual crap. Get in shape, cut down on drinking, watch less TV, etc, etc. This year, well who knows? I resolve to stay sane, and to do whatever it takes to stop Debra from leaving. *Whatever it takes.*

The park makes me feel worse. Everywhere I look, there are couples, families, people who are content in each other's company, people who have something to smile about. Kids shrieking. Dogs running around. It reminds me of when we used to bring our two here. When I was part of a proper family. I can barely remember what it feels like to laugh, or even smile anymore. Not genuinely. I can't cope.

There's got to be more to life than this.

2.5 HOURS BEFORE

BRYN 1:30PM

I SINK to a bench and Sammy flops at my side. What I need is to hear a friendly voice. I tug my phone out to call Hayley. It rings and rings. My own daughter doesn't want to speak to me. Just as I'm about to give up, she answers.

"What's up?" Her voice is croaky.

"Sorry, did I wake you?" Though I'm relieved I have. It's more grounding than I thought it might be, hearing a familiar voice.

"No, it's fine. I need to shift from this bed. What time is it anyway?"

"About half one." I can picture her, with wild hair and panda eyes after a heavy night. I've seen it many times. Suddenly I wish she was back in her room at home. Maybe now, and only now, I can see why Debra's been so bereft at them both leaving. Particularly so close together.

"Bloody hell." Her voice changes. "I can't remember the last time I slept in this late. Anyway, Happy New Year Dad."

"Same to you. A good night was it? Better than mine, I hope." It's a good segway into telling her what's going on. She's got a right to hear it from me, rather than her mother's warped version. Or someone else's.

"Erm yeah, what I can remember of it. At least Carl left me alone."

"That's because I kept him occupied for you." Though I have to agree with her. Carl might be a useful contact for me, but him being my daughter's boyfriend is not something I want for her, no matter what happens from here. Especially now I know what he's really made of.

"What do you mean? How?"

"Oh we were talking on and off through the night. He came into the pub."

"Mum thought he might come looking for me. That's why she didn't ask me to work. Was that what he came in for?"

"I suppose he was looking for you to start with. He was thinking of going off somewhere else but I persuaded him to stay."

"What were you talking about then? Me?"

I suppress a laugh. She's just like her mother. Hayley always thinks it's all about her. "No, not really. Other stuff. You know, sport, beer, plans." As soon as I say the word *plans,* I'm aware I could have said too much.

Sammy's spotted a couple of dogs she'd evidently quite like to join in with. I tug her back, having no desire whatsoever to make polite conversation with other dog owners. Jovial small talk is something I can well do without. There'll be no one else spending the start of the new year in the same way I am.

As I suspected, Hayley jumps on my reply straight away. "What sort of plans?"

"Nothing much. Just with it being another year. That sort of thing."

"Are you OK? You sound weird. More weird than usual, I mean."

I take a deep breath. There's genuine concern in her voice and my eyes fill with tears. She probably knows me better than I give her credit for. If it's one thing I've got right in life, it's my kids. They're good, caring people, even if they come down on their mother's side most of the time. I can't allow our family to be torn apart by someone like bloody Jay.

"Dad? What's up?"

"It's..." I take a deep breath and it forms clouds in the air as I let it out. "Your mum's saying she wants a divorce."

"She's told you that *today*?"

"You don't sound very surprised." Hayley sounds more concerned about *when* Debra's told me than *what*.

"I kind of knew something was coming. I was there over Christmas, remember?"

"You did?"

"Yeah, I'm not daft. But that doesn't mean I'm not gutted. Surely you've tried talking her round though? All couples argue more at Christmas."

"Of course I have. I've done nothing else but try to talk to her." Sammy sits up and rests her head in my lap as though she can sense my misery. "But I'm no match for that bar manager she took on, am I?"

"Jay? I suspected as much. I asked her about him the other day."

"Did you? Why haven't you said anything then?" No doubt, Hayley will be all for her mother. No matter what the woman does she always comes up smelling of perfume. "What did she say to you?"

"In case you haven't noticed Dad... I've had more than enough of my own crap going on lately, with bloody Carl stalking me." She's turned it back around to him. She'll be fishing for more information on what we've been discussing. Even Debra was asking me. "And," she continues, "I thought it best to keep out of whatever's going on between you and Mum."

"She's leaving with him."

Hayley falls silent for a moment which suggests this information *is* completely new to her. "But... but he's going travelling, isn't he? Abroad?"

"Yep. And now she reckons she's going too."

"But how can she? What about us? Me and Lance? And what about the pub? She can't just *leave*."

What about me? I want to add, but I don't. I should support my daughter, not be laying it all on thick to her. But I can't help it. Who else can I talk to? I don't have any proper friends, just acquaintances in the pub. I don't have any family, only Debra and the kids. What a shitty mess I'm in. And I'm about to get in even deeper. As soon as I send that text...

"Can *you* talk to her for me Hayley? I don't like to involve you, but I'm running out of options."

"When was Mum planning to tell *us* that she's leaving? God, I can't bloody believe it. After what she went through with her own mother as well."

"I know. I thought that. It's like history repeating itself."

"Except we're not eleven years old, like she was. Anyway..." Hayley's voice lifts, "she won't go Dad. I'm telling you. Not when it comes to it. She'll just be flattered that some younger man's flirting with her. That's all it will be."

"It's far, far more than that. I walked in on them last night. *At it,* I mean." Debra will *kill* me for telling Hayley this, but if I don't, someone else will. I think I saw some of her mates in there last night, from what I can recall of last night, that is.

"What! You mean *at it*... No!"

"Like I said. My new year couldn't have got off to a more horrendous start."

"Ugh. That's awful."

"I really need you to talk to her for me."

"I can try. Whether she'll listen..."

"You've got to get her to see sense." A couple walk past, arm in arm. I can hardly bear to look at them. Debra and I were once like that.

"But what happens if she leaves? What then? She hardly knows the man."

I can tell Hayley's thinking of herself here but at least we're on the same page. "I don't know what happens love."

"We'll do everything we can to stop her. Me and Lance."

"Can you speak to her soon? Like, *now* really. Can you ring her now? Honestly Hayley, if we can only get her to change her mind, I'll treat her like a queen, I swear I will."

"Well, can I get a shower and a brew first?"

"I'm not being funny but time's really running out." I shiver and pull my jacket tighter. My backside is numb, sitting here.

"What do you mean? Why? When's she planning on going?"

"I'm not sure. But soon by the sounds of it." My voice cracks. I've held it together well so far, but really, my entire world is falling apart and if she doesn't see sense, then...

"Dad, are you alright? You're not crying, are you?" I'm suddenly reminded of when Hayley was a little girl and I'd given myself a belt whilst doing some re-wiring. The concern in her voice now brings that little face that once looked up to me for everything, back into my mind. I could kill Debra for what she's doing to our family.

I wipe furiously at my face with my scarf as a couple of elderly passers-by look at me curiously. Until Hayley asked me, I didn't realise that I was crying.

"I'm sorry." My voice cracks. "I'm really struggling at the moment, that's all. I'm so sorry to lay this on you." This is the longest conversation I've had with my daughter in ages.

"I'm not surprised you're struggling. Look Dad. I'm going to get off this phone and try to speak to Mum. Will you be OK?"

"I don't know love. I don't know what to do." The tears are coming faster than I can wipe them away. I don't think I've ever felt this horrendous.

A woman pauses in front of me. "Are you alright?" She passes me a tissue. "Is there anything I can do to help?"

"Thank you. I don't suppose you've got a magic wand..." then to

Hayley, I say. "Look, I'll get off the phone and pull myself together. All this will get sorted."

"I'll ring her straight away."

"Will you let me know what she says? You're possibly the only person who might change her mind. Once she hears your voice."

"I'll be back in touch as soon as I've spoken to her."

"Bye love..." I look up. The woman's still standing there. She reminds me of my mother. She's about the same age she'd be now. A lack of a mother for both me and Debra was something we had in common. She had a decent relationship with her dad, though he had no time for me. About as much as my own father. If it wasn't for Hayley and Lance, my dad wouldn't have anything to do with me. "Thanks for your concern," I swipe at the tears flooding my eyes again. "It's in short supply right now."

Then wrapping the dog lead around my fist, I set off again. It's good to have people being kind to me but it's more than I can bear at the moment. Sammy walks a bit more happily than before. She probably thinks I'm taking her home.

And she's a good listener as we do a lap of the park. Then another. Then another. I keep checking my phone. Has Hayley managed to get through to her mother? Finally, it beeps. I slide it from my pocket, praying it's Debra. That she's come to her senses, that she's not going to leave, and that she loves me after all. But it's not. It's Hayley.

> I'm really sorry Dad. I'm furious with her. Mum reckons this is something she needs to do. She says me and Lance should be old enough to understand. She even had the nerve to be mad at you for telling me about it. I'll ring you later. When I'm less hungover and have got my head around it all. Some start to the new year this is. xx

I read the text three times, searching for a crumb of *anything* that can talk me out of what comes next. But there's nothing.

I feel sick again. If Debra won't even stay for her kids, then I've no chance of changing her mind. But as I very well know, she wouldn't just up and leave on her own. Without someone to run to. Or should I say, someone to run off with. She's never been on her own. She went straight from living with her dad to moving in with Kevin. Then, when I met her, she was seeing someone else. Someone her father approved of. But in the end, she chose me.

I deliberate for a moment whether to call Lance. He's always had his mother in his pocket. If *he* begs her not to leave, she's definitely more likely to listen.

But his phones off. *What to do? What to do?* I try again. And again and again.

It's time to send the text. The text that will set everything going. I don't know what else to do. For the last hour, I've been putting it off. I've tried reasoning with Jay, then with Debra. I've even got Hayley involved. Everything I can think of. There's nothing else for it.

Two words. Two words that are going to change everything. I take out the old Nokia I'm using to see this through. Then take a deep breath and glance around, not that anyone cares what I'm up to. And even if they did, they couldn't possibly sense what I'm doing.

It's on.

I wait a few minutes. Nothing. I need to know he's seen it. That it's still on for him too.

"Why are *you* ringing?" The voice is sharp, hostile.

"Just checking everything's set."

"I already told you it was last night."

"Right. Good. It's just..."

"I got your message. But other than that, we said no contact."

"This'll be the last time."

"You just need to do your bit now. No more talking. We need to stay away from each other. And certainly no more texting. This *has* to look like an accident."

"We haven't planned it this carefully for it to fail." I sink to a bench and stare into the sky. It's clear and blue, at complete odds with the conversation I'm having. "It should be cut and dried."

"It better be. Your mess certainly isn't worth doing time for."

"It won't come to that," I blurt. "All you have to do is strike a match and get out of there. I'm not planning to do time either."

"Have you sorted the money?"

"Yeah."

"Two grand?"

"That's what we agreed, isn't it?" Debra hasn't noticed that I never banked the December takings whilst she was away. She's been too preoccupied with having sex with the bar manager to get involved in the minutiae of her business.

"Well, until I get the money, there's no deal, like I've told you all along."

"It'll be exactly where I agreed."

"Cash?"

The enormity of the situation hits me so hard it almost winds me. "I'm trusting you. You'd better not let me down."

"It's me taking all the risk here. *You'd* better not let *me* down."

"Like I said, you'll be quids in after this. You'll be getting a good share of that insurance money too."

"A third, you said. And three grand on completion?"

"Yep."

"Right so that's it then. Afterwards, I'm going to lie low until the dust settles. Pardon the pun."

I catch amusement in his voice. As if there's anything remotely funny. This is serious. Deadly serious.

"No contact from now," he continues. "Nothing. Afterwards, I mean."

"I know."

"I'll get in touch with you."

"Right."

"Delete our messages. And delete this number." Then he hangs up.

"Shit. Shit. Shit. Shit. Shit." A couple of lads watch me as I rise from the bench and lumber past them, dragging a startled Sammy along behind me. "It's happening Sammy. It's really happening. Life as we know it. It's over."

An adrenaline rush has replaced the sickness.

This is it.

2 HOURS BEFORE

BRYN 2PM

"Where's my wife?" I'm met with three startled pairs of eyes as I charge into the bar. Stephen scuttles back to the kitchen, saying nothing. He's probably taken Debra's side.

"Hey. Don't leave on my account," I call after him.

"You mean Debra?" Jay raises an eyebrow.

Jennefer busies herself in folding towels, avoiding my eye.

"I mean my wife."

He slowly turns away, back towards whatever he's doing at the dishwasher without answering my question. I want to punch him. He's ignoring me, carrying on as normal, even after being responsible for blowing my life to pieces. I don't think I've ever hated anybody so much.

"Hey." I grab him by the shoulder.

Jennefer slams a towel onto the pile. "Bryn. Cool it."

"I'm still the landlord here and when I ask you a question, I expect an answer."

"Since when are you the landlord?" Jay shrugs me off.

"Since *never*." Debra's voice cuts into the tension that hangs between us all. "It's my name above that door."

I've heard that line a million times. It will be the epitaph on her gravestone.

She's got so much make-up on, I could scrape it off with a trowel. And even though she's at the other side of the bar, I can taste her perfume in the back of my throat.

"Are you still here Bryn?" She looks at me as though I'm diseased. I'd give anything for her to look at me like she looks at him.

"Why do you have to be so nasty? Haven't you done enough damage?"

"I'm not getting into this again." She turns from me to Jay, her earrings rattling with the motion. "I'm off to see my dad."

"Done up like that?" I don't trust a word that comes out of Debra's mouth. "Where are you really going?"

"I want to say Happy New Year. Not that it's any of your business Bryn. Not any more."

I don't know why she's bothering. Jim won't know whether it's New Year's Day, Easter Sunday or Halloween. Nor does he even know who Debra is - I've visited with her once and that was enough. The place was depressing beyond belief, after all, it's where we're all going to end up. I've not set foot in there since. If Debra really is visiting her dad, I reckon it's to say goodbye before she buggers off with this arse hole.

"Jennefer, you might as well get going." Debra's using the pathetic, syrupy voice she reserves for when she's out to impress people.

"But I'm supposed to be on until four."

"I'll pay you till four. But there's no point in two of you being behind the bar, giving up your bank holiday when it's so quiet."

"It's not like I'm in a rush to get home to *him*. But the kids would be glad to see me."

"Had he calmed down? By the time you got home, I mean?"

She's trying to pretend like she cares now. As if. The old Debra might have done. But the new Debra doesn't give a shit about anyone other than herself. And Jay.

"He was out of it thank God. Anyway, enough about my dramas." Jennefer flushes as she looks around at us. "You all heard enough last night." She gives me a look which leaves me in no doubt that she's referring to my little speech as well.

"You know where I am." Yeah, Debra's kindness personified with everyone other than me.

"Thanks. You have a good time with your dad."

"We're having afternoon tea apparently." Debra clip-clops in her heels towards the door. Afternoon tea. Who the hell does she think she is?

"Hang on. What are you doing with the dog?" I dash round to the other side of the bar, noticing Sammy for the first time.

"I'm taking her with me." She twists to face me, wobbling on her ridiculous heels. "Have you got a problem with that?"

"She's only just been out." I reach for Sammy's lead.

"You don't get to tell me what to do Bryn. Those days are over." She tugs the lead away from me. The low hum of conversation becomes a funereal silence as the few punters dotted around the pub watch our altercation over the bloody dog.

"Since when do you ever take the dog to the care home?" Sammy cowers as I raise my voice. I don't know whether to be sad or angry at this.

"There's a lot you don't know about me or what I do actually."

"You don't say." I could laugh if the situation wasn't so dire. "I don't trust you one bit."

"I don't care. And if you must know, the other residents, and the staff love me taking Sammy into the care home, so I'm taking her. And you can't stop me."

Perhaps this is part of her grand plan. To drop Sammy off with someone so it's easier to take her to wherever she's running off to. She's wrecked the rest of my life as I know it. No way is she having the dog.

"You're leaving her here." I hold my hand out for the lead. "She doesn't need to be walked again."

"Get lost Bryn." Then she looks at Jay. "I won't be long." She's speaking to him like she should be speaking to me. I won't be long. She's one completely heartless bitch.

She starts towards the door, then turns back. "Don't forget what we arranged, will you?"

Jay winks. Bastard.

"What do you mean, what you arranged? Are you off? Today? Is that what it is." I'm just playing a part here, for as I very well know, she won't be going anywhere with him. "Come on. I've got a right to know."

How Jay's got the nerve to have even turned up today, I do not know. But though it pains me to say it, he's exactly where I want him to be. And for the next couple of hours, I have to keep him here.

Jennefer, even though she's friends with Debra, shoots me a sympathetic look for once. As the door bangs, I slide a glass from the shelf above the bar. I need a hair of the dog, Dutch courage and whatever other friendly term I can give to the double whiskey I pour. It's do or die.

The liquid hits the back of my throat, then burns all the way down to my stomach. Perhaps I should just walk away, but I can't, I just can't. She's my wife and I'm not just going to stand back and let her leave. Besides, everything is set.

"How are you doing Bryn?" Jennefer follows me out from the bar, so I pursue her towards the staff room. The door creaks as it falls closed behind me.

"How do you think?" I sink to the sofa. Although I am grateful for the crumbs of sympathy. If only this wasn't all I ever got from anyone. Crumbs.

"I'm sorry this is happening to you both. I have tried to talk to her." She reaches up to the pegs and unhooks her coat.

"You knew?" I rise from the sofa and step towards her. "You knew about them carrying on all along?"

She shrinks back. "I didn't want to get involved Bryn. Besides, it's not been going on that long."

"You could have bloody warned me. Why didn't you?"

"I'm sorry. I couldn't. I..."

"They made a right fool of me last night. And I'll never get rid of that image of them in there screwing."

She tugs her handbag from the cupboard under the sink. "Look, I've got enough going on in my own home life right now without taking on other people's problems." She slides her arms into her coat, untucking her hair from the collar.

"And of course, you stand to gain if it's *you* my darling wife asks to manage this place. You'll probably want me out of the way as much as she does. Yeah, I get it. That's why you didn't tell me."

"It's not like that at all. Besides, she's not said a word along those lines."

"So you say." I don't believe her. Women stick together. I've found that out time and time again over the years.

Jennefer checks her phone then drops it into her bag, whilst I stare out of the patio doors. Then another thought occurs to me. Jennefer's always been friendly towards me. *Over* friendly, some might say.

"Is it *you* who's taking the flat on?" Without giving her the chance to reply, I carry on. "Maybe, you know, if me and Debra really are history, if I really can't get her back, when all this is over, you know, me and you, we could..."

Maybe, if I'm in with a chance with Jennefer, I could think twice about what I've set in motion to stop Debra from leaving. After all, it's only a matter of time until Jennefer leaves her husband. Especially if last night's little display is anything to go by. If she sets up here, maybe I won't have to go anywhere. We could even start off in separate rooms if she wanted to take it slowly.

"You've got to be joking." She actually looks to be stifling laughter. "Are you still drunk Bryn? As if you're suggesting that!"

Women. I'm sick of the bloody lot of them. "What's so wrong with me?" My fists bunch at my sides. I've had enough.

"Oh Bryn, where do I start?" Jennefer wipes her eyes. "Thanks for that. I was having a crappy day before you propositioned me."

"I'm fucking sick of people laughing at me, do you hear me? Fucking sick."

Footsteps march along the corridor. Jay pokes his head around the door. I should slam it on him. "You OK?" He looks at Jennefer.

"Get back in there." I jerk my thumb in his direction. "I was talking to her, not you."

He doesn't move.

"Are you deaf? I said get back to work, in fact, you can ring the bell for last orders."

"I don't take orders from you Bryn." I've seen the same defiance in Debra's eyes recently. I'm nothing. A nobody. I'll show the lot of them how seriously I should be taken.

"Fine. I'll do it then. No service after two and I want everybody out for half past. Do you hear me?" I stride back behind the bar and ring the bell until its sound reverberates around the insides of my skull. "Last Orders now please."

"Already?" Gareth slams his glass on the bar. "I'll have another one of these then."

I ignore him and knock into Jay as I head back to the door.

"Hey - watch it."

"No, you watch it."

I push the double doors into the kitchen where Stephen's leaning up against the counter, messing about with his phone. "Sorry boss. How's things?" He slides the phone to the far end of the counter and strides towards the sink. He's still calling me boss. So that's something.

"How do you think? You were here last night."

"That's why I'm asking."

I look around the kitchen. "Is there nothing much doing today?"

"I reckon everyone's too hung over to eat. It's been mainly Ploughman's that have been ordered. But there's been nothing for half an hour."

"You can head off." I've got Jennefer out of the way. I need to get Stephen out, as well as the punters.

"But I'm supposed to be here until four."

"You'll be paid. Just go."

"I just need to load up the dishwasher."

"I'll sort it. Get yourself gone."

1.5 HOURS BEFORE

BRYN 2:30PM

I NEED to know what this arrangement is that Debra was on about. I can't imagine there'd be many flights on New Year's Day so they can't be leaving right away. Maybe it's to do with her seeing the kids to tell them she's leaving. Or perhaps she's going to the care home so she can let her dad know whats going on. Maybe the plan is for Jay to meet her there.

I can speculate all I want. The most important thing, however, is to make a hundred percent sure that Jay remains exactly where he has to be, for what I've got in store to succeed.

I return to the staff room and slide the old Nokia from my jacket. Then feel around for the scrap of paper with Jay's number on it. I scribbled it down from Debra's staff and suppliers book. It's time to send the message I've meticulously planned. I've been holding it in my head for days. One advantage I've got over Jay is I know exactly how my wife writes texts. He knows sod all about her really. Apart from how to get her knickers off.

> Only me. I'm on my dad's phone. Mine's nearly out of battery. I forgot to say - can you get the year end account finished. The accountant's asked for it. I need to get it through to him asap as he's going away too. I'll be back in a little while.
> Xxx

I stare at the screen for a few moments. No reply. I need to get back in there. Make sure he sees it. He *has* to be in that office. And he has to stay there.

There's only a handful of people remaining as I return to the bar. I pour myself another double and ring the bell again, spotting Jay's phone as it flashes next to the till.

"That's it now. Bar Closed. Happy New Year." I load a fake joviality into my voice as I glance around the startled faces. "Haven't you got homes to go to?"

Lucky sods. My time of having a home looks to be running out. No matter what happens from here, I'm going to have to start all over again. Hopefully it will still be with Debra. That's what I'm doing all this for.

I watch as Jay reads the message. He smiles as he types a reply. *Gotcha.* The Nokia vibrates in my pocket. I stride around to the other side of the bar, out of his vision. Once around the corner, I check the phone.

> Change of plan? Ok dokes. I'll text you on this number when I'm done, then we can...

Yeah, I can imagine what dot, dot, dot, means. The slimy bastard will be planning to get into my wife's knickers again. I scroll down.

> Bryn's just closed the bar so I'll get on with it now. See you soon sexy.

Then a winking emoji. The sleaze ball. However, it's worked. It's really worked. I allow the anger to dissipate. When I was first thinking all this up, there seemed too many variables, things that could go wrong. But everything's falling into place. What's meant to be always finds a way.

"That's it. Drink up." My voice sounds manic as I stride around the pub, but I don't care. Time, as they say, is of the essence here.

"There are surely better ways to spend a Bank Holiday. You've got a family at home, haven't you?"

"Hey! I haven't even finished that pint."

"You have now."

"Bryn. That's enough." I glance up. Jay's heading towards me.

"No. What you've done is enough. And I want to know what this arrangement is with my wife." I square up to him. "What were you on about before she left?"

"You'll have to speak to her." He walks back to the bar. "I'm not dealing with you." He wipes it down without looking at me, like I'm not even here.

"I'll finish up. Just get out of my sight will you?"

As the last two punters leave, I slide the bolts across the front doors, then double lock them before dropping the key into my pocket. It's a relief to drag the heavy curtains across the windows - to be in smi-darkness. It matches my state of mind. I'm glad to be alone, after all the staring and gossiping about the state of our marriage, the state of our lives. Well, I'm alone apart from that pillock who's banging about in the office. Normally, I'd have thrown him out on his ear. But today is far from normal.

I rub at my head. The whiskey has eased the pain somewhat. Another should sort it out completely. I head back to the bar. After necking another double in two glugs, I glance around, recalling the first time I ever stepped foot in here. That day was in total contrast to this one.

It was the middle of summer and the place felt like home the minute I walked in. It helped that Debra told me to make myself at home. I fancied her like mad regardless, but when I discovered she had her own pub, it was the cherry on top. I had to bide my time, but really, I couldn't propose to her fast enough. Who wouldn't want to swap an inner-city, rented terrace in Leeds for a lively pub in the sticks. I could never lay claim to the place though, as much as I tried. First, my credit rating was shot, and second, Debra was incredibly possessive about 'her baby' as she called the place. She'd sunk everything her dad had freed up for her, all her own savings, and borrowed even more, well beyond her means to buy her ex out. It had needed a ton of work doing, she told me, and tempting people to travel further for a good evening out took longer than expected.

We were out for dinner one evening when she broached the prospect of a pre-nup. One of her dad's ideas apparently. Initially, I balked. But, I'd have signed anything for the life I've been able to lead all these years. Until Jay began sniffing around, that is.

I jump as the landline rings. I go to answer, but he's got to it before me.

His voice drifts from the office. I stand, still as a stone, next to the bar door, trying to listen. But I can't make out what he's saying or who he might be talking to. Probably Debra. It should be me she's speaking to.

The man's taken everything from me.

And I'm about to return the favour.

1 HOUR BEFORE

BRYN 3PM

THE CUPBOARD under the stairs looks undisturbed since I stashed what will be needed in here. Debra used to go on about sorting it out. It's like Jenga. Pull one item out and the rest will fall. Thankfully, what I'm after is within easy reach. Matches, lighter fluid, napkins. I slide an ashtray from the pile. We kept them from the days when smoking was allowed. Debra and I smoked then, eventually using patches to wean ourselves off. We supported each other through it, just like we supported each other with everything in those days. I can't believe I used to smoke so heavily. Maybe it's just as well Jennefer turned me down before. She reeks like an ashtray most of the time. Imagine playing tonsil tennis with that. The thought's enough to remind me of my nausea.

My last job in the pub is to empty the bin from behind the bar. I need the rubbish for the staff room. I drain my glass before pushing it against the optic again. It's a triple this time. I'm going to need it. Hair of the dog has very much given way to Dutch courage. I carry the stuffed bag into the staff room and empty it into the bin in front of the patio doors.

Then pause. Am I really, really going to do this? I dart back to the door. Check in the corridor. A light is visible under the office door, and I can just about hear the low hum of the radio.

Jay must have finished on the phone. I glance into the utility room, blinking away images of what I walked in on last night. As long as I live, I'll never forget it. She's my wife, she's married to me. She's mine.

I return to the staff room. After assembling the napkins across the top of the rubbish, I douse the lot in lighter fluid. The pathetic Christmas tree in the corner catches my eye. Debra trots it out every year for the staff room. I slide it next to the bin and empty what's left of the lighter fluid over it. This is the tree's final outing.

Next, I unlock the patio door, then draw the heavy curtains across, pushing the tree and the bin against them. Lastly, one-by-one, I drag several boxes from the recent drinks delivery from the stockroom into the staff room as quietly as I can. Thankfully, the office radio seems to be loud enough to drown my activity out.

I could never have predicted what sort of end this would all come to, but here we are. It's the end of an era. We agreed I'll leave it until the last possible moment to ensure Jay doesn't suddenly decide to leave here before I do. There's a few minutes to kill before I leave for the final time so I head up to the flat for a last look around.

I inhale the scent of home like it's oxygen. I hope I'll be able to recall it when it's gone. Then I'm stopped in my tracks. Debra's left her phone on the kitchen counter. Lately, it and she can never be parted. I tap the screen. Off, of course. I hold the power button down. Nope, the thing is as dead as our marriage. Still, it's weird. It's not like her to leave her phone behind. When I sent the text to Jay before, I didn't need to pretend her phone was running out of charge - I could have said she'd forgotten it.

My eyes flit to the overflowing bin and unswept floor. She hasn't even complained about the state of the kitchen or the stuff all over the lounge. Another sign that she's checked right out of our home life and marriage. She'd normally go berserk.

Tears fill my eyes as I spot the marks on the back of the pantry door. Hayley, four, Lance, six. There's around thirty marks at varying stages of them growing taller. Debra thinks I dismiss them. She thinks I'm glad they've moved out. But she's wrong. I just don't weep and wail like she does. Nor do I go running off abroad with the first person who crosses my path.

I haven't been into the kids' rooms for a while, not since Debra put the brakes on me turning them into something else. *If they want to come back*, she said, *I want their rooms exactly as they left them.* Yet now, she's buggering off and leaving them completely. At least she thinks she is.

In the lounge, the Christmas tree bears ornaments the kids made at school. I don't know whether to fall in front of it and weep, or hurl it across the room. Life's never going to be the same again. It's all his fault. I never wanted it to come to this. I glance at the clock and sink to the sofa. Just a few more moments and then I need to be out of here.

I'm going to let myself out by our private entrance, lock up, then leave the key under the plant pot. I'll go to the front and hang around for several seconds in front of the camera, just to make sure I'm picked up leaving. It would have been better if Sammy had been here, then I could be picked up on camera on the main road. It would look as though I was taking her for a walk. Debra never takes Sammy to visit her father, so I didn't pre-empt that one.

Suddenly, I have a brainwave. The perfect purpose to go out at three-thirty in the afternoon on New Year's Day. A reason to close up early and usher everyone out with such urgency. I can't believe that I didn't think of it before. I'm going to drive down to Lance's. After all, he's in a right old state after being dumped by his girlfriend. And nobody understands how he feels better than me.

That's it. I'm going to jump in the van and head down to Leicester. Completely out of the way. I'll just text him.

And it's time to send the *let's go* message. Take the plan to the final stage.

I'm about to hit send on the second text, when footsteps approach the door of our private entrance.

30 MINUTES BEFORE

BRYN 3.30PM

I DART from the lounge onto the landing. "What are you doing here?"

"Erm. I live here, don't I? What sort of question is that?" Debra reaches the top of the stairs and the door at the bottom bangs behind her.

"I thought you were with your dad? Where's the dog?" If she sticks around now, everything's ruined. Her next move will be to go down to the office to find Jay. She might even discover what I've set up in the staffroom. It's a miracle she hasn't smelt the trail of lighter fluid in the downstairs corridor. All the way from the staff room to the office. Her perfume must be masking it. She probably sprayed herself with the entire bottle this morning.

"I'm just picking my phone up." She reaches for her phone and drops it into her bag. "Sammy's still with my dad."

"What's the urgency with the phone - is it so lover boy can get hold of you? Is that it?" I can't resist having one more dig.

"He's in the office, isn't he? If I want to speak to him."

"You've no idea what you've done. To me. To all of us."

"Oh don't start again Bryn. I've had just about enough of you." She stands with her hand on one hip, like she's really something.

"And I can't believe you involved Hayley. Fancy getting her to ring me."

"She told you that?"

Debra comes towards me, but I push her back. This is her last chance to put a halt to everything.

"Let me through. Now. I mean it." Her face hardens as she tries to get around the other side of me. "I need to go back to my dad's for Sammy."

"You can still stop this. All of it."

"Have you been drinking again?"

"If I have, it's because you've driven me to it."

"That's right Bryn. As usual, you take no responsibility." Her lip curls with the disgust I've come to expect. She makes me feel like a piece of shit.

"Why should you get to be happy when you've done what you've done to me? You've ruined my life."

"Not as much as you've ruined mine over the years. Do you want to know what I call you?"

"No. But I expect you're going to tell me."

"Manchild." She laughs.

I want to knock her head off. I'm sick of being laughed at and called names. Especially by her.

"What did you say?" I step closer, the rush of blood in my ears.

"You heard." A hint of a smirk plays on her lips, winding me up even more.

"You bitch. You utter bitch." We're literally nose to nose, so close I can feel her breath in my face.

"Ugh. You stink. Do you know that?" She recoils.

My blood finally reaches boiling point. I grab for her throat, then ram her back against the freezer. "I've heard enough of your constant insults."

"Get off me." Her voice is a gurgle.

For a moment, I contemplate squeezing tighter. But something comes over me and I let her go. "I'm sorry. I'm sorry. It's just..."

She edges round me. "You've lost the plot, you have." Her voice is full of fear. "And you wonder why I can't stand to be around you anymore."

I dart back to the door, blocking her way through again. "I just wanted to talk Debra. Let's sort this out. Please!"

"No chance. Let me past."

"Look, hear me out. Just give me five minutes of your precious time."

"Bryn. It's over. Do you hear me? Let's not allow things to go any further than they already have."

"What's that supposed to mean?"

"I want you to leave. This is your last chance. Get a few things together and go. I mean it."

"Oh yeah." I laugh wildly. "And where do you suggest I go exactly?"

"You're a grown man for God's sake. You know people. Your dad..."

"What planet are you on? I'm going nowhere. I've told you. And since you won't see reason, neither are you."

I pluck my phone from my pocket.

I hit send.

PART III

HAYLEY

TIME

HAYLEY 4PM

"YEAH IT'S ME." I let the door close behind me. I might as well wait out here for the taxi. The fresh air will do me good, the way I'm feeling. Ropey barely covers it. "Happy New Year bro. Have you heard from Mum today?" I pull my scarf tighter.

"She rang me before." Lance sounds flat, worse than he did when I last saw him on Wednesday.

"Are you alright? You sound like crap."

"She's told me what's going on. The lot. I can't believe she's buggering off. It's the last thing I expected. Happy New bloody Year."

"I know. I can't believe it either." I glance down the street. There's barely a soul around. All nursing hangovers, I guess. Not only is it New Year's Day, it's also a Sunday. Everyone's in hibernation. Plus, it's getting dark. It's barely four o'clock in the afternoon and the sun's gone down already. I hate this time of year. Drawing the curtains before the afternoon's even done.

"Have you tried talking her round?"

"She wasn't listening."

"She wouldn't listen to me either. She was going on and on about how she still loves us but it's her time now."

"She said the same thing to me. It's like she rehearsed it."

"How long have you known?"

"Only since today," I reply. "Dad asked me to speak to her." I picture Mum now, all hairspray and heels lately. No matter how angry I am, if she goes through with this, I'm going to miss her like mad. But, much as I love my dad, I can understand why Mum's had enough. She's always nagging at him to help her but he does sod all. And he gets into some awful moods. Luckily, Lance and I have always known when to keep out of his way.

"All this has certainly taken my mind off my shit with Sophie."

"It was obvious things had got worse with Mum and Dad on Christmas Day."

"I know. But I noticed nothing between Mum and Jay."

We fall silent for a moment. I inspect my nails. I had them done just before Christmas. The polish is chipping away already. Mum was laughing because I'd had them painted black, rather than a 'nice, festive red.'

"Jay of all people," Lance blurts. "He's only a few years older than us."

"It's gross, isn't it?"

"I'm not being funny but what's in it for him? Mum's nearly bloody fifty."

"Ugh. I can hardly stand to think about it." I reply. "Dad reckons it's her money."

"How is Dad with all this? I've had a message saying he's coming to see me. I don't know whether he means today, tomorrow or what. Has he said anything to you?"

"Nope. We were only on the phone a few hours ago and he didn't mention it. He must have decided since then." I'm not sure about him foisting himself on Lance. But maybe it's for the best if Dad gets out of the way until things settle down.

"I tried ringing him to find out when he means," Lance says. "But he's not answering."

"I've tried him too. Not so long ago actually. Several times. I'm a bit worried to be honest. He was in a right state earlier." As soon as I say this, I regret it. There's no point in Lance being as worried as I am.

"Have you tried Mum?"

"Yeah. Same."

"She'd be answering if she was at the pub, wouldn't she?"

"God, as if we're having to babysit our sodding parents like this. I should be laid on the sofa stuffing my face with pizza and getting over this hangover."

"So what now?"

"I'm going to try speaking to Mum. I'm just waiting for a taxi. I need to make sure for myself that everything's OK. Then I'm off back to bed."

"Why a taxi?"

"I'm too rough to ride my bike up there." Glancing into the porch window, I get a glimpse of my wild hair. I look a right sight - I haven't even put any make-up on.

"I reckon I might have more chance of getting some sense into her, face to face. If she's back, that is."

"Back from where?"

"Jay said she was with Grandad."

"Jay. So he knows where Mum is, and we don't."

"Something like that. And he said Dad was at the pub when I asked him."

I sink to the doorstep. Where is this bloody taxi? I tug my coat more tightly around myself, shivering as I connect with the concrete. Maybe I should have waited inside but Gemma has been doing my head in, going on and on about last night, and asking questions about my conversation with Jay. She started the moment I got up, as though she couldn't wait to tell me what had happened. Apparently Dad was plastered. He climbed onto the bar and was making all sorts of wild threats. Saying he'd give everyone something to really talk about.

Lance doesn't need to know about this. He'd be mortified. And more worried than he is already. He's had enough anxiety recently with settling in at uni and being away from home. On top of that, there's Sophie dumping him. Me and Lance have fought like cat and dog over the years, but I've always been super protective of him.

"You spoke to Jay? Why?" Lance sounds as shocked as I felt when Jay agreed to speak to me. Really, I think his curiosity won out.

"Like I said, I rang the pub and it was Jay who picked up. I wanted to speak to Dad really. When I got Jay, I asked him to call round here. It seemed like the right thing to do in the moment."

"And he came?"

"To be honest, I expected him to say no. But I've always got on reasonably OK with him. Until all this, anyway."

"So he came to your house? Does Mum know?"

"I asked him not to tell her. Or Dad. But I bet he does. I don't really want them to know I'm meddling. To be honest though, Dad's that desperate, he'd want me to do whatever it takes."

"Poor Dad."

"He said to me that he knows he's been wrong and that he'll change. He said he'd treat Mum like a queen if we can get her to change her mind about leaving him."

"I know he can be a total pain but I also know first-hand what it feels like to be dumped. Who'd have thought we'd be comparing notes?"

"It'll be a right pity party when he gets to yours." That was too sarcastic. "Sorry Lance. I meant nothing bad."

"It's not as if you have much more luck with relationships, is it sis?"

"Fair point, well made." It is. My usual heaviness returns to rest in my belly.

"Did you get anywhere when you spoke to Jay?"

We've gone completely off topic here. "Not really. Though he doesn't sound as serious about the relationship, if you can call it that, as Mum seems to be."

"Is that what he told you?" There's a hopeful note in Lance's voice. Our parents are far from perfect, but it'll be awful if they split up.

"He's letting her set off with him."

"Set off where? Abroad?"

"Apparently. He says she's a grown woman who can do what she wants."

"What about us?"

"He seems to forget that she's our mum as well. He doesn't give a toss."

It really shocked me when Jay turned up. Part of me had thought he was messing about when I gave him the address. But he's probably getting off on all the drama. I never realised what a smarm-ball he really is until today. He roared up outside my house on his motorbike like he was some kind of movie star. Leather jacket, boots, the works.

He followed me into the lounge.

"I'll cut to the chase here Jay." I made sure Gemma got out of the way, much as she wanted to be nosy. "My mum's told me what's going on. And I want you to leave our mother alone."

"Yeah, she mentioned she was going to tell you." He grinned. He actually grinned.

"What are you playing at? She's married. And double your age."

"It's not what you think," he replied, sinking to the sofa. I didn't invite him to sit. "Sure, there's an attraction between us, but it's all just a bit of fun."

"Do you know what you're doing to my dad? They're having their silver wedding anniversary soon." Not that she'd shown any enthusiasm when he mentioned it on Christmas Eve. I was surprised at that. She's been going on for years about wanting an eternity ring. However, there wasn't even a mention of that when she had the chance. "They had plans, they did. You're ruining everything."

"Your mother's been after me since the day she took me on as her manager." Jay's face relaxed into a wider grin. "If it hadn't been me, it would have been someone else, you know. Anyway, is that the reason you asked me here? Why aren't you talking to your mum?"

"I wanted to ask you, no, to *tell* you, to back off and leave her alone."

"*Tell* me?" He laughed.

"I mean it Jay. I will not stand back and watch you break up their marriage. They've been together for years."

"And why should I do what you tell me?" He folded his arms, his leather jacket creaking with the movement. "Surely your mother's entitled to make her own decisions."

"Because they're my parents." I raised my voice then. Maybe by getting upset, I could get through to him. If he could see that it wasn't just Dad he was hurting. "I'm hoping there's a decent human being somewhere in there. Someone who'll let them sort their marriage out in peace."

"There's no marriage to sort out. Come on. You're not stupid." He pointed at me. "You're studying for a law degree aren't you? They haven't been happy for ages. Debra might not admit it. But she's just been waiting for a way out."

"They were perfectly fine until you turned up." That's not strictly true, but I said it anyway.

"That's what you think. They weren't *perfectly fine* in the slightest. You only saw what you wanted to see." He looked out of the window, then back at me. "Your mum deserves to be happy too, you know."

"She is happy."

"She's wiped yours and your brother's arses for long enough.

And now you've gone - you're getting on with your own lives. Why shouldn't she grab everything life has to offer her?"

"Like you?"

"Like everything. She's still an attractive woman."

I couldn't believe he was saying such a thing to me. "So do you love her? Do you?" I sank into the armchair facing him.

He laughed again.

"I'll take that as a no then."

"She's a very special lady, and..."

"Do you want to stay with her? Or are you going to dump her from a great height and hurt her? After you've got what you want, that is? We both know she's got a few quid."

"I don't think our relationship is any of your business. So, if you've quite finished." He rose from the sofa.

"I can see right through you. So can my brother."

"I should get back to work."

We went round and round in circles for a few more minutes until I told him to piss off.

I could see what Mum saw in him on the outside. Yes, he's good-looking and all that, but there wasn't even a hint of regret at what he was doing to Dad. Or to us. I read somewhere that grown-up kids of divorcing parents, can be even more affected than younger ones.

"It takes a certain kind of bastard if you ask me." Lance's voice jolts me back into the present. "To be messing about with a married woman old enough to be his mother."

"I nearly threatened him with Carl," I reply. "He would have a not-so-friendly word if I asked him to."

"What, even though you've broken up?"

"I'm sure I could persuade him."

"I'd stay well clear of him Hayles."

"I know. I was only saying."

"Wait till I see that bloody Jay. He was all friendly with me over Christmas. I even talked to him about Sophie."

"I don't think you'll get a chance to see him. According to what Dad's been saying, it sounds like they could clear off over the next few days."

"You're joking! *Days!* Jay isn't supposed to be setting off until next month. He told me he still needed to save more money."

I blow onto my hands. There's still no sign of this taxi. "Mum's probably paying what he's short. That's the main reason she'll be tagging along, no doubt."

"I completely agree." Lance's voice hardens. "Surely between us, we can get her to see sense."

"For what it's worth," I continue. "If Mum goes with him, I reckon she'll be back with her tail between her legs. Once he's had what he wants from her. He'll certainly give her a taste of her own medicine."

"That doesn't help Dad now though. Or us. What an absolute idiot Mum's being."

"I know."

"I told her so as well. When she rang me before."

I laugh for the first time today. Not that anything's funny. "She won't have liked that. Listen, Lance, the taxi's here. I'll ring you as soon as I get to the pub and have made sure everything's OK. And I'll talk to Mum again."

"Make sure you do. And I'll let you know if Dad turns up here."

30 MINUTES AFTER

HAYLEY 4.30PM

"Double fares today, I'm afraid." The taxi driver meets my eye through his mirror. His eyes remind me of Dad's. Heavy. As though he could do with a good night's sleep.

"No problem." I'm so desperate to make sure things are alright, I'd pay triple fare. I can't even be arsed complaining about how long he's kept me waiting. At least it gave me the chance to talk to Lance.

"Where are you headed?"

"*The Dales Inn*, please."

"It's not actually open, you know."

I glance at my watch. "It's supposed to have been open eleven till four today."

Thankfully, I got out of being roped into helping behind the bar this year. Mum's way of keeping me out of Carl's path. I laughed when Gemma told me she spent her New Year's Eve collecting glasses, instead of me. Until I found out she got triple time. I'd have been lucky to get time and a half if it had been *me* working last night. I'll be taking that up with Mum, I will.

"Well, I was in there for some lunch with my missus right before I came on shift earlier, and we got booted out by the landlord. We'd barely finished our drinks."

"By the landlord?" I wonder whether he's talking about Dad or Jay. It must be Dad. Jay doesn't even look old enough to be a landlord.

"Yeah. He'll get himself a bad name being rude to his punters like that. I won't be going back. Do you want me to drop you off somewhere else instead?" He glances over his shoulder.

"Erm no. Thanks. What did he look like?" I'd better make sure who he's on about. "The landlord, I mean?" It must have happened whilst Mum was with Grandad. She'd have gone mad, getting back and finding the place closed on New Year's Day.

"Middle aged. Bald. Dressed like a teenager. What difference does that make anyway?"

"He's my dad." I sigh. "And he's found out over the last day or so that my mother's leaving him."

"Oh damn." He catches my eye again in his mirror. To his credit, I see a genuine apology in them. "I'm sorry for what I said about him. I take it back."

"Yeah, well, think on. You never know what's going on with people." I glance out of the window. We pass by the row of local shops, all in semi darkness. I'll be glad when this so-called festive period is over and we can get back to normal. Whatever that will look like now. *Will Mum even still be here?*

"You've got a wise head on young shoulders. I wish my daughter was more like you."

"I've needed it lately." I say it more to myself than to him, but he jumps on it anyway.

"Do you want to talk about it? I'm a good listener. Ask my daughter."

It must be nice to have a dad who'll listen. Mine never has. And he leans on me more than I lean on him. Still, the taxi driver doesn't need to know this.

"Nothing much to talk about really. In any case, I've got rid of one of my problems."

Hopefully, I can say this now. I've had a reasonably quiet couple of days as far as Carl's concerned. I told him straight what I thought of him a month ago. Since then, he's veered between appearing outside my house, and wherever I'm working, professing his undying love, to issuing threats of what he'll do if I keep ignoring him. And the police have done nothing about it.

"You sound as though you're referring to some lad there. Your boyfriend?"

"He wasn't really my boyfriend. More like some stalker who thought he owned me. I thought he was alright to start with. Then I realised he was weird. Seriously weird."

"Sounds like you're well rid of him."

"Yeah. He still goes in my parents' pub though."

"And they let him in?"

"They don't know the full story. There's enough going on with them at the moment without me adding my problems to the pot."

Though I don't say it now, knowing he was speaking to Dad last night fills me with a certain dread. I can't quite put my finger on it. I might have a limited knowledge of Carl, but his interests didn't seem to include sport or cars, as Dad mentioned. But it's these *plans* Dad hinted at that worry me more. I only hope they don't involve me.

"Who'd be having a bonfire on New Year's Day? Especially at this time of day?" I wrinkle my nose against the smoke. The windows of the taxi are closed, yet I can still taste it in the back of my throat. It must be one hell of a bonfire. Smoke's hanging in the air at every turn. People will complain about it in the local Facebook group, especially if they're letting off fireworks. There's not much they don't complain about on there.

I lean back in my seat, making the most of my final moments of peace before we arrive - who knows what I'm about to walk in on? Jay was going back after we spoke, so there's bound to be a right atmosphere. At times it feels like I'm the parent and they're the children.

"That's no bonfire. Oh my God." The taxi driver pulls up sharply at the side of the road. "No. No! It's not safe to get out." He swings his arm towards the door and there's a click as he applies the central locking. But he's not quick enough. I'm already out of the door and running from the car with the words *come back* ringing in my ears.

Swirling blue lights illuminate the darkening sky as I hurtle towards the front doors. Flames leap from the upstairs windows and my eyes ache in the glare of them. Oh my God. Oh my God.

Sirens echo in the distance. Then, a huge explosion.

My ears are stunned for several seconds. I stand, rooted to the spot. Voices and screams soar around me. Everything's gone into slow motion. Then, as the sound ricochets into the dusk, I finally find my voice.

"My mum," I shriek at a fireman as he jumps from the cabin of his engine. "And my dad. They might be in there." Then I remember Sammy. "My dog! Sammy! No! Noooo!" Again, I lurch towards the entrance of the pub. Our pub. The place that's been home for my entire life. My jumbled brain tries to reassure me that Mum's still with Grandad, even at this time. And Dad's on his way to see Lance. Maybe Jay changed his mind about coming back here. Maybe there's no one in there apart from Sammy. "Sammy!" I can't get through the main door, so I dart to the right of the building. I've got to get her out. Somehow, I've got to get in there.

"Get back. Stop! Now!" The thud of boots pursues me and a heavy hand lands on my shoulder. I shake it free and bolt forwards again. But the heat beats me back.

"Come here love. Come on. They're doing everything they can." Strong hands grip my arms and I'm turned into the chest of the taxi driver.

"I don't know what's happened. What's started this? Please. I've got to get in there. My dog..."

"I can't let you go." His fingers tighten on my arms. "If you manage to get in, chances are you won't be coming back out."

"If my parents are trapped, I might as well die with them! And my dog." The initial shock gives way to tears as Lance's face flashes into my mind. How the hell will I break all this to him? Especially if the worst is happening here? If Mum or Dad are trapped.

"I need to find someone." I literally howl the words at him. "Let me go!" I have to tell someone about my dog. "Sammy!" I'm screeching now. It's up to me to get her out of there. I don't care if it's the last thing I do. I spring away from the taxi driver as he loosens his hold, but he catches my arm again whilst I'm in mid-flight.

"Just let them do their job." His fingers loosen again as the fight drains from me. "They're trained and equipped to go in there. You're not. If there's anyone to be rescued, they'll get to them."

Another explosion scatters sparks into the dusk. A cry goes up amongst the crowd that's gathered behind us.

"No. No. No! Sammy!" My voice fades as the reality of what's happening envelops me. All I can do is sink to the edge of the kerb and watch helplessly as firefighters run this way and that, some firing water into the flames, others darting in and out of the pub. They're all in breathing gear. Vehicle doors slam and shouting echoes all around. Please. Please. Please. If there is a God...

We're herded further back along the lane as they stretch police tape from one lamppost to another.

"That's my home, my family." I can't stop sobbing. Mum's face appears in my mind with such an intensity, it's like a punch in the stomach. Then Dad's. I can't lose them. I just can't. In the distance, I'm certain I hear a dog barking. Sammy. My poor Sammy. I'm consumed by a grief I've never known. "Please God. Please God." My eyes burn and my throat's raw - a combination of smoke and screaming. I start to cough. I can't stop. I can't breathe. Please. Please don't let anyone be inside. As Mum's always said, things can be replaced. People can't.

"It'll be OK." The taxi driver, still standing beside me, pats my back. Someone else passes me a bottle of water and drapes a blanket around my shoulders. "They'll get them out, if there's anyone in there, you'll see."

"How can you say that? You can't possibly know that." I turn and shout into the taxi driver's face.

I don't know how much time passes as flames continue to lick the roof from the flat upstairs. Downstairs is in darkness. Smoke billows from smashed windows. Perhaps downstairs has been dampened down. If anyone was in there, I can't see how they could make it out alive. I can only pray that maybe Mum was taking Sammy for a late afternoon walk, or had stayed longer than normal with Grandad. But Jay said she wouldn't be long. And that was ages ago.

Watch this space, Dad apparently said last night. Surely he didn't mean something like this. Gemma said he was paralytic, and I know better than anyone that he comes out with all kinds of bull when he's drunk.

Something's happening in the doorway. I attempt to pick out the shapes through the smoke and the shadows. What's going on?

"No! No!" I leap up from the kerb. I hold my breath as four firemen hoist a stretcher out of the pub. They lay it down in the front car park. Paramedics race forwards, surrounding it, obscuring my view. There was someone in there. *There was someone in there.* Hysteria rises like bile. But who? I'm too far away. It's too dark to make anything, or anyone out.

After a few minutes, a fireman emerges from the crowd surrounding the stretcher. He shakes his head at a colleague. In a gap between paramedics, I watch as a sheet is lowered, blanketing the entire body of the person on the stretcher, including the head. That means... That means....

A blood-curdling wail reverberates through the air. Everyone in the crowd turns to look. Then I realise the sound is coming from me.

1 HOUR AFTER

HAYLEY 5PM

"I'M NOT GOING ANYWHERE. I need to know! Please! You must be able to tell me *something*."

"We'll need to do a formal identification with the next of kin."

"But that could be me! I might be the next of kin," I shout at the police officer. Then immediately regret saying it. It's like I'm accepting a reality that the body is one of my parents. "There's a slight chance it could be my mum or dad." I add.

Perhaps it could have been someone else in there. Stephen might have been doing some cleaning in the kitchen. Jay said *he* was coming back after speaking to me. Mum might have arranged for Janice to do a clean, or it could be Jennefer. Gemma told me Jennefer's pig of a husband turned up having a go last night. Maybe she was waiting for Mum to come back, so she could have a drink and a chat with her?

Bloody hell. What sort of bitch am I, wanting to inflict the reality of who that body is onto one of the staff? Anyone, so long as it's not one of my parents. And there's still no sign of Sammy. I've been told they're looking for her. The policewoman has got kind eyes, surely I can get her to put me out of my misery here. "As soon

as we're able to, you'll be the first person we give information to."
She squeezes my arm. "I promise."

I point at the tent. Figures are moving in and around it like
ghosts. "You must be at least able to tell me if it's a woman or a man
you've found?"

"We can't release anything just yet." She shakes her head and
looks from me to the taxi driver. "I'm really sorry. If you could just
wait here behind the cordon, we'll get some proper information
from you as soon as we can."

"But this is my family. That's my home." I gesture towards the
smouldering building. "*Was* my home."

I keep expecting to wake up. For this to be some kind of a
nightmare. I'd be able to warn Mum, Look, *stop seeing Jay.*
Something awful might happen. I had a bad dream about it. I pinch at
the skin on the back of my hand, just in case. No, it's real. It's
happening. I turn and search the crowd for familiar faces. Mum.
Dad. Both of them. Turning up. Feeling the same horror as I am,
finding *this*.

My phone's ringing. I tug it out and stare at the screen, hoping
and praying the whole time. It's Lance. No, I can't face talking to
him, not yet. I should allow him to stay unaware of this for a while
longer. It stops. Then rings again. And again. What the hell can I
say to him? How can I tell him what's happened? He'll go to pieces,
and I'm not even there to look after him.

"Are you not going to answer that?" I'm grateful to the taxi
driver who's stuck around to support me. He didn't have to. But like
he said, he's got a daughter my age. I'd be well and truly on my own
without him. The press have already been sniffing around. He got
them off my back.

"It's my brother. I don't know how to handle it." My throat is so,
so sore. My eyes are burning. And I feel really, really sick. "I don't
know what to say."

"Would you like me to speak to him for you?"

"No. Thanks. But this is better coming from me." I hit the button to call Lance back. I just need to get this over and done with. And I'll have to do it sooner or later.

For a moment, I don't speak. I don't trust my own voice.

"What's going on sis? You said you'd ring me. Why haven't you been answering?" The familiarity of hearing my brother speak makes me want to bawl like a toddler down the phone. But he'll be looking to me for support. Especially if the worst has happened here. I can hardly lay my grief on him. "Hayley. Talk to me."

"I'm sorry. I've..." my voice trails off. How can I tell him? Saying it out loud will make the whole thing more real. There is a chance that our parents are dead. Our dog might be dead. Our home's gone.

"You're scaring me now sis. What's going on there?"

"I don't know what's happened," I finally cry out. "Someone here is dead." Then all at once, the sickness I've been trying to hold back comes rushing up. Dropping my phone, I lurch into the bushes at the side of the lane, crying as it all forces its way up my throat and splatters around my feet. I want my mum. I just want my mum.

After I've regained my breath, I step away from the mess I've made, disgusted with myself. Everyone's watching. I look away. Try to compose myself. I've got to speak to Lance. Looking in the opposite direction of the pub, I try to pretend none of it is happening. But with the taste of vomit permeating, the memory of Mum looking after me during childhood tummy bugs fills my mind. Then another memory of her holding my hair back when I had a disastrous teenage encounter with vodka and orange. I remember another instance of her turning up at my halls of residence with Dad when I'd managed to poison myself with undercooked chicken, not long after I started at uni. And now she might be dead. I can't cope without her. No way.

The taxi driver's speaking into my phone and with his other hand, he passes me the bottle of water I left on the kerb.

"Get that down you." Then. "No, we don't know yet." He's taken over speaking to Lance. Maybe it's just as well. "She's been trying to find out... Yes... She's in a complete state... Are you able to stay with him? Look, give me your number so I can get directly in contact if I need to... And I'll pass it on to the police... Yes. I'm looking after her... Right. I'll let them know that... What time was it? But he's not turned up there yet? And he's tried calling? His mum as well... Right you are. OK, I'm going to see to his sister. You sit tight for a few minutes and one of us will ring you back." He turns to me. "That was your brother's friend I was speaking to there."

"I'm sorry." I wipe the water away from my mouth with the back of my hand. "It's just a combination of you know, being really hungover, and the smoke, and well, it's not every day a body's brought out of your home and you don't know if it could be one of your parents.... My dog." I yell into the smoke. "Have you found Sammy?"

"What sort of dog is it?" The taxi driver passes me the blanket I dropped on my way to throw up. "I'll ask them now."

"She's, she's..." I can hardly bear to describe her. "A little black spaniel." My poor Sammy. I want her. I *need* her.

"Everybody needs to get further back please." Two police officers force us all backwards. "We're clearing the lane completely. Come on. Right back."

"What are you all gawking at?" I turn to the sea of faces behind me. "Do you get off on other people's misery?"

"I'm really sorry love." A middle-aged woman comes towards me. "I just live around the corner and heard all the commotion."

"There's nothing to see," the taxi driver adds. "You might as well go home."

"That's my family in there," I yell out again. "You're all rubbernecking bastards."

A man elbows his way through. "McKenzie Marshall. Yorkshire Star. Did you say it's your family? What exactly happened in there?"

"You know what you can do?" The taxi driver holds his palm towards the reporter. "Come near her again and I won't be responsible for my actions."

"Is my brother OK?" I ask the taxi driver as we head towards the far end of the lane. "What's your name by the way?"

"It's Allan. And he's in shock, by the sounds of it. Struggling to take it in. He's got a friend with him who took most of the call thankfully. I've saved his number."

"The worst bit is the not knowing." I stare into the smoke-filled sky, feeling utterly spaced out. I still haven't accepted this is really happening. "I should be doing something."

"What's your brother's name?"

"Lance."

"Right. The lad I've just been speaking to told me that Lance had a message from your dad?"

"When?" Hope rises. Maybe he's sent another one.

"Earlier this afternoon." Then it falls again.

"I already know about that one."

"Well, he hasn't arrived yet. But Lance is apparently adamant that he's going to."

I try to assemble my thoughts. "Well, it's at least a couple of hours on the motorway." I point at the tent. "So that can't be him in there. Which must mean that's my..." I clasp my hand across my mouth as I allow the reality in again. "No. It can't be..." This is the stuff of nightmares. As if they won't tell me one way or another. I've got the right to know surely? "Mum!" She'd be here, right here, if she was alive.

It'll be all over Facebook that there's been a fire. It might even be on the local news by now. This place is ancient - it's a listed building. *Was* a listed building. I start back towards the pub. If that's Mum, I've got a right to know. "Mum!" Several heads turn to look at me as I rush towards the cordon and screech into the darkness. I'm sick of everyone gawping at me. It's as though I've become some kind of freak show this afternoon. "I need to know if it's her. Is that my Mum you've brought out?"

Allan races after me, catching me just as I get to the cordon.

"As soon as we find out who it is, we'll get you away from here." He looks thoughtful and I wonder what on earth he could be thinking about. There's certainly nothing that could help what's happened here. "Have you got anywhere else you can stay? Do you want to come back with me?" He passes me my phone. "Let me give you this back. No doubt your brother will be in touch again shortly."

"I've got my own place. I've already left home. But, no. Thanks. I'm staying right here."

I'm back on my phone again. I try Mum's number first and then Dad's. Mum's goes to voicemail. Dad's rings, then goes to voicemail. That's a sign. Maybe a good one. If he's on his way to Lance's, he'll be driving. "Did you find out exactly what time Lance got the text from him?"

"Twenty past three, his friend said."

"And he's not heard from him since?"

"I don't think so."

I glance at the time on my phone. Dad will practically be there if he set off straight after texting him. There'll hardly be any traffic today. I haven't been since the journey we all made down there. When Lance first moved into his halls of residence. I actually cried when I got back into the car with Mum and Dad. And after we'd left him there, it felt like someone had chopped my arm off. I wish to God he was here with me now. I didn't mean what I said before about wanting to go with Mum and Dad if that fire's killed them. At least I don't think I meant it. No matter what, my brother still needs me.

I slump back onto the kerb. Any minute now, Lance will let me know that Dad's arrived. All I can do is pray with every fibre of my being that it isn't my mother inside that tent. And all I can do is wait.

2 HOURS AFTER
HAYLEY 6PM

"IF YOU COULD all move to the side, please." I jump as a siren blasts from behind me. Like herded sheep, we all follow the instruction. An ambulance crawls past us towards the cordon. If that body is dead, then why an ambulance? I don't understand. Unless, there's someone else in there. Or the person who was dragged out isn't dead after all. But then why did that fireman shake his head? This is horrific. Why won't anybody tell me what's going on? Surely I've got a right to know?

A police officer lifts the cordon and beckons the ambulance on. A moment later, the officer who was speaking to me earlier says something to a paramedic, gesturing in my direction as she does. I hold my breath as I realise she's heading my way. Oh God. Oh God. This is it. This might be when my life changes forever.

"We can speak to you now." She nods to me. "Myself and my colleague. If you'd like to come this way."

"They want to speak to me." I grip Allan's arm. "What if..."

"Do you want me to come with you?" Allan says.

I let go and start towards the policewoman. "I should be OK." I call back over my shoulder. Though in the absence of any family, he's been an angel. Especially since I hardly know him. I turn my thoughts back to reality. What the hell are they going to tell me? I'm wondering whether I should call on one of my friends to support me, or at least let Grandad, Dad's Dad know. Though what would I say to him? *Mum or Dad might be dead.*

No, until I know exactly what's happened and exactly who has died in there, me and Lance going through this is terrible enough. I just hope he's being well looked after by his friends. Despite what I initially thought about him going back to Leicester, at least he's at a distance from all this. I'm glad he's there.

The policewoman gestures towards the crowd. "Sorry to make you wait, but the priority was to bring the fire under control."

"It is really under control?" I can't see a thing through the smoke and the darkness, just the outline of what was home. And swirling blue lights, wherever I look. I think I'll see them every time I close my eyes after this. Everything in there is probably burned to a frazzle. Me and Mum once had a hypothetical conversation about three things she'd save from a fire other than people. I can't remember what else we both said, other than photographs. They'll be gone. All gone. I said *Sammy,* and she said, *Sammy is family.* I agree. She's as good as a person.

"The fire's out," the policewoman tells me.

"My dog," I reply, my voice calm now. It's as though the fight's drained from me. "Did they find my dog?"

"I don't think so." She shakes her head as she lifts the cordon. "But the building is still under the control of the fire service. They'll be doing a thorough search. They know about it now."

"*Her,* not *it.*" I stare at the dark shape in the distance through the smoke. The way the flames were leaping from those top windows, I can't imagine how anyone could be found alive. Yet, somehow, it feels safer not knowing. Not for certain, about Mum, Dad and Sammy. Whilst I still have hope of them all being alive, I can just about hold it all together. Yet I can't force the sound of the dog barking from my mind.

"If you'd like to come this way." I follow them towards the

ambulance. The other police lady turns to me as we reach it. "What's your name lovely?"

"Hayley. Hayley Ford."

"My colleague has got some tea, Hayley, if you'd like a warm drink. You look as though you could do with one."

I nod gratefully as they help me up the step. At least it'll take the taste of my being sick earlier, away. My legs are shaky. The blast of warm air burns against my freezing face as I move inside. I didn't realise how cold I was. And it's so bright in here. I've never been in an ambulance before and have often wondered what it's like. Now I know. Aching adds to the stinging of my eyes as I come out of the darkness. One of them gestures to a seat. As I sit, my teeth are chattering madly and my whole body is shaking, not just my legs anymore. I seem to have lost the blanket they gave me outside. Perhaps now I can let go, and stop trying to be brave and hold it together. There're people around whose job it is to catch me. One of the ambulance crew wraps a foil blanket thing around my shoulders, the sort people get after running a marathon.

"So, you're the daughter of the licensee?"

I nod. Who knows whose daughter I am anymore after what's happened. I could be an orphan. The thought brings more tears.

"Debra Jayne Ford." She's looking down at her notepad.

I don't like the way she says Mum's name. It's too matter-of-fact. "Have-have you found her in there?"

"We don't know yet." She sounds as apologetic as before. "Look, Hayley, I know how horrendous this all is for you, and I'm sorry we need to do this now."

"Do what?" Panic grips my chest. Maybe they're going to ask me to look at that body.

"We need to ask you a few questions if that's alright..."

"But I need..."

"And obviously we'll tell you what we know so far. But it's not a great deal at this stage."

"OK." Although part of me is still happy not knowing. I really know what Grandad meant when he used to say *no news is good news.*

"Right Hayley, my name's DCI Jacqueline Leonard. I'm leading the investigation into what's happened here today, along with my colleague."

"I'm Sergeant Rachel Ellis." She gives me an attempt at a smile. "I'm going to make some notes whilst you're both talking, but first let's get you that drink, and get you warmed up." She turns towards the paramedic, who shuffles towards me with a steaming flask cup.

"Tea. I've put some sugar in it. It's good for shock. Try to get it down you Hayley."

I try to smile at the kindly looking woman as she offers me the cup.

"You look freezing. I'm Nancy by the way. I'm one of the ambulance team."

I take the cup and attempt to hold it with my shaking hands. It's no good. I'm slopping it all over me, all over the floor. It should burn my legs but I can't feel a thing. I bet I'm making the whole ambulance shake. I just can't stop. DCI Leonard plucks the cup from me and rests it on the stretcher next to where I'm sitting. "It'll stay warm for a few minutes. Let me know when you want it back."

Nancy rubs at my hands, the same way as our dinner lady might have done in the playground when I was small. It's a kindly gesture, and invites more tears to my eyes. This has got to be the worst day I've ever known in my life.

I don't feel like I'll ever stop shivering. Then a wave of nausea overtakes me. "I'm sorry. I'm going to be..."

Nancy hurriedly passes me a bowl. It's one of those that looks like a cardboard hat. When Lance was in traction with his leg when we were kids, I made him laugh, dancing around with one of these on my head.

I retch for a few minutes. I've not eaten today and really thought I'd thrown up everything I had in me next to the cordon. Normally

I'd be embarrassed, puking like this in front of people, but this is a far from normal situation.

"How are you feeling sweetheart?"

When I'm done retching, Nancy gently takes the bowl from me and touches my shoulder with her other hand.

Even more tears spring from my eyes at her concerned tone. "I'll be OK. I'll have to be, won't I?" Nancy reminds me of Mum. What I wouldn't give for Mum to appear in the doorway of this ambulance right now. If she's gone forever, I don't know how I'll cope. She is still my mother, even though she's been treating Dad badly by carrying on with Jay. I'd a hundred times over prefer to know that she's somewhere at the other side of the world, enjoying herself - not this. I feel guilty now for being angry with her.

Nancy holds the cup in front of me. "Can you manage some tea now Hayley? Take the nasty taste away. As I said, it'll help with the shock too, I promise you."

"I'll try." I take the cup from her again, and manage to lift it to my lips without spilling it all over myself this time. Right now, I feel more like twelve than twenty-two. I glance through the windows out into the dusk, hoping they don't send me back out there, amongst that crowd. I want to stay here, with this foil blanket wrapped around me, hot tea, and people asking me how I am in gentle voices. To be somewhere where I still don't know if my parents and my dog are dead.

"We could really do with asking these questions now Hayley." DCI Leonard follows my gaze through the back doors, then swiftly back to me.

"Are you up to answering questions right now?" Nancy looks me over with concern swimming in her eyes. "If you're not, just say."

"I think so."

"I'll be in the front then. Just holler if you need anything. I'll be back after the police have spoken to you. I'd like to check you over."

"Why? I'm OK. I wasn't in there."

"We'll just monitor the shock - that'll be what's making you sick, and also you might have inhaled some smoke. So, I'll see you in a few minutes."

I nod. I won't bother telling her I'm as hungover as I'm shocked. If she wants to look after me, I'm not going to argue.

"So Hayley. Firstly, how old are you?"

"I'm twenty-two." Why my age should have anything to do with this is beyond me.

"And what's your father's full name?" DCI Leonard glances out again. Is she looking at the tent? By looking at that whilst she asks Dad's name, does she know something?

"Bryn David Ford."

"And you still live here, at home with your parents, I take it?" She gestures towards the pub, or what's left of it. I'm struck by the madness of her words. No one lives here. Not anymore. I don't know if anyone will ever live there again.

"I moved out to go to uni a few years ago. Now I'm renting a place with two of my friends in the centre of town." I reel off the address. The other officer writes it down.

"Have you got any brothers or sisters? Anyone else who's still living at home?"

"No. My brother Lance has just started uni in Leicester. In fact, my Dad's on his way to see him right now."

"Really? Are you sure? How do you know this Hayley?" DCI Leonard frowns.

"My brother got a text from our dad at twenty past three this afternoon. Saying he was setting off to Leicester."

"Twenty past three." DCI Leonard sounds thoughtful as she glances at her watch. "Can I have your brother's number Hayley? And your dad's? We'll get this checked out straightaway."

DCI Leonard averts her attention from me and onto her colleague. "Can you get an officer onto this Sarge? Right away."

"Just a second. PC Haydock." Sergeant Ellis stands and calls from the ambulance door. "Over here."

"How would your dad have been travelling?"

"Either in his van, or in our car."

"Did you notice either of the vehicles outside there?" She jerks her head in the direction of the still-swirling blue lights. "The car or the van?"

I shake my head. "To be honest, I wasn't really looking for them. I was too busy trying to get inside. Besides, there's car parking around the back too." But I give her what I can remember of the registrations, which isn't much.

"We'll check around the back now and, if they're not there, we'll look them up on the system. PC Haydock," DCI Leonard nods at both police officers in turn. "If either of these vehicles are missing, we need an ANPR check done on them right away. Between here and all routes to Leicester."

2.5 HOURS AFTER

HAYLEY 6:30PM

"WHEN WERE you last inside the pub Hayley?"

An image of the cosy lounge bar emerges in my brain. With the annoying Christmas decorations, the cheesy music, and the fire I loved to spend hours beside. I've missed having a real fire since I moved out - the irony.

"Yesterday. I called in to see my mum. It was in the afternoon but she wasn't back."

"Back from where?"

"Leicester."

"She's been to Leicester? And now your dad's going there?"

"She was spending a couple of days with my brother. His girlfriend dumped him over Christmas and he was in a bad way." All this seems completely trivial now. Especially when there's a body laid out in the pub car park. But I guess they've got to know everything about our family. It's the only way they'll be able to piece it all together.

"Did you see your dad instead? When you called around yesterday afternoon?"

"Yes." His angry face fills my thoughts. He was probably the angriest I've ever seen him. Should I tell them this?

"And how was he when you saw him? What did you talk about?"

I hesitate. I somehow feel like I'm betraying him by telling these officers the truth.

"If we're going to get to the bottom of it all Hayley, we need to know *everything*."

If they're asking me these questions, perhaps they suspect something. Something really awful. However, I can't let my mind go there at the moment.

"He was in a terrible mood. So I didn't stay long." Should I tell them about why he was in such a bad mood? Should I? I've got to tell them. They'll hear it from someone else, if not from me. It sounds like the entire universe knows anyway. So I run through it all, prompted by DCI Leonard, right down to Dad walking in on Mum and Jay when the bar was closed at midnight. I can't imagine how shocking that must have been for him. I wish I'd been more sympathetic on the phone now.

DCI Leonard asks all the questions whilst Sergeant Ellis scribbles down my answers.

"OK, so next we need the details of everyone who works here Hayley."

I reel them off. "There's Stephen, the chef, but I don't know his surname; I only know that he lives somewhere in Addleton. And Janice Baxter, the cleaner, who lives with her mum at the edge of Tipley. Again, I don't know her address. Why would I? All the staff records are in the office. *Were* in the office."

Like there's going to be anything worth finding in there now. It dawns on me that if Jay came back here like he said he was going to, the office may have been where he died. Where the body they brought out was found. I'm able to tell them where Jennefer lives. I've been to her house with Mum often enough over the years. Then, there is Jay. Bloody Jay. I really don't know a great deal about him. I don't know his surname, or where he lives. Mum could give them chapter and verse, no doubt.

"Do you know who's likely to have been inside when the fire broke out?" The most important question of all.

I shake my head. "According to the taxi driver, Allan, who brought me here, Dad had thrown everyone out early and closed up. He was in a right state over Mum's affair."

"Right. We'll need to get a statement from Allan as well," DCI Leonard says to Sergeant Ellis. "Do you know how we can reach him?"

"He said he'd wait for me." I point towards the crowd. "He's been really good to me today."

"Did he tell you what time this happened? Your dad throwing everyone out?"

I shake my head. "Around lunch time - that's all I know. It was supposed to be open until four. But I think he'd had enough. He was really, really stressed when he rang me earlier." My voice is wobbling. I can't seem to steady it. What I'd give for him to ring me now. He's a lot of things, I know he is, but he's still my dad.

Though I have a sense that he's safe. They'll spot his car or van on the cameras soon. In fact, he's probably got to Lance's by now. I just pray he has. I choke back a sob as I close my eyes. But please don't let it be Mum in that tent. Let it be one of the others, no matter how awful a person this makes me for thinking it.

"OK Hayley. That's enough for now. We'll let you get checked over." DCI Leonard rises from her seat.

"But, but what now? You said you'd tell me what..." My voice trails off.

"Over the next day or two, and when we know more, we'll take a full written statement from you."

"But what can you tell me about who you've brought out?" I need to know. They can't walk away without telling me if Mum's dead or not.

"I can tell you, as you've witnessed, that one casualty has been recovered from the fire. So far, that is the only casualty, but the fire service are still conducting a thorough search of the building. Obviously, we'll keep you posted if anything else is found."

I wonder why she says *anything* rather than *anyone*. She probably means Sammy too. "When will they be finished?"

She looks at me, sympathy swimming in her eyes. "It's difficult to say. The building's extremely unsafe. But as soon as we know more, we'll let you know too."

"What about the person in the tent?"

"Unfortunately, this person is deceased."

"What about my dog?" If I keep asking them repeatedly, they might tell me something.

She shakes her head. "There's no news yet. But like I said, some parts of the building can't be entered just yet for safety reasons."

"Can't you tell me anything more?" Really, I want to scream at her. *How would you feel if this could be one of YOUR parents? Or YOUR dog?*

"The body we've recovered is too badly burned to say anything more definite, I'm really sorry." In her defence, she looks genuinely sorry. "We're going to be relying on DNA and dental records to do any formal identification."

I once saw a burning body on a horror film. My mouth fills with saliva again, as it dawns on me that the awful smell that's been mingled in with the thick smoke is possibly one of burnt human flesh.

"You're joking. How long will that take?" Though really, if we don't get hold of Mum within the next couple of hours, we'll be able to draw our own conclusions about who's died today. I take out my phone to try her again. She normally answers within a few rings when it's me or Lance - she always has done. I've got an awful feeling, a really awful feeling.

"It will speed things up if we can get a DNA sample from you. That will at least prove a family connection, or not, with the deceased, so then we'd be able to say if it was one of your parents."

The deceased. One of your parents. I close my eyes. Though it still could be Jay in that tent. If he went back to the pub after we spoke, it really could be. That's what he said - it's definitely what he said. *I've got work to do.*

"When do you want the sample? How soon will you know?" I need to hear the words, *there's no family connection.*

"We can take you to the station after Nancy's checked you over if that's alright. And I'm sure we'll know much more within the next twenty-four hours." She rests her hand on my shoulder. "We'll be transporting the victim from here shortly, so we can begin the identification process as soon as possible."

Twenty-four hours. How I'm going to wait that long, I don't know.

"Will I have to identify the person? Actually see them?" I think of the crime dramas I usually enjoy watching whilst sitting with my parents. I don't think I'll ever watch them again after this. "If you think it's my mum or dad, I mean?"

She shakes her head. "Unfortunately, the injuries are too severe for a visual identification. So no. We won't be putting you through that."

"Whoever it is must have died in agony." Much as I despise Jay for blowing my parents' marriage to smithereens, he didn't deserve this.

4 HOURS AFTER
HAYLEY 8PM

"THERE'S STILL no sign of Dad - he's not answering." Lance sounds hysterical. "Where are you sis? Are you still there? At home, I mean?"

Home. What the hell does the word mean any more? Wait until he sees the state of the place. He won't be calling it *home* then.

"I'm at the police station," I tell him. "The police brought me here."

"Why? What are you doing there?"

"Giving a DNA sample. And a statement." There's an engine roaring in the background. "Where are you?"

"On the M1," he shouts. "JJ's driving me back."

"Right." Part of me wants to protect him from all this. The other part of me needs my little brother like never before. "How long will you be?"

"About an hour. What are you giving a DNA sample for?"

"I'll tell you when you get here."

"I've left Dad a note to ring me when he turns up at the halls. Maybe he's stopped off for something to eat."

Something plummets within me as I glance at the clock. It's nearly four hours since Dad sent the message. "He'd have been there ages ago if he was heading to you Lance. And there'll be nowhere open for food - it's New Year's Day."

"He might have had a puncture."

"Yeah. Maybe." I'll let him hang onto his hope. "The police are checking out the registration anyway. They're going to let me know."

"Ring me as soon as they tell you anything. Promise me."

"Of course I will. I'm glad you're on your way Lance." Just talking to him is a comfort. Tears prickle at my eyes. We've always had each other's backs. We always will. And somehow, we'll help each other get through this, whatever the outcome.

"He'll be fine sis. And so will Mum. I'd be able to feel it if something awful had happened."

That's what I thought to start with. Lance hasn't asked about Sammy so I don't mention her. If by some miracle all three of them have survived this, I'll never take any of them for granted again. Every single day, I'll walk Sammy, and buy her some new toys. I'll laugh at all Dad's jokes. I'll book a spa day for me and Mum. Maybe Mum and Dad will appreciate each other again. As if it could take something like this to bring them back together.

"I'll come straight to the police station, shall I?" Lance's voice slices back into my thoughts. "Is it the one in Tipley?"

"I don't see why they needed a statement from me as well," Lance says as we leave the police station. "I was miles away when the pub caught fire."

It's a relief to swap the stifling pumped out heat for the freezing evening air again. My cheeks are burning.

"I thought we would never get out of there. But I guess you were the last person to hear from Dad."

"Don't say it like that Hayley." Lance zips his coat up. "You make it sound as though he's not coming back."

"Are you going to call your friend to pick us up?" Tucking my coat under myself, I lower onto the wall of the police station. They offered to let us wait inside whilst we got ourselves sorted. DCI Leonard offered a lift but said we'd be waiting half an hour before an officer would be free to take us. I just wanted to get out of there. I stare into the sky. The smoke is still hanging in the air. I'll probably taste it in the back of my throat forever.

Lance raises his phone to his ear as he sits beside me, then crosses one foot over the other.

"New trainers?"

He nods.

"They look expensive." Then I immediately feel bad for noticing something as normal as my brother's new trainers.

"Yo. Bro. Can you come get us? Yeah... I'll tell you soon. In a bit."

With the extent of my brother's telephone conversations, he wonders why I never ring him whilst he's at uni. He always starts with *yo* and ends with *in a bit*. And he makes me laugh with how he calls everyone *bro*. I link his arm with mine as we sit side by side. Him just being here is keeping me sane right now. I've got to keep it together for his sake, and to be honest, some of his positivity is rubbing off.

A Corsa pulls up alongside us with a screech.

"I can't believe he's driving like a nutter outside a police station." Lance laughs as he rises from the wall and opens the passenger door. "You were quick."

"I was parked up nearby." The lad replies in his Brummy accent as I slide into the back behind Lance. He thumps at the stereo's off switch. "I don't know it round here, do I?"

"Hayley, JJ. JJ, Hayley."

"Good to meet you Hayley. How are you doing?"

"You know."

He twists in his seat to look at me. "Sorry, silly question... I can't imagine what you must both be going through."

"Where to?"

"I want to look at the pub," Lance replies.

"You sure bro?" It sounds strange hearing someone else calling my brother *bro*.

"I'll direct you." I lean forward between their seats. "At least we can check that nothing else has been found." I can't use the word *no-one*.

"I can't believe we have to wait until tomorrow for that identification." Lance droops in his seat. "But hopefully they'll both be in touch tonight - Mum *and* Dad. And one of them will have Sammy with them." He wipes at his face with the back of his hand. I reach forward and squeeze his shoulder. My little brother has done far too much crying lately.

He visibly stiffens in his seat as we pull up in front of the road closed sign. "I kind of didn't believe it before," he says. "This can't be happening."

"Can we park up and walk?" JJ switches the engine off.

"Stay here, I'll find out."

It's the same officer as before, PC Haydock. "Can we go through?" I call out as I walk towards him. "My brother's here now. He wants to see what's happened."

"I'm sorry. I'm under strict orders not to let anyone through." He stands there, legs apart, as though he's someone really important. "It's really not safe."

"I thought they'd put the downstairs out."

"There was another explosion, after you'd gone, I mean. I'm surprised you didn't hear it."

"You're joking." *Joking?* What a stupid thing to say.

"They think it's the water heater tank that went. Whatever it is, they've called off the inside search until daylight."

"But, but what if...". My voice trails off. That's three explosions. If anyone was in there besides the body that's been brought out, it's not looking good. A sob catches in my throat. "Look," I step closer to him, "no one's telling me anything. Me and my brother," I glance back in response to the car door banging. "We need to know. Surely you can tell me something?"

He shakes his head. "I can't..."

"He won't let us through," I say to Lance as he approaches us.

"I can't let you though," PC Haydock replies. "Look, I'm really sorry."

"You would be if it was *your* mum." Lance stares into the distance. "*Your* dad. *Your* home."

All falls silent between us. For a moment I have an urge just to run for it. Run in there. See what's happening. But what good will that do? We still won't know.

"And dog," I add, my voice almost a whisper.

"Sammy!" Lance's voice rises into the darkness as he breaks into a sprint.

16 HOURS AFTER

HAYLEY 8AM

I'VE HEARD people talk about that first few seconds in the morning. When you wake after something dreadful has happened. There's a moment, just a moment, when everything feels normal. Then it all comes flooding back. A tiny piece of respite before everything hits with the force of a tsunami.

I lie for a few moments, staring at the ceiling, not wanting to face the day. I move my attention to the window. The sun seeping around the edge of the curtains is not welcome. This is the day when we might find out that one or both of our parents has died. This is not a day for sunshine.

"Lance." I reach across to shake one of his size eleven feet. We haven't slept top and tail since he was scared of the dark when we were kids. "Wake up." I reach for my phone and call Mum's number. I haven't tried it since three am.

This is Debra Ford. Sorry I can't take your call right now but please leave your name and number and I'll get back to you as soon as I can.

"Mum, this must be the millionth time I've rung. Please, please, please call me back. I just need to know you're alright."

Then Dad.

This is Bryn Ford. Leave a message.

"Dad, it's me. Again. Please, please be OK. Please just be drunk somewhere. Call me back the minute you get this."

Lance still doesn't move. Maybe I should leave him in his land of wherever he is for a few more minutes. Sleep is the best escape.

I send Jay another message through social media.

> You must have heard about the fire. Have you heard from my mum? I need you to let us know as soon as you get this. We're really worried.

He's showing as not having been active for one day. So is Mum when I click through to her profile. The fact they're both inactive is surely a good thing? It could mean they're together somewhere. But they must have been on the moon not to have heard what's happened here. Or to have smelt the smoke last night. Just so long as she's not trapped in the burnt out wreckage of that pub.

And maybe Dad *did* have car problems on his way to Leicester and checked into a hotel somewhere. He perhaps wouldn't have thought to let me or Lance know - it's not as if we're still living at home. My heart sinks again at the word *home*. I might have moved out now, but *The Dales Inn* was all I ever knew as home until starting university.

Another thought intrudes into my mind. On the day after Boxing Day, Mum was on and on at Dad to get the car serviced, so perhaps something really has blown on the motorway. That's why she and Lance went on the train down to Leicester. The police said the car's gone from the pub and there's been no sign of it so far anywhere. It's probably stuck in a garage between here and Leicester whilst Dad sunk a few beers in a hotel bar last night.

No matter what, someone is dead. However, whilst we know nothing for certain, we can still have hope that it's not either of our parents. And that's what I'm clinging to. I'd go insane otherwise.

"Well?" Lance sits bolt upright as though our reality has just clobbered him. He reaches for his phone too. "There must be something by now. It's the not knowing that's killing me." He rubs his eyes with his other hand.

"Me too." I swing my legs over the side of the bed, resisting the urge to mention that he's looked dead to the world whilst I've been tossing and turning most of the night. "Look, let's get sorted and get back down to the police station. They might have those DNA results back. If not, we'll wait there until they do. Will JJ drive us?"

"Yep. I'll go and wake him." Lance puts his phone beside him on the bed. "I can't go on like this sis." He draws his skinny legs up from beneath the duvet and hugs them to his chest. "I keep thinking that if I hadn't got myself into such a state over Sophie, I'd have still been at home and it would never have happened, and..."

"Stop it Lance. How can what's happened be your fault? Or mine? For all we know, it might just be some electrical fault - Mum was on at Dad to fix something, wasn't she?"

"Yeah, but he wasn't listening."

"Let's try not to panic again. Mum, Dad and Sammy might all turn up today."

"God, I hope so." Lance looks thoughtful for a moment. "Though I have to say, the more time that goes on, the more I think they won't - unless..." he pauses, "was Jay definitely cashing up at that time?" A flicker of hope crosses his face, and if I know my brother correctly, he'll soon be feeling as guilty as I do for thinking such a thing.

I nod. "He was definitely going back to the pub. I've gone over and over it in my head. With it being the month-end, and year-end, he probably had loads of work to finish. Especially if they were planning on leaving soon. Accounts, wages, ordering, that sort of thing."

I've helped Mum several times with all this. Jay might be a lot of things but he's been a good bar manager. Though that's not necessarily why Mum hired him.

"Did you tell all this to the police?"

"Yeah. Course I did."

"It's not looking good, is it Hayley? None of it. What if it is... *was* Jay that was brought out, but Mum, Dad and Sammy are still trapped in there somewhere?"

"Surely they'd have found them by now. They've been searching, haven't they? They know what they're doing, what to look for."

"But they stopped the search overnight."

"They'll have started again by now, I reckon, what time is it?" I tilt my watch towards me. "Yeah, it's been light for over an hour, and according to the police, as long as the building, and each room was safe to enter, the fire crew won't stop searching until they're absolutely certain there's no one else in there."

"Come on. Let's get moving."

At first I think I'm seeing things. There, on the road at the end of my path, Mum is locking up her car as though nothing has happened. She's wearing make-up, her hair is damp from the shower and she looks, well, normal, really.

"Mum!" Time stands still as I bolt towards the door.

As Mum opens the boot, Sammy leaps out and comes hurtling towards me. I bend to make a fuss of her as she leaps up, squealing in delight and licking at my ears, something I'd never normally allow her to do.

"Oh my God. You're both safe. Mum! Oh my God."

With Sammy still jumping around my heels, making all her excited noises, I run towards Mum and give her the sort of hug I'd have given her when I used to think she'd abandoned me at school, but then came back again.

"Now that's what I call a warm welcome." She laughs, but it's weak. I can tell from her face that she's heard.

"Where have you been Mum?"

Sammy's running around our feet, still going berserk. Lance

comes running out next, rubbing his head with a towel. For a moment, he just stands there, gaping at us all.

"Well, you're a sight for sore eyes," he eventually says. Bless him, he looks as though he's going to cry.

"Come here son." Mum finally speaks and lets go of me with one arm to stretch it towards Lance. He's not usually one for public displays of affection but he strides over and hugs Mum like he possibly never has before.

"Where've you been all night?" Lance echoes my question. We both look at her.

"I've only just heard about the pub." She looks down at the floor. "Or I'd have been here earlier."

"Oh Mum. It's been awful. Everything's gone. And Dad..." my voice trails off. If we don't allude to the fact he might be dead, he won't be. I'm still clinging to the illusion that the body is Jay. Yes, Mum will be gutted but we'll look after her.

I know it isn't Stephen, Jennefer or Janice because I've spoken to them all. Jennefer came round last night in absolute bits. Stephen turned up at the pub just after they took the body away, and Janice rang me in tears. They're all as much in shock as I am about it. None of them had any way of getting hold of Jay when I asked them, and all were getting the same response as us when trying to contact both Mum and Dad. Nothing. The body is either Dad or Jay.

I've been opening Jay's Facebook page non-stop since last night. We're 'friends' so I've been able to check on him suddenly becoming active on there. I don't know if he's got any family - apparently his mum died when he was a teenager, and he's mentioned no one else. He's always been a closed book. But if Mum's seen him since the fire, then I guess we have our answer. So I dare not ask her. There's no one else it could be. Other than Dad. Unless someone broke in. I crouch to make a fuss of Sammy. She won't have any idea of what's going on.

"Dad messaged me yesterday," Lance tells Mum, the hope still very much alive in his voice. "He was on his way down. But you've got the car so..."

"On his way down, where?"

"To Leicester. To see me. Yesterday." Lance looks how I feel. Hair all over the place and he's not even tied the laces on his trainers.

"Have you heard from him Mum?"

She shakes her head. "My phone's been off love. After all, I thought you two were OK. I only spoke to you both yesterday. Some start to the new year..."

Tears blur my vision as I stare at her. Maybe she doesn't mean to sound so casual about it. Perhaps she's in shock, like I've been. After all, the pub's gone, Dad has disappeared into thin air and she's standing there wearing probably the only clothes she has left.

So I've got to ask her. I have to know. I take a deep breath. "Have you seen Jay Mum? Is that where you went to last night?"

She looks uncertain for a moment and her silence is maddening.

"Just answer Mum."

As she opens her mouth to reply, a police car pulls up behind our Golf. It's the two officers who spoke to me in the ambulance yesterday, DCI Leonard and Sergeant Ellis. It's strange how long ago yesterday feels. Emotionally, I've gone to hell and back since Nancy, the paramedic, checked me over and finally let me go.

What are they going to tell us? What the hell are they going to tell us?

17 HOURS AFTER

HAYLEY 9AM

THE TWO OFFICERS stop short of our huddle of three on the footpath. "You must be..." DCI Leonard begins, looking at Mum.

Sammy darts to greet them. All is well in her world. After all, three out of four of her humans are here.

"Debra Ford. I'm Hayley and Lance's Mum."

"Bryn's wife." Sergeant Ellis seems to raise an eyebrow. "It's good to see that you're safe after everything that's happened."

"Thank you." Mum's tone is so light, I wonder if she's mistaken what the police officer just said as a compliment.

"I'm DCI Jacqueline Leonard and this is my colleague Sergeant Rachel Ellis."

Sammy slinks back, dejected, as neither of them take any notice of her. "Clearly, it will be necessary to ask you some questions, Mrs Ford, but first, we need to have a word with you all together."

"Is this about Dad?" Lance looks at his feet. It appears as though the *no news is good news* mantra we've been reminding each other of since yesterday, is about to be flipped on its head.

"Can we go inside?" Sergeant Ellis glances around. Already, curtains are twitching. One or two neighbours have even stepped from their front doors, probably at the sight of the police car. I want to tell them all to bugger off. The fire is all over the local news. Though the neighbours here don't know me well enough to connect me to it. Yet.

"Yeah. Sure." I spin on my heel as everyone's footsteps tail me. My heart is thumping. This might be the final moment of having hope that my dad is still living.

Gemma's brushing her hair in the hallway mirror.

"Can you give us a minute Gem?"

"Course I can." She squeezes my arm as she makes her way to the foot of the stairs. "It's so good to see you Debra." She squeezes Mum's arm too. "I hope..." Her words fade out. There's nothing she, or anyone else can say of consolation if what they're about to tell us, is what I think they're about to tell us. "I'll take Sammy with me, shall I?" She catches her collar and heads up the stairs.

"I'll just be in the kitchen." JJ emerges from the lounge and darts past us.

I lead everyone into the lounge, then nod to the policewomen. They lower themselves onto the edge of the sofa in response. Mum sits in the armchair facing them. Lance and I stand in front of the fireplace. I glance at him. He looks frozen to the spot. Silence hangs between us all. The officers have a really serious air about them. More so than they did outside.

Surely they'd be smiling if they were here to tell us that it isn't actually our dad who is dead? There again, maybe not. After all, if it isn't Dad, someone has still died. Maybe they're here to let us know it's Jay - that's if they've already told his family. I glance at Mum. She didn't get a chance to answer us before. If it's Jay, then between us, we'll look after her. She and Dad will either rebuild the pub, or find another, and then everything can get back to normal. Maybe a new start is what's needed.

"As you know," DCI Leonard begins in an even voice. "The fire service recovered someone from your public house yesterday. And that person was unfortunately deceased." I stare at her trousers with the big crease down the front. Her boots are hideous, but look really comfy.

"Sierra Oscar to one two nine." Sergeant Ellis's radio bursts into life.

She leans towards it. "If you could just give us a few minutes. We're with the Fords at the moment."

"Yes." Lance has moved closer and we're gripping onto each other. It reminds me of when we got back from being on holiday when we were younger. Lance was sixteen, I was eighteen. Our GCSE and A-Level results were contained in two long white envelopes, waiting for us on the doormat. Mum and Dad opened an envelope each, and we didn't know who had whose results. Thankfully, as we'd looked from one face to another whilst they scanned the papers, it wasn't long before both faces broke into smiles. If we hadn't got good results - Lance and I, we'd have never heard the end of it from Dad. At least he had something new to boast about in the pub.

Mum and Dad had their moments, but often, I felt relief that I was in the minority amongst my circle of friends. I was one of the few with parents that were still together. It's literally only in the last few months that everything started to go really wrong. Dad joked about the menopause to start with, which did Mum's head in. He was out of order though. He shouldn't have said the stuff he said in front of people in the pub. He shouldn't have said it at all. Things like *get on the HRT and do us all a favour. Or is your wife as monstrous as mine now that she's drying up and shrivelling away?*

Then in recent weeks, things have become much more serious. At least now we know why. Bloody Jay. Dad probably wouldn't have thought in a million years that Mum would ever betray him. She was his, and he was hers, as far as he was concerned. I've never wished anyone dead before but if it's a choice between Jay and my father...

"As a result of the DNA sample we took from Hayley yesterday,"

DCI Leonard says, "as well as the dental records, we've now been able to check..."

This is what the words *time standing still* mean. I notice the washing piled high on the other armchair. I need to sort that out. The curtains need washing and the floor needs hoovering. When the police have gone, I must tidy this place. Get some control back over my life. And get rid of that bloody Christmas tree. It's the new year now. Some new year. I've a good mind to put the tree in the bin.

"We've been able to verify the identification of the deceased and are really sorry to bring you the news..."

Don't say it, don't say it, don't say it.

"That it's unfortunately your husband, your father, Bryn David Ford, who died in the fire at *The Dales Inn*." She looks from Mum to us, sympathy etched across her face.

Lance tightens his grip on me and I pull him closer. It's my job to protect him. Just like I always have.

"No. You must have got it wrong," he says. "Dad was on his way to see me." He lets go of me and slides his phone from his back pocket. "Look, I'll show you the message." He pummels at his phone. "Look."

"We're really sorry." The sergeant keeps her gaze on Lance's face. She looks tired and I wonder whether she's even been home since they took the scrape from the inside of my cheek at the station last night.

Why do people always say *sorry* when someone has died? Anyone would think *they'd* started the fire.

"Are you absolutely sure?" Mum sounds calmer than I'd expect her to be. It's probably for our benefit that she thinks she needs to be strong. Or maybe she's only relieved that it isn't Jay.

The sergeant nods slowly. "A hundred percent. Please accept our sincerest condolences Mrs Ford."

"Is there anything we can do?" The other woman asks. "Anyone we can contact for you?"

Bring my dad back. Please. This. Can't. Be. Happening.

Mum shakes her head. "I don't think so." Then, "Where is he now?" What a stupid question. Like that makes any difference.

Lance crouches down onto the rug, hugging his knees again. He looks utterly lost. I don't know how we'll get through this. Do I even want to? All I want is Dad back. Any moment at all, he's going to come racing up this path saying it's all a big mistake.

"He's in the pathology department at the Yorkshire General," Sergeant Ellis replies. "He's been there since last night." She makes it sound as though he's visiting. If only. They must have this wrong. They must have.

"Have you any idea how it happened?"

"Not yet." DCI Leonard shakes her head. "But we'll find out."

"There must be easier ways to do it, than what he's done."

"Do what?" Lance looks up at her.

"He was very depressed," Mum continues. "Our marriage was breaking up. He'd made threats, like he wouldn't live without me."

"We'll talk to you at the station about this, Mrs Ford. We'll have to get it on record."

Lance's jaw stiffens in the same way Dad's would in temper. "If you're saying what I think you're saying Mum." It's years since I've heard Lance shout. He's normally so easy-going. "Dad would never choose to leave us. So shut up."

"I know you're upset but I won't have you talking to me like this. Don't you think I had enough of it from your father?"

"Stop it, both of you." I clasp my hands over my ears. Dad's dead and they're bickering like a pair of kids.

"Will I be able to see him?" Mum asks after a few moments of awkward silence.

"That won't be possible, I'm afraid." DCI Leonard glances nervously down at Lance. She's already told me it's because of the state he's in after the fire, but Lance doesn't need to know this. I try to catch the officer's eye, to give her a look, as if to say, *please don't say any more.* I can almost smell what I thought was burning flesh again and a wave of nausea washes over me.

"But I'm his next of kin," Mum continues. "I want to see him."

"Maybe you should have thought about that before you went off with Jay," Lance shouts at her. He sounds broken. "It's all your fault. *Next of kin!*"

I drop beside him and wrap my arms around him as he sobs. Mum stays rooted to the spot, as though she doesn't know what to say, or what to do.

PART IV

DEBRA

18 HOURS AFTER
DEBRA 10AM

"THEY'VE OPENED OUR LANE AGAIN." Hayley stops dead and Sammy sits beside her.

"Not that it's *our lane* anymore." Lance stops as well.

"Look, I'll sort everything out, I promise you." I reach towards him but he pulls away. I'm trying to respect his space, after all, he'll be struggling to process it all, especially Bryn's death - they both will. And on some level, Lance is blaming me.

"I don't know if I can go back there." Hayley turns to me with tears in her eyes.

"It guts me to know that you saw it all sweetheart." I put my arm around my daughter, and draw her near. The bobble on her hat tickles my nose as she melts into me. It's not very often she lets me hug her these days, but this is certainly no ordinary set of circumstances. "I'd do anything to have made sure you didn't have to go through that."

She gives me a squeeze which draws heat to the back of my eyes. "It's not your fault Mum."

"I know. Though I can't help but feel..."

"I want to see the pub." Lance looks into the distance. "I won't believe it's all gone until I see it with my own eyes. They wouldn't let us near last night."

"I know what you mean. I feel the same." I let go of Hayley and reach for Lance, finding his bony arm beneath his thick coat. But again, he tugs away.

"Do you want to wait here for us love?" I turn back to Hayley. "If you can't face it. We'll only be a few minutes. I don't think we should hang around here for long."

She hesitates. "No. I'm going to come too. It might help me accept it all a bit more."

"Maybe they'll let us go inside," Lance says. "There might be a few things worth saving. Not everything will have burned, surely?"

Having seen pictures of the pub on the news, it's unlikely, but I don't say this. They're both suffering enough as it is.

Hayley links my arm and passes Sammy's lead to me. "Come here you." She reaches for Lance, who allows her to link his arm with her other hand. Together, we head towards the place that was home for so many years. It's the longest I ever lived anywhere, after my childhood home with Dad. Sammy trots alongside, probably thinking she's going home. Perhaps we shouldn't have brought her. Bryn was a bad-tempered swine, but Sammy still adored him.

"There won't be any photos left of me and Lance when we were growing up, will there?" It's true what people say about photographs. They're irreplaceable.

"Don't worry, Grandad's got them... some of them. He's got loads of photos of you both in his albums at the care home."

Neither of them reply, both suddenly transfixed on the horror in front of us. I raise my eyes from the ground to look at it too, noticing torch light coming from within. It's ten times worse in the flesh than it was on a TV screen. I bury my nose under my scarf. Smoke still clogs the air. The policewoman said before that it had gone up really quick. By the looks of it, Bryn didn't stand a chance. If it wasn't for the cordon with the police guard, I'd have liked to have gone in to have a look too. But there's a fire service car and a police car parked a few yards from where we're standing - they must still be investigating.

"Oh Mum. I can't stand it." Hayley turns and huddles against my coat. "Poor Dad."

"Look, his van's right there."

We follow Lance's gaze beyond the police tape closing off the entrance to the car park. The only vehicle remaining - the burnt-out shell of Bryn's works van. Not that he ever drove the thing. I force the thought away. This is no time for bitterness about anything he did or didn't do.

"Where was the tent?" Lance steps away from us. "Where they put him?"

"At the front, just there, but it's gone, thank God. You really wouldn't have wanted to see that." Hayley points to the left of the pub and closes her eyes, her long lashes brushing the top of her cheeks. "I'll never forget them bringing him out and laying him on the ground." Opening her eyes again, she turns to me and grips my arm. "And I thought it was you Mum." Her voice catches which breaks my heart. "They wouldn't tell me a thing. Until you showed up this morning, I was terrified it was going to be you."

There's nothing I can say to make her feel better. Either of them. Only time can do that. *Time heals* is the biggest cliche on the planet. But it's true.

"As if the place is still smoking," Lance says.

People in white suits and masks are visible through the blackened holes in the walls, once windows. They're in and out of the building, swarming around it like flies around decaying meat.

"It was a huge fire," Hayley replies. "You've never seen anything like it."

The day before Christmas Eve, I cleaned all the windows. I always have a mammoth clean in both June and December. I feel somewhat peeved that all that time has been wasted. Then I berate myself for being so shallow. It's strange how your mind jumps around. What it considers at a time like this. As if I'm thinking about time spent cleaning windows.

"What exactly will they be looking for Mum?" Hayley's cheeks are turning pink in the cold, making her eyes look bluer. It warms me to be needed by her so much again. It's a shame it took something so drastic. Lance seems to have gone the other way. All I can do is give him some space. He'll come around.

"I'm not sure to be honest love. But I guess they'll need to be certain of how the fire started and how it spread."

"They might be looking for electronics too," Lance adds.

"What for?"

"Any evidence. Apparently hard drives can survive a fire."

"Believe me," Hayley sniffs. "Nothing would have survived that fire. You've seen pictures of it in full swing on the news, haven't you?"

"I suppose so. Did you see the pictures Mum? Is that how you found out what had happened?" Lance's tone has softened. It's as though he's forgotten he's mad with me, for whatever reason.

"No. I haven't watched any TV since I was staying with you. I stay away from the news these days, it's all so depressing."

"So how did you find out about this?" He points at the pub.

"When I got all your messages. When I plugged my phone in." It devastated me, reading what they'd sent me. Both kids frantic with worry, needing to know I was safe. Just one word would have been all it would have taken to reassure them. So I've got a lot of making up to do.

"Do you think Dad was asleep Mum? When the fire started? Is that why he didn't make it out?" Lance tugs at my sleeve, in the same way to what he might have done ten years ago. If a silver lining exists here, it's that it's going to bring the three of us closer again, no matter how fleetingly. I'll never take it for granted.

"No. We had smoke alarms. They'd have woken him."

"From what the police said." Hayley sinks to sit on the kerb. "He tried to get out, but the fire trapped him on the staircase to the flat."

"It's not the fire that kills you normally, it's the smoke." Lance drops beside her. I've never seen a sadder sight. My two kids, sprawled on the ground in front of their burnt-out childhood home. Thank God though that they've both got somewhere else to return to. But they've lost their father - something that's going to take a lot more getting over than losing this place. Even though Hayley and Lance were never quite good enough for Bryn, and they were always on the edge of wariness with him, they loved him and it was obvious that his approval of them mattered.

I'm lost in thought as I continue staring at the pub. Until my attention is averted to the flap of cellophane from the rows of flowers beneath me. Against my better judgement, I bend to read some cards in front of the cordon.

Rest in Peace mate. Gone too soon.

It's one of the regulars - he was in the other night. Our final night.

Hayley and Lance see what I'm doing and jump up to join me.

I wish you'd have talked to me Bryn. Would have been here for you.

One of his electrician friends. Not that they ever did much 'electrician-ing' between them. Just plenty of drinking.

Hope you're at peace now Bryn. So much love to Debra, Hayley and Lance.

I can't read the signature on that one, but it must be someone who knows us all.

And they go on. From the tone of most of them, there's a definite consensus that he's taken his own life, just as I suggested back at Hayley's. It might calm Lance down to know I'm not the only person saying it. He wasn't there on New Year's Eve. He didn't hear Bryn's threats when he climbed onto the bar.

"Sorry about your dad." I turn to the last voice I want to hear.

18.5 HOURS AFTER

DEBRA 10:30AM

FROM HER EXPRESSION, Hayley feels the same. Together, the three of us turn to face Carl.

"Thanks," Lance says stiffly, glancing at Hayley. One wrong word from Carl, and I expect Lance will fly at him, especially with the mood he's in. But he's all gangly arms and legs. He's certainly no match for Carl.

"Me and *him*. We had unfinished business." Carl looks pointedly at me.

"What's that supposed to mean?"

"He owed me money."

"My dad's lying in a morgue, and you're here, tapping my mother up. Do one, will you?" Lance squares up to him. "I don't care what he owed you. He can't pay anyone anything now, can he?" His voice cracks and his shoulders slump.

"Is that what you and my dad were talking about the other night?" There's an accusatory edge to Hayley's voice. "Money?"

"What do you mean?" Carl turns towards her, and Hayley straightens up, clearly keeping her distance from him. I notice with pride that she's completely different with him now, to how she used to be. There's a confidence in her stature. And she's looking straight at him as she speaks. I will not stand back and watch her make the same mistakes I did. But perhaps I won't need to intervene here. She's handling it well enough herself.

"My friends saw you both talking."

"Just a business thing." He looks at me. Clearly he expects me to pay him off. As if.

"I need to know what it was. It's important."

The tone of Hayley's voice must slightly soften him as his tone changes.

"It's nothing for you to know about."

"I've got a right to know. You saw him after I did." Tears are rolling down her face. "It's not fair. You got to talk to my dad face to face on his last night alive. I didn't!"

She lunges forward and for one awful moment, it's as though she might attack him. I grab for her and pull her towards me.

He continues to stand there. Really, we need to get rid of him. I don't want him around Hayley, especially whilst she's in such a vulnerable state. Men like Carl will always take advantage, and he's repeatedly proven how callous he is.

"Would you mind leaving us alone?" I pin my shoulders back and try to exude a confidence I'm not feeling. "Everything's quite raw right now, as I'm sure you can appreciate." Part of me expects him to offer a comeback at my dismissal, but he just stares at me for a moment, with an expression I can't quite read.

"You heard her," Lance says. "Get lost."

"You haven't heard the last from me."

Hayley watches after him as he walks away.

"You'll keep," he calls back over his shoulder.

"Let him go love. He's utter trouble."

"I know, it's just... I really want to know what him and Dad were on about."

"So do I," Lance says. "Do you think it's worth mentioning it to the police?"

"Possibly. But your Dad was really drunk. Not a lot of what he said that night will be worth investigating." It's true about how drunk he was. It's a miracle he didn't crash off that bar and break his neck.

Hayley gazes back at the smouldering shell in front of us. Lance and I follow her gaze and we all just stand in silence for a few moments, staring. Sammy flops to the ground with a sigh. "What about all your things Mum? Your furniture? Your clothes?"

I grip Sammy's lead tighter. "You're both OK. And Sammy. That's all that matters."

"But not Dad. Why aren't you more upset about Dad?" Hayley looks at me with wide eyes and a pained expression. Then her tone changes. "I suppose this means you're free to do what you want with Jay now, doesn't it?"

"I haven't even thought about that yet," I lie. "And I'm not in floods of tears as things just haven't sunk in yet. I feel numb to be honest." It's true. I do. "Besides, we've only just found out that it's Dad."

"Where are you going to live Mum? You and Sammy?" She bends to stroke Sammy, now laid at my feet. Her ears are flat to her head and I wonder if she somehow knows Bryn has died, and that our home has gone. Dogs can sense things like this. "Do you want to stay with me?"

"You're not still going to go away, are you?" There's a sharpness to Lance's tone, almost daring me to say yes. "With *him*?"

"We need you here Mum. More than Jay needs you to go away with him." Trust Hayley to tighten the guilty screw.

As I deliberate how to reply, our attention's averted to movement at the doorway of the pub. Well, what's left of the doorway.

"Look... Hayley. I was right about the hard drive thing." I follow Lance's pointed finger to one of the officers, who appears to be carrying a laptop in a polythene bag. They must have got into the office safe. To where the laptops and the takings were kept. They asked for the code earlier. The safe has certainly lived up to its water resistant and flame retardant promises.

"I bet they're looking for the CCTV back up," Hayley says.

21.5 HOURS AFTER

DEBRA 1:30PM

"THANK YOU FOR WAITING DEBRA. Is it alright if I call you Debra?"

"I suppose so." I want to ask this sharp-voiced police officer why she was calling me Mrs Ford whilst breaking the news about Bryn this morning, then this afternoon has decided it's Debra. Maybe because I'm now on her turf.

"Thank you Debra. I'll start the interview by announcing who's present today, and then we'll get some basic details from you. Is that OK?"

The detective's finger hovers over a button on her remote control, as she squints at me beneath the fluorescent overhead lighting. What a dreadful room. Not only are the furnishings, if they can be called that, fastened to the floor, everything is in varying shades of blue. My mind flits back to when we were upgrading the interior of the pub about ten years ago and I did some work around the psychology of colour. Blue is the colour of truth.

I tug my scarf more tightly around my neck and shiver. Which is strange because it was boiling in here when I first arrived. What's that saying... *someone's walked over my grave?* A saying which suddenly has resonance. I still can hardly believe Bryn's no longer here.

If anyone had asked me how I'd cope with the death of my husband a few years ago, my answer would have been *I'd go to pieces*. Back then, it would have felt like my right arm had been cut off. Yet knowing he's gone, whilst it feels kind of eerie, has a sense of liberation about it.

The long beep echoing through the silence reminds me of the crime dramas that I'd have once curled up with Bryn to watch, in our happier times. I usually guessed the whodunit correctly, he nearly always disagreed. We should have taken bets. Bryn would joke that the key to a happy marriage is *rule one is the wife is always right*. Then he'd say, *and rule two is when the husband believes he's right, he should refer to rule one.*

But in recent years, everything changed. I was always wrong; he was always right.

Now he's not here, I'm being bombarded with happier memories. Before everything went sour. It wasn't an overnight thing - more a gradual decline - a slow sliding of a once satisfactory marriage disintegrating into a pit of despair. A pit where happy memories couldn't reside. And now they're back, I don't want them. I certainly don't need them.

"Today is the second of January, the time is one-thirty-three pm, and my name is Detective Chief Inspector Jacqueline Leonard of Yorkshire Police. This interview is being carried out at the Dales Police Station. Also present is," she nods towards her colleague who clears her throat.

"Sergeant Rachel Ellis, also of Yorkshire Police." She leans towards the voice recording equipment as she speaks, and nods affirmatively. The woman doesn't look old enough to be a police sergeant, but maybe that's just me. Today, I'm exactly two months away from my fiftieth birthday and *everyone* looks young. Maybe

I'm just envious, especially now I've got a younger man to keep up with. And today I feel especially saggy and old. I didn't exactly sleep well last night.

"We are conducting this interview with..." DCI Leonard looks at me with a pointed expression. Everything about her is pointed. Her nose, her chin, even her bony fingers which she interlaces on the table between us. Rings sparkle from her wedding finger; they're not dull and weathered like mine. My right hand instinctively reaches for my own rings, and twists them as I reply. Whilst it doesn't seem appropriate to wear them anymore, I've worn them for so long they've become part of me.

"Debra Jayne Ford." Will I keep the name Ford? Now Bryn's gone? And the kids are grown up? Perhaps Jay and I... *Debra Manningham.* Bloody hell. What an idiot. I'm here, talking to the police about my husband's death, and I'm fantasising about being married to Jay.

"Thank you Debra. Can you also confirm for the recording, your date of birth and your current address?" She looks uncomfortable for a moment, and quickly adds, "where you are staying at the moment?"

Her question hits me like a thump in the chest. There is no current address. I've lost nearly everything. I reel off my date of birth. At every turn I'm taunted by how close to fifty I am. Maybe once my birthday has passed, I'll be less obsessed with it. People tell me it's fairly painless, then laugh and remind me it's half a century. I only hope Jay will want to stay with a woman of half a century. I'll get my kids through this nightmare and Jay will get me through my own.

"Where did you stay last night Debra?"

"With a friend who lives in Moorton." As soon as the words are out, I realise I've said them too quickly. Too nervously.

"Would this friend be your bar manager?" DCI Leonard surveys me with cold eyes. Who is she to judge? She's probably as bored in her marriage as I was in mine.

I reel off Jay's address. "I don't know if I'll be staying there again tonight though." *No matter how much I want to,* I refrain from adding. Perhaps this is what's known as being of *no fixed abode.* Except most people of this dreadful status wouldn't be anticipating the huge insurance pay out I'll hopefully get after the investigation.

I haven't spoken to Jay since I left this morning. We've texted a bit, but we've agreed it's best if I focus on Hayley and Lance today. Jay being around would probably upset them even more. What happened yesterday is massive. So perhaps I'll stay with Hayley tonight. As the reality of Bryn's death sets in, I've got to focus on the kids. Make sure they're OK, before I go anywhere with Jay. He's told me he'll wait.

"Thank you Debra. We've asked you to attend here at the station as part of the ongoing investigation into a fire at the public house where you are the licensee. This is known as *The Dales Inn,* Yorkshire, in which your husband, Bryn David Ford, lost his life yesterday."

Hearing his full name spoken out loud strikes misery into the centre of my being. Another intrusive memory floods my mind. *Do you take Bryn David Ford to be your lawful wedded husband? Till death do us part.* I don't know whether I'm supposed to respond. What she said seemed like information more than a question. So I stay quiet.

22 HOURS AFTER

DEBRA 2PM

"Can you tell us about your marriage?" DCI Leonard looks at me through narrowed eyes. Are they narrow with interest, or suspicion?

I take a deep breath. Here we go. "Bryn and I were married for nearly twenty-five years. We've got two grown-up children together, Hayley and Lance, as you know."

I pause, knowing she probably wants a lot more than that. She'll be digging for dirt and wouldn't have to dig too deep to find it. Especially if she's been talking to any of the regulars. They've heard row after row between Bryn and I in recent months. I'm also aware that I've referred to our marriage in the past tense. But it's been coming to an end for a while.

"But things haven't been going so well between you lately, have they Debra?"

She obviously *has* been talking to the regulars, and tilts her head to the side like a dog waiting for a bone. Except I won't be throwing her one. But I will be honest about how rocky things had become. Up to a point.

"Erm no."

"Can you tell us more?" There's an impatient air about her.

Probably because she's having to grind every bit of information from me. But I need thinking time. I'm struggling to process everything. Who wouldn't be?

"To the outside world we probably seemed like a normal couple, with the usual ups and downs. But behind closed doors, Bryn could be a bully." I stare at the table.

"Oh? What do you mean by that?"

"He could be really controlling, to the point of being nasty - not only with me, but with the kids too."

"They haven't said anything about that, have they?" She glances at her colleague, the sergeant, who shakes her head. She might as well be telling me they don't believe what I'm saying.

"They wouldn't, would they? Now he's died, both Hayley and Lance have suddenly got Bryn on a pedestal. To be honest, they had him on one, even when he was alive."

"How do you mean?"

"Well - I was the consistent parent, the one who looked after them, whilst Bryn," I pause as a wave of guilt washes over me for talking like this, now he's dead. "Well, the kids were often chasing him, needing his attention, wanting his approval. He wasn't there for them like I've always been."

"OK. We might come back to that. But for now, can you give us some examples of Bryn being *controlling and nasty*? Just so we can get a picture of how things were for you?" DCI Leonard's voice rises as though she's genuinely interested. Really, she'll be wanting to get this over and done with so she can get home for her dinner.

Home. At least she's got one. Though maybe, just maybe, me losing mine will eventually feel like a price worth paying. After all, even though it's too early to appreciate it, for the first time since my early twenties, I've now got absolute freedom in every area of my life. I'm no longer shackled to anything or anyone.

"It's just, well, I had to account for every single move I made; Bryn didn't trust me. This got worse and worse, especially over the past year. He was constantly checking up on me, following me, questioning me, accusing me."

"Go on."

I feel like saying, *isn't that enough?* Evidently not. "We shared the car between us, as there was little point having two. Bryn had a work's van."

"Yes. We've seen it."

What's left of it, I don't say. "He hardly used it though. Really, we should have got another car, as every time I took it, he'd ask where I was going, and he even clocked the mileage of my journeys."

"Really. Why?"

"I don't know. To check I was where I said I was going, I guess. He'd ring me all the time, even if I was just having a coffee with one of my friends. If I didn't answer, he'd keep ringing until I did. Sometimes he'd follow me." It's true. No matter where I was, it was as though Bryn had a secret ability to locate me. It would astonish me sometimes, when he popped up at the window of a cafe, a bar, or a shop.

"It sounds like things were very difficult. For all of you."

"That's an understatement." I laugh, despite the circumstances. "Bryn was just so insecure. He hated that it was *my* pub, *my* name over the door and *my* graft that had given us the lifestyle we had."

"But you were married. Surely that would make your home and business automatically half his anyway?"

"It was *my* home and business long before Bryn came along." I feel rotten continually emphasising the word *my* but it's how it was. "I'd taken a mortgage out for *The Dales Inn* with a man I was once engaged to. When that relationship fell apart after a couple of years, my dad helped me buy him out. And it was my dad who persuaded me to get a pre-nup agreement when I was marrying Bryn."

"I see."

"He signed without issue at the time, but I think Bryn often felt emasculated by our situation. This only got worse as the years went on."

"What made you think this?"

Question after question after bloody question. I don't know why this DCI wants to know chapter and verse about absolutely everything, but if it helps things draw to a close more quickly, then so be it.

"He'd constantly put me down."

"In what way?" DCI Leonard's voice is gentle, but sceptical.

As if I'd lie about all of this. I've been utterly foolish for allowing it to go on for so long as it is. I've always thought couples who stay together for the sake of the kids are misguided. But it's easy to make assumptions until you're in that position. "In every way. My appearance, my age, stretch marks, level of intelligence, you name it. In the end, I only had to open my mouth for Bryn to jump down my throat." A vision of his twisted face when he was on at me, fills my mind. "You ask my kids."

Although that might be fruitless, as right now, since he's died, he's really become *Saint Dad*. Though at least Hayley's convinced, and Lance is starting to be convinced, that Bryn's death was probably self-inflicted. In some ways it's a shame they weren't there on New Year's Eve to witness Bryn's speech in all its glory. When the searching is done, everyone, including Hayley and Lance, will have to accept that the fire was deliberate - that Bryn brought this on himself in a final act of anger and control over me.

"So tell me more Debra."

How much more does she want? Though at least questions like these aren't too difficult to answer. "Bryn never wanted us to break up. He wouldn't do, would he? After all, he had it pretty comfy. He had a roof over his head, bed and board, access to the pub night after night, and he barely lifted a finger for any of it."

It's somewhat ridiculous saying this aloud, after all, it was me who allowed things to get like this. I should have pulled the plug years ago.

"Did Bryn not have his own business too?"

I laugh - a hollow sound which bounces around the concrete walls. "If you can call it a business. He worked occasionally, and I mean occasionally. When he felt like it - which wasn't very often. To be honest, money, and me doing all the work was what we argued about the most."

This is obviously a noteworthy point. There's the scratch of pen against page as Sergeant Ellis writes this down.

"OK." DCI Leonard nods and looks almost sympathetic. Almost. "So moving on slightly... when did your affair with your bar manager, Jay Manningham, start?"

I was wondering when we'd get back around to Jay. This is, admittedly, slightly embarrassing. I can only imagine what must be going through the minds of these police officers. Probably the same thing that's gone through the mind of everyone. Cougar. Mid-life crisis. Empty nest syndrome. He's only after your money, etc, etc.

"About a month ago."

"And the relationship..." DCI Leonard shifts in her seat. "I'm sorry to be so personal, but is it a physical one?"

I cannot see what this has to do with Bryn's death but I'll answer her question anyway. Surely they'll let me leave soon. I've had enough. I want a coffee. In fact, I want a gin. And I want to speak to Jay.

"We didn't actually sleep together until the night before Christmas Eve."

I refrain from adding, though we've done little 'sleeping.' I've never really understood the term, *sleep together*. Last night was the first time we've stayed in the same bed for an entire night, though after Jay had fallen asleep, my mind was going round and round all night, like a game of ring-a-roses.

"We've heard from other witnesses that Bryn had discovered the extent of your affair with Jay. He found out the night before last. Is that correct?"

"Yes. On New Year's Eve."

"He walked in on you, and Jay?"

"That's the polite way of putting it."

"How would you say Bryn reacted to this discovery, Debra?"

What a stupid question. "How do you think?" I realise how sarcastic I sound, so I change my tone. The last thing I want to do is rub these officers up the wrong way. The sooner all this is over with, the better. "Badly, of course. Very badly." The memory of Bryn flying at Jay like an angry wasp floods my mind - However, Bryn wasn't what he used to be, with his wasted muscles and his beer belly, and Jay literally held him against that wall with one hand.

"What did he actually do?"

"He went for Jay. There was a scuffle between the two of them, but Jay held him off. Then I asked Jay to leave us for a few minutes whilst I talked to Bryn." The memory of my new lacy knickers spreadeagled on the floor makes me blush.

"*Talk* to him?"

"Yes. I needed to make him accept that our marriage was definitely over."

"I'm sure he already had that message, loud and clear." Sergeant Ellis raises her eyes from her notepad, for the first time in a while, a trace of a smile threatening to break out.

DCI Leonard frowns at her. "What happened next Debra?"

"Well, as you've probably heard from many of the customers you've spoken to, Bryn stormed back into the pub and made his threats in front of everyone... he climbed onto the bar and let them all know he was going to give them something to really gossip about."

"Yes, we've heard that from several witnesses," DCI Leonard says. "But the next morning, when he'd calmed down... yesterday morning, what then?"

"He hadn't calmed down at all - I don't know what makes you think that. In fact, he was making more threats. Directly at me."

"Tell us about those, Debra."

Her constant use of my name is both irritating and patronising in equal measure. I wonder if that's just her way, or whether it's an interview tactic designed to upend the supposed balance of power. "At first Bryn warned me I either ended things with Jay, and got rid of him from behind the bar, or he would. Then, he said, it would be my turn if I still tried to go through with leaving him."

"When he was saying it, did you not suspect it was an empty threat? Against Jay, and you, I mean? Especially with him being so angry?"

"He said if I thought I could just walk out on twenty-five years of marriage, and make an idiot of him, I had another thing coming. But when that didn't work, he had to try something different."

"Go on."

"He was making threats to end his own life."

"Can you tell us exactly what he said?"

"That *if I didn't want him, then he's had nothing to live for,* and the other thing was that *he couldn't go on without me.* I just thought it was emotional blackmail. Usually people who make those threats don't go through with it, do they?"

"I couldn't comment. We'll leave that school of thinking to the experts on suicide, shall we?" DCI Leonard falls silent for a moment, as though pondering her next question. Between the conversation, it's so quiet around here, it's almost possible to hear the silence. But at least she used the word *suicide.*

This pause between us lasts for so long, the question of whether I need to contact a solicitor begins to form itself. But surely the answer will be no?

I'm better off not asking, not yet. It'll only hold things up, and well, it makes me look as though I've got something to hide. And it's not as if I'm under any suspicion; I'm only here so they can conclude whatever they need to conclude, before *the case,* as she's called this situation, our reality, goes to the Coroner. We've already been told there will definitely be an inquest with it being a sudden death. The Coroner needs to be satisfied that the only foul play involved was from Bryn himself. Then it will be *case closed*. Those words cannot come soon enough for me.

"Can I ask Debra..." There's a new hint of satisfaction to DCI Leonard's voice. "Where were you between three and four pm yesterday afternoon?"

22.5 HOURS AFTER
DEBRA 2:30PM

I suppose that being asked to confirm one's whereabouts is standard practice when an incident as huge as this has taken place. Though Hayley and Lance have already given recorded accounts, and haven't mentioned being asked to confirm theirs, as far as I know. It's probably with our marriage being so on the edge, that I'm being asked this question.

For a moment I don't trust my voice. Are they accusing me of starting the fire? I need to reply. Now.

"I was visiting my dad in Castle Hill Nursing Home. I wanted to wish him a Happy New Year."

Bryn had even sneered at that.

"And how far is the nursing home from the pub?"

"About a mile. So it's only a few minutes in the car."

"We'll need the address." DCI Leonard raises an eyebrow. "Were you on your own?"

"I'd taken our dog with me." Referring to the dog causes the slightest pang of guilt. "But other than that, yes."

Sammy's already pining for Bryn, no matter how much of a fuss Hayley and Lance are making of her. Hayley mentioned hearing a

215

dog barking when the fire was at its height. She'd apparently tried going in to rescue her.

Hayley venturing into the fire was a scenario I hadn't foreseen. Visualising it makes me feel sick. I'd purposefully not asked Hayley to help in the pub at all over the new year to make sure she was well out of the way. Which worked out well initially, as she was avoiding Carl. I had the perfect excuse. When I'd spoken to her earlier in the day, I'd made sure she had no plans to go anywhere near the pub. I hadn't needed to make the same provision for Lance as he'd returned to uni.

"Can any of the staff at the care home vouch for you visiting your father, and confirm the times you were there?"

"Of course. They all saw me when I arrived, and again when I left. You have to sign in and out, so the exact times will be there."

DCI Leonard nods at Sergeant Ellis. "Have you noted down the name of the nursing home? If you could get in touch when we've finished here."

Sergeant Ellis's eyes are heavy as she nods back. Mine usually would be at this time in the afternoon. However, the adrenaline coursing through me over the last couple of days has been akin to the force of the Niagara Falls. At least DCI Leonard has just used the word *finished*.

"I was there for three hours or so," I continue. "In fact, I stayed for afternoon tea. The two care staff who brought that round will also vouch for me."

Thank goodness I could afford for Dad to live in one of the garden suite rooms, one with its own patio doors, where I've been given the code to switch the alarm off whenever I'm there. On warmer days, I wheel Dad outside to feel the sunshine on his face. On colder days, I always open the door, even if just for a couple of minutes. It's nice to bring the outside in for him, as well as to circulate the stale air that's always the norm in a care home.

I can tell by the expression on DI Leonard's face, what she's thinking, *you're drinking afternoon tea, and meanwhile, your husband, your home and your business are burning to a crisp.*

Sergeant Ellis stifles a yawn as she continues writing. I've nothing to worry about on the alibi score. Mine will check out just fine. No one will know I cut through the park to slip back to the pub. I went as soon as they'd brought afternoon tea round, having left my phone at home as a decoy. Sammy had opened one eye from where she was sleeping at Dad's feet as I left, but to my knowledge, I left the care home by the back entrance, and returned without being seen by anyone. Other than Bryn, of course.

If I hadn't overheard Bryn's conversation with my own ears on Boxing Day, I'd have never believed it. Thank God I *did* hear it. Bryn couldn't have pocket rung me at a better time. It's not the first time he's rung me without realising. We've laughed about it in the past, especially the time he rang me whilst in the loo. However, the conversation I was able to listen in on was anything but laughable.

Bryn had planned to trap Jay in a fire he was paying someone else to start. As I'd listened to the one-sided conversation, he wasn't finalising things at that stage. It appeared Bryn was setting things up, ready to put it all into motion as a last resort, in an attempt to prevent me from leaving him.

They'd got as far as establishing the fire would be started in the staff room, one of the few areas of the pub not covered by CCTV. Bryn would set everything up, leave the patio door ajar, and give the person he was talking to a final signal. Jay would be in the office. And from Bryn's side of the conversation, I gathered it was all going to happen after closing on New Year's Day.

But I'd put paid to their carefully concocted plans. I'd really put paid to them. For all Bryn's snide remarks about my so-called lack of intelligence, he seriously underestimated me. I got the impression they'd already discussed money, therefore was disappointed when no figures were mentioned for me to undercut.

A counter-attack was already forming in my mind. One which involved me discovering the identity of the arsonist and offering them more money than whatever Bryn was paying. More money to do things *my* way. But in the end, I went one better even than that.

Bryn discovering me and Jay in the utility room on New Year's Eve is seemingly what pushed him over the edge. A vision of him, staggering about on top of the bar, proclaiming to the whole pub what he was going to cause fills my mind. It would be Jay lying charred and unidentifiable in that mortuary if Bryn had got his way. The evil, drunken, balding, bullying, jumped up... I could go on forever. He deserved everything he got. It's taken going over and over it to these police officers for me to get the anger back. Thank God I have. Anything else is counter-productive, to the verge of being dangerous.

The catalyst that forced him to hit the 'go button' was discovering I was *really* going to leave. And that he also needed to. What happened yesterday was all totally Bryn's fault. I'd never, ever have done what I did without him setting it all in motion in the first place. Not in a million years.

I realised Bryn would go through with the fire as I watched him staggering around on the top of the bar after finding me and Jay. His intent became even more obvious with the barbed comments and veiled threats that came my way as I was getting ready yesterday morning. *You're going to regret this* was one. But the biggest one, *either you get rid of him or I will* was the red flag.

When I returned to collect the phone I had 'forgotten,' Jay appeared to be in the office. The low hum of the radio and the strip of light beneath the door would have led Bryn to think that too. To avoid disturbance when cashing up and processing wages, whoever was doing them, me or Jay, would lock ourselves in there. Put the *do not disturb* sign up. Not that Bryn would try to disturb him. As far as he was concerned, Jay was exactly where he wanted him.

However, it was incredibly risky going back in when I did. Especially since I had no exact idea of Bryn's timescale. But I had to make sure he was in the flat, and going back gave me the chance to re-check every possible escape from there was blocked. I had all the keys to the windows. We never normally lock the door at the bottom of our private staircase, so Bryn wouldn't have noticed that I'd already removed the key from his keyring.

The Dales Inn was a nineteenth century building, filled with many fixtures and fittings in keeping with that era. Though perhaps not in keeping with today's fire regs. Another advantage, or disadvantage, depending on how it's viewed, is that we're well out of town. Emergency services take far longer than they should to reach us.

But it was a dicey situation on so many levels, and by going back there, I was really risking my neck. Literally. I rub at it now. When Bryn got hold of me yesterday, he had a fury in his eyes I've never seen before. As though he was going to strangle me. I was lucky to get out of there. Our violent altercation cemented my decision though. Backing out of the plan by then was unthinkable. Not only was Bryn willing to let Jay burn to death to get him out of my life, he'd shown physical violence towards me, to add to the verbal, mental and emotional I was already so accustomed to.

He'd told me repeatedly throughout our marriage that he'd never *ever* let me go. *I was his, and he was mine,* as though people are commodities to be owned. I would never be free of him without this action. Ever.

23 HOURS AFTER
DEBRA 3PM

"W<small>HY DIDN'T</small> you return to the pub after visiting your father?" DCI Leonard is frowning again. I suppose the normal thing to do on New Year's Day would be to spend the evening at home in front of the telly. Recovering. Sleeping it off. Whatever.

I've pre-empted most of their likely questions. And laid awake half the night rehearsing possible answers. The questions are no different really from the ones I've already had to answer to Hayley and Lance.

"The mood Bryn was in, I'd already decided to stay away for the night before I left. I'd spoken to both my kids earlier in the day, so didn't think they'd be looking for me. And I had the dog with me, of course."

"Had you taken some things with you?"

"Yes. Just an overnight bag, the essentials." They might search Dad's room. If they do, many of the things they'd find there, I could pass off as his, such as the photo albums.

"What about the pub? Would you not normally have to get back there?"

"We only ever open for lunch on New Year's Day." I'm heavy as I say this. *We only ever open...* If only the pub hadn't been forced to become a casualty in all this.

"So you went straight to the home of your bar manager, Jay Manningham? After being at..." She looks down. "The Castle Hill Nursing Home."

"That's correct. He rents a room in a shared house. I went straight there." No matter what had happened, it felt safe there last night, squirrelled away from reality, in Jay's temporary bachelor pad.

"What time would this have been?"

"I'm not too sure. It was dark though. Maybe about five o'clock. Something like that."

"And how did you travel between the two places?"

"I drove."

"You must have noticed the smoke? You could see it and smell it for miles last night."

I pause. All this makes me look like a right cow. The way everyone will see it is that my husband's burning to death, whilst I'm heading off to my toy boy.

DCI Leonard repeats, "For the benefit of the tape Debra, can you confirm whether you noticed any smoke whilst leaving your father's nursing home?"

"I don't remember any. My car was at the front of the building... on the road. I went straight to it." At least when they check Castle Hill's cameras, they'll see me coming and going from the main entrance, well outside the timings of the fire. They should probably have CCTV on the garden suite exits, but they don't. Not that I'm complaining right now. Hopefully, on the footage, I'll have my nose burrowed into my scarf as well. Which will go some way to explain me not noticing the smoke.

Neither of them say anything, so I carry on. "Like I said, my dad's already a mile or so from home. Where Jay lives is another twenty-minute drive. And I was probably too wrapped up in my own problems to notice a right lot yesterday."

"Exactly when did you find out about the fire Debra?" DCI Leonard is frowning again. Probably because my alibi is pretty watertight. She'll know she's on a hiding to nothing, questioning me. As the afternoon wears on, I'm thinking more and more that I have nothing to worry about. As long as Jay holds up when they question him. He's got too much riding on this not to.

"Not until this morning. As soon as I woke up and charged my phone."

"I find it difficult to believe that you didn't hear about what had happened last night. Surely you must have spoken to Hayley or Lance?"

"My phone had died." Again, I worry I've answered this question a little too quickly.

And I've possibly answered with an unfortunate choice of word. *Died.*

"Most people would know if their phone was out of charge within the timescale we're talking about here. Your phone appears to have been off since just after noon yesterday until twelve minutes past seven this morning."

It's on the tip of my tongue to say, *I'm not most people.* And it's true. Until Jay came along, I didn't bother with my phone a great deal, unless it was the kids. I prefer to actually live my life, rather than miss things because I'm trying to video them. I'm quite old-school that way.

"It was zipped up in my bag."

"You didn't look at it, *at all*?"

"I was busy." I feel my face colouring up as I say this.

By the way the two officers look at each other, that was the wrong thing to say as well. "Look, without going into too much detail, I didn't think to plug the phone in until this morning. I suppose part of me didn't want to. I didn't want Bryn trying to get in touch."

"What about your kids?"

"Like I keep saying, I'd been in touch with both Hayley and Lance. As far as I was concerned, they were both nursing new year hangovers." And coping with the news that I was leaving, but I don't add this.

There was no way I'd have charged my phone last night. After all, people can be tracked from their mobile phones. All I wanted was to be cocooned, away from it all, with Jay. It was our first ever night of being completely alone. We ate together, had a bath together, watched a film and had more sex than a pair of honeymooners. It was as though the incident a few miles away had never happened. Wine helped, of course. And as the hours with Jay passed by, it became easier and easier to pretend the outside world really didn't exist. On the one occasion he tried to bring it all up; I distracted him in the best possible way.

However, if the truth be known, it became more difficult to suppress my itch to just plug my phone in. Check for messages or news reports. See what was going on. Especially when Jay finally fell asleep in the early hours - that's when the enormity of it all hit me. I still didn't know if Bryn was dead, if Carl had turned up, or anything.

I'd been hoping to separate from Bryn without having to drag Jay into it all. I would not say a word about what I'd overheard on Boxing Day, instead I'd put it down to Bryn's anger and frustration. Yes, Bryn might have wanted Jay out of the picture, but him torching our home and my business was just stupid talk. There are easier ways.

Though, from what I can gather, Bryn already tried some of these so-called easier ways whilst I was in Leicester with Lance. He'd tried reasoning with Jay to start with. *Man to man,* Jay told me. When that didn't work, Bryn had apparently offered Jay money to leave the pub and get out of my life.

It was only when Bryn flipped after catching us in the utility room; I realised he might really be capable of carrying out the plan I'd overheard. Especially if someone other than him was going to take the bulk of the risk.

And Carl, to my mind, has always been capable of anything. Especially if the price is right.

13 HOURS BEFORE

DEBRA 3AM NEW YEAR'S DAY

JAY and I had sat up until after three on New Year's Day morning.

"What the hell was all that with Bryn?" Jay pulled the bolts across the door after the last customers. "Do you fancy a coffee?" He flicked the switch on the coffee machine. Coffee would be good. I needed to get my head straight. There could be no more alcohol.

"He's planning on torching the place."

Jay stared at me. "What? No! What do you mean?"

"It's what he was getting at when he said *he was going to give them all something to gossip about.*"

"By setting fire to the pub? Nah. He wouldn't have the balls." Jay tugged a pint of milk from the fridge beneath the bar.

"Maybe not himself. But he's paying someone to do it for him." I'd been steeling myself to tell him the full story since Bryn's performance. "I overheard him on the phone on Boxing Day."

"To who?"

"I'm not sure, but I have my suspicions. Have you noticed him with Carl tonight?"

"I haven't really paid much attention to him. To be honest, I've only had eyes for you." He winked as he poured milk into our cups. "What would be in it for him anyway? Who'd get the insurance?"

"Me, I guess. But he probably thinks that by being married to me... Look, never mind all that - can't we just *leave*? I can't stand it anymore." I was fighting back the tears.

"When are we talking?"

"Tomorrow. As soon as possible." I was deadly serious. Bryn's little act tonight had been the final straw. "He said *New Year's Day, after closing,* when I was listening to him. We can't hang around waiting to see what he's going to do."

"You're joking." His eyes widened and his tone changed. "That soon?"

"Yes. And I wish I *was* joking."

"Why didn't you say something sooner? You've known about this since Boxing Day?"

"I don't know. I should have done. I guess I was working out how to handle it. What to do." Jay was right. I should have said something. I should have gone to the police. *Should have. Should have. Should have.* But like always, I buried my head in the sand.

"I can't believe you went away with Lance without telling me any of this."

"I've been trying to find out who the other person is."

"Why? What difference would that make?"

"So I can undercut Bryn." I looked towards the spot where he'd been in cahoots with Carl. "And now I've got my answer, I'm sure of it. I didn't see Carl leave, but I'll sure as hell be getting hold of him over the next few hours."

"And then what?"

"I'll message him through social media. I stalked him when Hayley first brought him home, so I know he's on there."

My instincts about Carl when Hayley first introduced him were spot on. Though I could never have imagined the extent of how unhinged he is. To agree to something like Bryn has put in front of him - whatever the price. That was assuming it was *definitely* him.

"Anyway, what do you mean by *undercutting him*? I don't follow. You're talking in riddles Deb."

I took a deep breath. "I haven't told you everything."

"What do you mean?"

"He's planning to torch the place with *you* in it."

He let out a long whistle. "Bloody hell. You actually heard him say that?"

I nodded.

"Perhaps you're right then. We do need to get out. This is serious shit." He came around the bar, light into dark, and walked to where I was sitting.

"As soon as we can, as far as I'm concerned."

"Though I'm not there with what I need. To leave straightaway, I mean." He lowered himself to the stool - the only man I know who can make sitting down look sexy.

"I don't follow."

"I'm on about the funds Deb."

"I've got funds, haven't I?"

"I'm listening."

"I've got close to sixty grand in the business account, if we need it. What would we need?"

"Just enough for flights and somewhere to stay really." Jay seemed to light up with the prospect.

"How much?"

"I'm not sure. I can have a look though."

"The sooner, the better."

"Just say the word and I'll sort it for us. I can sort the transfer from the business account, the tickets, a hotel, *everything...* if you want me to, that is?"

His use of the word *us* spread a glow within me. "But where would we go?" My brain felt foggy. The stress, the previously consumed alcohol and the fatigue was closing in on me. "I can't think straight at the moment. I need some sleep."

"I'm happy for you to leave it all to me Deb. Just give me the account login and I'll sort the lot. You've had enough to deal with this week."

He put his coffee down and reached for my hand across the table, cupping one of mine in both of his. Suddenly I felt protected and supported. Like there might be a future for me after all. When Lance had gone to uni, all I could see was daily drudge. Not to mention growing old with a man I couldn't stand.

"You still haven't said where we'll go." Despite the fear and the fog, a surge of excitement shot through me. After years of conforming to expectation as a wife and a mother, I was going to do something just for *me*. Jay and I were going to take off from here. Before Bryn got the chance to do anything to stop us. It was the best way forward. Perhaps the only way forward.

"Anywhere. As long as it's well away from him."

Jay tore a beer mat in half and slid a pencil from his pocket. "Write the instructions for the login, will you? Let's get on with this if we're going to do it."

I took the pencil from him but hesitated as an attack of reality hit me. Would I really be able to leave Hayley and Lance?

"What's up?"

"Oh, I don't know. Like you said, this is serious shit. Much as I want to run away, I keep thinking I should go to the police."

"I'm pretty sure it's all Bryn's jealous bluster." He took a sip from his cup. "Plus, you saw how pissed he was earlier. I don't think for one moment he'll do anything, but we should take it as a sign to get out of here."

"I've got no proof of anything even if I *did* go to the police."

"Come on Deb, you've planted the seed now. You and me. Right now. Well, over the next couple of days. And just think, you'd be saving my life as well." He winked at me again. In the short time we'd been together, he seemed to have realised that winking turned me to putty.

"I want to go. Really, I do. It's just... what about my kids?"

"They're not kids anymore Deb. You've done your time as a

hands-on mother. They'll understand. You're entitled to a life too."
He squeezed my hand. "Even Bryn will eventually calm down,
you'll see. And everyone will move on - including us."

"What do you mean? You want us to stay together, for your
whole trip?"

"Yes. Of course I do. You're the only woman who could have
possibly changed my mind about it. So let's get out of this toxic
cesspit right now."

"You're right. I know. It's just a wobble I'm having."

"It's quite normal and I love you even more for it."

"You do?" My stomach flipped. He'd never said that before.
"Love me? Really?"

"I'll tell you every day once we're out of here." He nudged the
beermat towards me again.

"You need to say it again if you want the login."

"Debra Ford. I right love you."

Grinning, I scribbled down what was needed for our tickets to
the future. Username. Account number. Memorable information.

"I love you right back." I would never forget this moment. Here,
in the semi-darkness. The first day of the new year. The first day of
the rest of our lives. "Anyway. I could do with some sleep. Much as
I'd like to stay up and plan it all with you. My head's pounding."

"Go on then. It's a shame I can't come with you."

"I know. But this is the last night of things being like this." I slid
the beermat back to him.

Jay stood from his stool. "I'll lock up and go home. Ring me the
minute you wake up. Then we'll get sorted."

"I can't wait."

8 HOURS BEFORE

DEBRA 8AM NEW YEAR'S DAY

I TRIED to get a bit of rest in Hayley's old room, but did little sleeping. Eventually, I must have dozed off for a couple of hours, as I woke suddenly to Bryn's snoring. It was vibrating through the flat like a JCB. I felt like going in there and smothering him with a pillow - a fury I'd never known and didn't welcome. Eventually, when my anger was at fever-pitch, I gave up on sleep and went to make a coffee.

I needed to get well away from him, so took my drink down to the office. Closing the door behind me, I paced the floor for a few minutes. Jay and I were going to leave. He'd said *I love you* to me. We were really going to have a future together. I glanced at the clock. He'd probably still be asleep. Maybe I could have a look at New Year's Day flights myself. There'd be some going out today, surely? I fired up the laptop. And thank goodness I did. It was still logged into Bryn's Google account. I gasped when I clicked into his search history.

. . .

On the third time of trying, Jay picked up the phone.

"Sorry Deb. I was asleep. I laid awake for ages after I left you. My mind's been spinning."

"Mine too. Can we meet? I've found something."

"Give me half an hour. Usual spot."

The roar of Jay's bike seemed louder than normal, especially so early in the day. I stared across the deserted park and shivered inside my coat.

"You're still in last night's clothes." Jay laughed as he tugged his helmet off and came towards me. "You're officially doing the walk of shame."

"That's the least of my worries." I patted the cold steel of the bench beside me. "I've been on the computer to look at flights."

"And?"

"I came across Bryn's search history."

"Go on." He sat beside me, looking surprisingly fresh for 8am on New Year's Day. I hadn't even looked in a mirror before setting off. I probably had lines all over my face and mascara streaked across my cheeks.

"Right, not only has Bryn been looking up insurance procedure, he's also been on a site looking at what starts fires, and makes sure they spread quickly."

Jay looked thoughtful. "What's the date on the searches?"

"Yesterday. Last night actually, not long after I got back from Leicester." I tried to think what difference the date made. I guessed the more recent, the more likely. "You haven't heard the best one."

"What?"

"How quickly would someone die from breathing in smoke?"

Jay's expression was hard to read. No wonder. Bryn wanted him in that fire. He wanted him dead.

"What are you thinking?"

He didn't reply for a few moments.

"Come on Jay. Tell me."

"OK." He hesitated. "I say we play him at his own game. Not that it's much of a game."

"I don't follow."

He paused another infuriatingly long pause, then said, "What if Bryn was to fall victim to his own doing? What if we were to offer him what he wants for me?"

"I've still got to get hold of Carl though." I glanced at my watch. "And quickly."

"Forget Carl. You keep hold of your money. We're going to need it."

"I still don't follow."

"You heard what Bryn said last night. Everyone who was in that pub knows how desperate he is. And how volatile. *Watch this space*, wasn't that what he said?"

"Yes, but Carl..."

"And now we've got the computer search history to back everything up. Me and you are the *only* other people who can get into that computer. And the CCTV will show us in the bar at the exact time when the searches were done."

"True."

"Where is he now? Bryn, I mean?"

"Snoring away like an animal."

"You need to get that computer locked in the safe."

"Why?"

"To make sure he can't delete that history."

"But he can get into the safe."

"Change the combination to... I don't know... 0101. A number we can both remember. New Year's Day. The start of our new lives."

The start of our new lives. I liked that. "And then what? We need to do something, quick. I still don't know for sure that it's Carl he's been setting things up with."

"He said, *after closing*, didn't he?"

"Yes. That's if he's in any fit state for anything today. You haven't seen Bryn with a rip-roaring hangover. They take ages to get over when you're..." My voice trails off. Jay needs no more reminders of our age difference.

"Bryn's got a lot riding on me actually *being* there, in the pub, hasn't he?"

"You're there every day, Jay."

"Is he planning to lock me in somewhere?"

"I've no idea. When I was listening, I don't think they'd got that far as to plan the finer details."

"Right. OK. Here's what I'm going to do. I always cash up on a Sunday, so no difference there, yeah?"

"That's probably what he's thinking."

"Right. Well, as far as he's concerned, I'll be in the office. In fact, I'll be there for as long as it takes."

"This sounds really, really risky. I don't want anything to happen to you."

"Do you know which room he's thinking of setting the fire off in? If he's after *me,* it won't be the pub itself, will it?"

"The staff room, I think."

"Figures. How much charge have you got on your phone?"

I glanced at it. "Not a lot. Twenty-seven per cent."

"Good. Right. Let it run down, then keep it off. I'll keep mine on until about an hour before, then turn it off too. We can't have our phones putting us at the pub when it happens. The problem is just *you* now Deb."

"Charming." I raised my voice at him.

"I need you out of the way, but also able to give me the nod when it's time."

"But we don't know what time." I thought for a moment. "Though if I need to be out of the way, I could be at my dad's."

"Good. Good. I like it."

"And he's close enough, to cut back from through here." I gestured across the park. I only ever took the car to Dad's in the cold or rain. One reason for choosing Castle Hill was that it was a nice walk through the park for me to visit him.

"I like it even more."

I glanced at him. It all seemed so worked out. And Jay seemed so enthused, I wondered if he was thinking on the fly, or whether he too had been concocting ideas since we spoke last night.

23.5 HOURS AFTER

DEBRA 3:30PM

"INTERVIEW WITH DEBRA FORD recommenced at 3:30pm."

With a bit of luck, this is the final stretch. The two officers have been out and have returned to the interview room for the third time. DCI Leonard wouldn't tell me what they were doing in their absences. She looked at me as though I had two heads when I asked. If I were to guess, I'd say they'll have been checking that my story stacks up. At least I'm more assured than I felt a couple of hours ago. They'd have arrested me by now if they were going to. It's looking like a solicitor won't be needed.

"Are you aware your son and daughter thought it might be *you* dead in your pub?" The stern tone in DCI Leonard's voice rises a notch.

The sinking sun, just about visible through a slit in the top of the wall, which can hardly pass as a window. It casts an orange glow across the faces of both officers as they wait for my answer.

"They've had all night," she continues, "to turn themselves inside out about that possibility. *All* night."

"I'm aware now." I stare at my hands, avoiding eye contact with her.

That they've had this to go through without me, is what I regret the most. Perhaps I *should* have shown up last night, but I wanted one night, just one night, with Jay. I've been a cook, carer and counsellor for all these years and had decided to put myself first for a change. But having seen the state Hayley and Lance were in this morning, I know that decision was wrong. Totally wrong.

Really I knew, deep down, how much they'd need me. However, I forced this knowledge from my mind, repeatedly telling myself they had each other for support.

"Like I keep saying, I knew both of them would be nursing hangovers, plus I didn't want to face Bryn, so I went straight to Jay's." I look her straight in the eye now. What I'm telling her is all perfectly plausible. Which is partly why I've been laid awake most of the night. At least I've got my story straight. Jay and I had to lie low - it was the only way. Play dumb. Play ignorant. Most importantly, I had to get my head back together - I was so shocked that everything had gone to plan that I didn't trust myself not to say the wrong thing in front of the kids, the police, everyone. I still don't.

"What time did you last see Bryn, Debra?"

I think for a moment, my hesitation hopefully increasing my plausibility, despite having already rehearsed this answer. "It was just after two o'clock yesterday. I'd waited for Bryn to come back after he'd taken the dog out."

"Why was that?" DCI Leonard tucks a stray hair behind her ear. "If things were so bad that you didn't even want to go home last night, why would you wait for him yesterday afternoon?"

"It wasn't really *him* I was waiting for. It was Sammy, my dog. I wanted to take her to visit my father."

"I see." She flicks her pen against her chin a few times before speaking again. "Which way did you drive from the care home to Moorton?" She glances down at her notes. "It's been confirmed that you left Castle Hill at four thirty-five pm."

"Along the A40, mostly."

The care home have confirmed things! Phew!

What the police don't need to know about is the slight detour I made after leaving Dad. From the street behind the park, I could see the pub roof in the distance.

We've gone and done it, I'd muttered to Sammy in the darkness of the car. I had no way of knowing whether Bryn might have made it out, if Carl had ever been involved, or even whether Jay was alright.

All I knew was if Bryn wasn't finished in there, he'd try something else to hurt Jay, or me. Despite this, my conscience had threatened to overwhelm me as I watched the flames in the distance leap higher and higher, as smoke billowed into the air. I think I'll taste it in the back of my throat forever.

I watched for five minutes or so. There really was no going back. Then suddenly my solitude had been broken into by the screech of passing sirens and blue swirling lights.

Losing my pub in this way was devastating. However, I'll be able to start again. Perhaps after Jay and I return from travelling, we can use the insurance money to set up something else. We'll be free to do whatever we want.

"Quite an elusive character, isn't he?" DCI Leonard's voice jolts me from my planning.

"Who?"

"Your chappie, Jay. He's on all the systems." She runs a manicured nail tip down a list. "PAYE, DVLA, NHS, DWP...." She looks up at me, "as living somewhere else. It can be prosecutable, you know, especially with the DVLA."

"It's only temporary - the bedsit where he's staying. We're going travelling soon. Well, we're supposed to be." I add the last part quickly. It doesn't look good that I've no plans to cancel it. Then it dawns on me that I might be told to surrender my passport. No chance. Over *my* dead body.

"So I gather from your daughter." She frowns. "And presumably Bryn knew about this arrangement of yours?"

I nod. "Like I've already said, he was feeling pretty desperate about the whole thing."

At least the situation points towards Bryn deliberately starting the fire before submitting himself to it. They know nothing about Carl's involvement. It has to stay that way. What I need to do now is to walk away from it all. And if Carl has the audacity to demand any money from me, I'll laugh at him. He'll not get a penny.

Bryn would never have had the guts to set that fire going himself, that much I'm sure of, hence his reasons for paying someone to torch the pub in the first place. And who better than someone like Carl. From what I've gathered about him, he's of the *act first, think later* brigade.

And he's totally without conscience - the way he tried to control Hayley shows that. They always warn there's a risk of ending up in a relationship with a man like your father. Though it's the opposite in my case. My dad's a good man - it was my mother who didn't measure up. One positive side effect of Dad's Alzheimer's, however, is that his memories of my mother have become rose-tinted.

There were so many things that could have gone wrong yesterday. If someone had seen me leaving, or returning from Dad's patio door, that would have blown my alibi. As would any CCTV that might have picked me up, though cutting through the park kept me safe from that. If I hadn't managed to get away from Bryn when we were arguing, it might have been me that burned to death. If I hadn't been able to lock Bryn in the flat, he might have escaped before the fire took hold.

But if Jay hadn't managed to give me the 'go' signal in the first place, Carl would have got there first. The pub would have burned to the ground with no one even inside. Everything would have been for nothing.

But it all aligned in the end. As Dad would say when he was well, *What's meant to be will always find a way.* At least, that's what I keep telling myself. And I'll have to keep telling myself. Ending the life of my children's father will be on my conscience forever. But what's that other saying? *An eye for an eye.* It came down to a choice between a man I can see an exciting future with, or a bullying knuckle dragger I could no longer stand the sight of.

"So Debra, this morning, as soon as you heard about the fire, you went straight round to your daughter's?"

"Of course I did."

"If you don't mind me saying, you really seem to be taking the death of your husband, and losing your business and home calmly." DCI Leonard's words are once again laced with suspicion. "More than I would if I were in your situation."

I swallow. "Perhaps I might be calm on the outside, but really, I'm all over the place. I guess it hasn't sunk in. At least my kids are safe - that's the main thing."

"But not your husband." Sergeant Ellis gives me a strange look.

"Once I'm alone later and it all hits me, it'll probably be a different story, won't it, I don't know..."

I'm wittering away, jumping around with my words, petrified of what these officers might infer if I'm quiet. This is why we have solicitors, but to have asked for one would have been akin to hanging a big sign around my neck saying, *I did it. It was me.*

"Can I ask," DCI Leonard slides some bound sheets of paper from her folder. "Why the CCTV only covers the pub? Not your business or living quarters?"

"Bryn organised it like that. Years ago. He was saving money. I always meant to get around to extending the coverage but never did." I'm relieved for more than the obvious reason that there was no footage from the flat. The last thing I would have had the stomach for would be footage of Bryn, burning or choking to death.

"The CCTV really hasn't shown us much at all. Though it confirms what you, and other witnesses have said about Bryn climbing onto the bar." She points at a picture and then swivels the page around. "Can I ask about this gentleman?" She points at an image of Bryn sitting with Carl. "The recording shows them speaking at length... several times throughout the evening."

Misery hollows me out as I stare at Bryn's image. Rage and hate fuelled him, but at the same time, he was so full of life. It's me, my actions, and my decisions, that have snuffed out that life, once and for all.

"My daughter's ex. He and Bryn got on pretty well."

"When did Bryn discover the truth about your affair?"

"I'm not entirely sure. He was jealous of Jay from the moment I employed him."

"And rightly so. We can see his fears were confirmed, from footage he may have viewed from the early hours of Christmas Eve. Are you aware of the footage I'm referring to."

Luckily she spares me the embarrassment of seeing the pool table images. The CCTV would jump from location to location, capturing activity in and around the pub, so at least it won't have recorded the full thing, but still embarrassing. Who knows who else might see it though? If this is going to an inquest, even my kids might see it.

DCI Leonard shuffles pages for what feels like an eternity, running her pen down some of them, either looking for something, or checking things. Surely she's going to let me go soon? I'd have been arrested by now if I were a suspect.

As it stands, there are only three people in the world who know of my involvement. Me and Jay for starters. No, actually, there are four people if I count Dad. Not that he'll remember. He looked almost pleased when I returned to him and told him what was happening, and why. He always thought I could do better than Bryn. Right from the moment I introduced them.

The tea the care home staff had brought before I left was still lukewarm in the pot when I got back. I drank it whilst Dad and I looked at the photo albums of the kids together. Old photos are supposed to be great for people with Alzheimers. Dad was the most lucid he'd been in years. Ironically, it was one of the best afternoons I've spent with him in a long time.

"Right. I think we've got all we need from you for the moment." DCI Leonard closes her file.

"Really?"

"Subject, of course, to the scrutiny of CCTV. We'll also need to review the evidence coming in from pathology."

"And the Crime Scene Investigation Team," Sergeant Ellis adds.

"The Crime Investigation Team?" My voice wobbles. This is the first they've mentioned of this. I'm not sure if I'm imagining it, but they both seem to peer at me more curiously. I know they've got to do a thorough search but the word, '*crime*' hasn't been mentioned before.

"Yes. The fire service concluded their investigation a short time ago, as you know, and the property has now been handed to the police."

I want to say it's *my* property. But I know I relinquished that right the moment I took Bryn's plans into my own hands. Instead, I ask in a steadier voice, "What's left to investigate?"

"We have to ensure there's no further evidence of foul play. So clearly, we may need to ask more questions of you."

"OK. But I've told you everything I know. Which isn't really very much."

"We appreciate your help." DCI Leonard's tone has softened - a reassuring sign. "Well, we'll let you get back. I'm sure you've got lots to sort out." She leans forward for the remote control. "Interview with Debra Ford terminated at three forty seven pm."

Hopefully, I don't look too stunned as I stare at DCI Leonard. I could have got away with it here. I really, really could have got away with it. After all the name calling, Bryn's interrogations, the suffocation. I'm free. After all these years, I'm bloody free.

"Can I start the ball rolling with the insurance?" I'm not looking forward to yet more questions and investigations, but there shouldn't be a problem. After all, I'll be perceived as one of the victims in what's happened. Even to Carl, who will believe his money was usurped by Bryn himself, certainly not by me and Jay. Also, now the pub has gone, he's got no direct way to get to Hayley. Once she gets beyond all this, she's got her whole life ahead of her, hopefully as a barrister - I will not let someone like Carl hold her back.

"You can, but they probably won't process anything until the inquest has been concluded." DCI Leonard rises from her chair.

Sergeant Ellis follows. "I'll come to the desk with you. They should be able to give you a case reference number to be going on with."

Plucking my coat from the back of my chair, I also get to my feet, hoping that it doesn't take too long to sort this reference number out. I can't get out of here fast enough. I really want to see Jay. Find out how he's holding up. One of his parts in things was small, the other as large as it gets. First, he gave me the signal whilst I was with Dad that it was time to go. Then he waited and watched for my signal that Bryn was locked in the flat. Bryn had already prepared the staff room.

All Jay had to do was light the match.

After I've seen him, my place tonight is with Hayley and Lance. They're going to need a lot of support whilst I'm still here. And I've a lot of making up to do for last night. So I'll stick around for as long as I can. Yesterday, Bryn was still alive, and there was an urgency for us to leave, but now he's gone, we can take our time. Hopefully.

My mind fills with the fourth person who knows the whole truth. Tina from the train. Part of me regrets being so open with her - but the whole thing seemed so far fetched that I never truly believed it would even happen. The gin was flowing, and we'd made such a connection with each other, that I knew she was a safe person to talk to. It's not as if we knew each other, or would be likely to cross paths again.

24 HOURS AFTER
DEBRA 4PM

THE SECOND DAY of the new year is already darkening to dusk. I can't believe how drastically life has changed in the last twenty-four hours. Nor can I believe they've let me go. Just like that. No arrest. No charges. No bail. No passport demand.

We really can get out of here as soon as possible. Perhaps when the funeral is over and done with. After all, other than my kids, my dad, and my dog, there's nothing much to stay for. And it's not as though I'll be gone forever.

I'm shown through the exit with the words, *we'll be in touch* ringing in my ears. A couple of passers-by eye me inquisitively, as I descend the steps of the police station. They might have heard about the fire, but there's no reason they should connect me to it. I take a deep breath as I reach the bottom, the air so cold it stabs at the back of my throat. I won't be surprised if we see snow soon. Pulling my coat tighter, I head towards the car.

This time yesterday, I was with Dad. This time yesterday, Bryn was taking his last breath. This time yesterday, it was too late to stop what we had started. This time yesterday, I still had all this to face.

I'm convinced that I've faced the worst of it.

They've let me go.

I slam the car door, letting my stress sigh out whilst resting my head on the steering wheel. I can hardly believe we seem to be in the clear. The inquest will probably conclude suicide - I can feel it in my bones. And I could tell that by the questions and reactions during the police interview.

The insurance will pay out, and at last, I, Debra Ford, will live happily ever after. This is my reward for all the years I've tolerated Bryn. What I've had to cope with, listen to, and avoid. Like Jay said yesterday, the kids will come around to the idea of me going travelling, and hopefully, in time, they'll also accept me being in a relationship with Jay. In the last couple of days, he hasn't once mentioned the idea of me only *beginning* the trip with him. A couple of weeks ago, he repeatedly reminded me it was his trip, and I needed to respect that. But now, we've got this secret. The thing that will always bind us. And we'll need to support each other through the aftermath.

I start the engine and turn the radio up. *Perfect Year.* One of my favourite songs. Yes. And now, it has the potential to be one. My whole life suddenly has so much going for it. As soon as I hear the words *case closed* and all that insurance money hits, it's onwards and upwards. Life begins at forty... Nope. My life is going to begin at fifty.

I pull up outside Jay's with excitement fluttering in my belly. As I yank the handbrake on, I glance up at his window. It's in darkness. Perhaps he's fallen asleep. We were up until very late last night. I smile to myself.

My breath quickens. His motorbike isn't here. Perhaps the police have called him in, straight after I left. I expect the officers will be keen to get all the interviews done and dusted. They'll have boxes to tick, and deadlines to meet.

His phone goes straight to voicemail. The police *must* have called him in. I sit for a few moments, wondering what to do. I really wanted to see him before returning to the kids. It'll be difficult to get away once I'm back with them. I sigh again, surprising myself at how guttural it sounds in the silence of the car. My eyes fall on a pen on the dashboard. I rummage around in my bag for a scrap of paper. I'll push a note under his door. That's all I can do. He might not check his mailbox until tomorrow. Now I just need to get into the building.

Hi handsome. Hope you're OK. Call me as soon as you get back. Deb xx

I loiter outside for several minutes. I can't seem to make a straight decision today. My brain's turned to mush. It's no wonder really. Most people wouldn't go through this amount of stress in a lifetime, let alone in twenty-four hours. I push Jay's buzzer, just in case he *is* in there. I imagine his bedsit, sparse and tidy. Fading yellow patches on the ceiling. A ceiling which I spent half the night staring at, whilst he snored softly beside me. I used to seethe at Bryn's snoring, yet I was strangely grateful for Jay's last night. I'd forgotten what it's like to feel this way about someone.

I press a different buzzer.

"Hi." I lean forward. "I'm a friend of Jay's. Would you mind letting me in please?"

"He's not there." A male voice barks back. Then a click.

I try another button. No reply.

And another. Someone finally lets me in. I take the concrete stairs two at a time, landing outside his door. I knock. Nothing.

"Jay. Are you in there?"

Of course he isn't. The place is as dark as a graveyard. His bike isn't here and someone's already told me he's gone out.

I try his phone again. It doesn't even go to voicemail this time. Three beeps, then the line falls silent. It happens again. And again.

Shit. My stomach's coiling around itself. Something's not right here. I stand still for so long chasing my thoughts around in a circle, that the overhead light suddenly clicks off, leaving me shrouded in darkness.

I blink away an image of Bryn, charred and cold, now laid in a similar environment. I wave my arms and the light's back.

Then a door from the floor below bangs. There are footsteps on the stairs. Maybe it's Jay. I glance over the banister. It's a young girl with straggly hair.

"You looking for Jay?" She jerks her head toward his door as she reaches the top.

"Yes. Do you know where he is?"

"He's gone."

"I can see that. Did he say where?"

"Nope. Sorry." She turns on her heel to go back down.

"Hang on! Wait! Please! Did he mention when he'd be back?"

She stops. Looks at me with large eyes. "He won't be back."

"What do you mean?" Panic grips my chest. She must have got this wrong.

"He's moved out. He left the keys with me to hand back."

"He can't have done."

She shrugs. "He went this morning. First thing."

"Where?"

"Never said. Just left his keys."

"Can I see in there?"

"I've already handed em back to the landlord. They've gone. He's gone."

I stand, rooted to the spot, staring at her.

"I'm–I'm his girlfriend."

She looks me up and down. Then she laughs. "His *what*?"

I push past her, my heels clip-clopping on the stairs as I run down them. There'll be a simple explanation. He'll have the tickets. He'll be waiting somewhere for me. All I have to do is find him. He's probably looking for me right now.

I race back to the car. Try to call him again. Beep, beep, beep.

I press into Facebook to see when he was last online. He doesn't come up first like he normally would. I search his name. A string of Jay Manningham's come up. This means. It means... He's either deleted his profile or he's blocked me.

When I had to sign to accept the inventory of the safe at the police station, they said there was no cash inside. There should have been. The last month's takings should have been in there.

A cold dread creeps over me. I need to check the business account. Like the other staff at the pub, Jay's set up as a payee. And like an idiot, I've given him the login details for full access to all functions. I thought I could trust him. I thought we were in this together.

I type in the passwords and memorable information. My hands are shaking. As the site loads up, I close my eyes. I dare not look. Has he bought the tickets and accommodation like he promised? Or has he cleaned me out?

It's the latter.

There are no specific details of the transaction. Just 'Transfer £68,861.'

It's everything I have. It was everything I had.

I stare again at his window.

Everything I had has gone.

EPILOGUE
TINA

I USUALLY STAY clear of the news. My life is full of enough misery to wallow in. I can do without falling victim to the scaremongering and gloom the media perpetuates.

But today I'm compelled to hit refresh repeatedly. Until the report I've been waiting for finally lands. Finally. And now, I hardly dare read it.

Warring husband's pub blaze results in tragedy

"A betrayed husband intent on making his wife's lover disappear became a victim of his own making, a Leeds Coroner heard today.

Bryn David Ford, 52, was the only person present in Yorkshire-based *The Dales Inn* after ordering his customers to leave, prior to closing time on New Year's Day. He was described by one witness as, *'having something manic in his eyes as he threw us all out. He obviously had an agenda.'* Another witness described the desperation he must have been feeling over the breakdown of his marriage, saying, '*you got the sense that without his wife, Bryn had nothing to go on for - he wasn't thinking straight.*'

As the blaze took hold of the public house, a listed building, Ford is said to have believed Jay Manningham was in the office of the family-owned business, working on the year-end accounts. The fire is thought to have taken hold more quickly perhaps than Ford might have envisaged, trapping him in the eighteenth century public house, which over the years, had become the hub of the local community.

Pubgoers told police of how they had watched Ford just after midnight on New Year's Eve, into New Year's Day, making threats to everyone present that they would shortly '*see drama which would give them something to talk about.*' They were told to '*watch this space.*'

Suggestions of his death being a suicide were considered, but later dismissed by the Coroner. The inquest was told how Ford had checked in with the couple's commercial insurance policy only two days before the fire. In addition, Ford's internet search history offered confirmation of his intent to deliberately set fire to his family home and his wife's business. This collaborated, the Crown asserted, to suggest that Ford did not intend to take his own life in the inferno he caused. Instead, his actions were *a serious attempt on the life of bar manager, Jay Manningham, or at the very least to cause him serious harm.*

The inquest heard how Ford's estranged wife, Debra Jayne Ford had bought the licence on *The Dales Inn* twenty-five years prior to the incident. After her marriage with Bryn Ford, the couple and their two children had lived at the centre of their community for many years. But the relationship had become volatile in recent months, with Mrs Ford admitting to having an affair with her staff member. She had also told Ford of her plans to leave the family home, and accompany Mr Manningham on his forthcoming backpacking trip around the world. They had made these plans definite the day before the fire, and it was in his rage, and drink, that Ford took matters into his own hands.

Ford is said to have started the fatal blaze at around 3:45 pm on New Year's Day. The fire was started in a bin using a fire accelerant in the staff room, at the rear quarters of the public house. This quickly spread to the non-retardant curtains and other furnishings. The fire took hold when it reached the Christmas decorations around the room and the stacked boxes of bottles containing alcohol.

Police and fire crews were called by passers-by, but by the time they arrived, the building was well ablaze. When the emergency services gained access to the inside of the building, they found Ford's body on the steps of their private family flat. A post mortem examination revealed he died of smoke inhalation.

The police are not looking for anyone else in connection with this incident. Staff member Jay Manningham was not in attendance at the hearing, and Debra Ford declined to comment publicly when invited to by the media."

Until I saw the first news report on the evening of New Year's Day, I hadn't believed Debra would have the guts to go through with it. Although she never mentioned her surname when we met, I knew straightaway who the reporter was referring to. From the conversation we had on the train, I knew she felt trapped... but she could have just left, like I'd suggested to her. That's what I thought she'd do.

Debra reckoned that if she just tried to get out of the way, her husband would never have left her alone. She'd been wanting to leave for years, she said, and told me how he'd used everything from emotional blackmail, to threats of violence to keep her exactly where he wanted her.

She was also scared that their kids would be on his side - whenever anything had gone off within the family before, they always painted her as the villain of the piece. At least, that's what she told me. I only ever heard her side. For all I know, her husband could have been a decent bloke. She might have orchestrated the whole thing herself.

If she was telling me the truth about her husband's intentions, surely she could have gone to the police with what she knew? But, she had argued, when I suggested it, that she had no proof.

I asked her whether the man her husband had hired for 'the job' might testify against him, but Debra said there was no way, no matter what. In fact, she had said, the only way was to take matters into her own hands - to pay the man more money to do things her way.

When they flashed a photo of the husband with their two kids onto the TV screen, he didn't look the type to be as nasty as she'd talked about. But what does a so-called abusive bully look like anyway?

Part of me wants to reach out to Debra, to see whether it was all worth it. I wonder whether she feels guilty, or justified in what she's done. After all, her husband was planning to kill her lover in that fire. And by the sounds of it, he hadn't given a great deal of thought to who else might be caught up in it, or its aftermath...

I've searched for her on social media and though I don't know for sure, her feed suggests she's split up with the bar manager. It's full of 'woe is me' posts, 'how you don't know what you've got until it's gone' and how 'the only person you can rely on is yourself.' Many people have joined her pity party and anyway, she'll be due her massive insurance pay out soon enough.

I can't stop thinking that maybe for keeping her secret quiet like I have, it should entitle me to a piece of the pie. After all, a man is dead because of her actions and I could easily go to the police with what I know.

However, there's a good reason I'm forced to keep quiet.

When my son, Carl, came home reeking of smoke on New Year's Day, I knew he'd been up to something. I can always tell. It was only when I observed him glued to news reports the next day, and jumping every time the doorbell rang, that I accepted it was *him* who'd been paid to torch *The Dales Inn*. They say it's a small world, but this is ridiculous. Debra had told me on the train about her daughter having dumped someone, the same someone her husband had hired for the job. Carl never mentioned being *dumped*, but then he never talks about girlfriends. Not to me.

I glance back at my phone screen. *The police are not looking for anyone else in connection with this incident.* Something's gone awry though. Surely Carl would have been paid something? However, he's not given me board money for months now, continually pleading poverty.

Meanwhile, I'm stuck here with my mother, well, the shell of my mother, and two grown up kids. Neither of them can stand the sight of me. Then, there's the husband who no longer acknowledges my existence. He's too busy sleeping with one of his clients.

So maybe, just maybe, it's time for me to take Debra-style action too.

Before you go...

Thanks so much for reading Last Orders - I really hope you enjoyed it!

Join my 'keep in touch' list to receive a free book, and to be kept posted of other freebies, special offers and new releases.

One of the best things about being an author is being in touch with readers.

You can also join via https://www.mariafrankland.co.uk, and this is where you can also find out more about me, and my other domestic thrillers.

BOOK DISCUSSION GROUP QUESTIONS

1. What does the term empty nest syndrome mean? Discuss the possible emotions it might involve.

2. Look at the reasons for the affair having started between Debra and Jay. What were their motivations, and where did each of them see it going?

3. In a house fire or similar disaster, which five items would you choose to save?

4. Talk about the current likelihood of achieving a twenty-five year marriage. What can help and hinder a marriage lasting this long?

5. Which character did you sympathise with the most? Talk about your reasons.

6. What are the differing effects of marital break up on a couple's children, whether young, teenage or grown up?

7. Are there any circumstances in which you would divulge your secrets to a stranger? Talk about the pros and cons of doing this.

8. What was Debra's motivation for doing what she did?

9. Do you see the old year turning into the new as an end or a beginning? Talk about what this time of year can bring to the surface?

10. Talk about Tina's role in the story.

11. To what extent was justice done, or not done, in this story? What are your feelings about this?

12. What might come next for each character?

FRENEMY
PROLOGUE

I step back from the door, peering up at the house. The upstairs is in darkness, but the flickering TV is visible between the cracks of the blind. Is she *hiding* in there? Ignoring the door? She wouldn't have known I'd be calling tonight, so it can't be that.

I lift the flap of the letterbox and peer inside. Nothing. I check up and down the street. Deserted. I brush beads of sweat from my brow before creeping around the side of the house, picking my way through the bins and stepping over plant pots. The gate creaks as I push it open.

Curtains curl out of the open patio doors. As I start in that direction, my attention is diverted to a dark shape at the side of the shed.

It's... She's...

I drop into a crouch beside her. I reach for her hand. As my fingers search her wrist, I see a halo of darkness surrounding her head. Blood. Her hair flutters in the breeze. Her eyes stare back. Dead.

Available via my website

INTERVIEW WITH THE AUTHOR

Q: Where do your ideas come from?

A: I'm no stranger to turbulent times, and these provide lots of raw material. People, places, situations, experiences – they're all great novel fodder!

Q: Why do you write domestic thrillers?

A: I'm intrigued why people can be most at risk from someone who should love them. Novels are a safe place to explore the worst of toxic relationships.

Q: Does that mean you're a dark person?

A: We thriller writers pour our darkness into stories, so we're the nicest people you could meet – it's those romance writers you should watch...

Q: What do readers say?

A: That I write gripping stories with unexpected twists, about people you could know and situations that could happen to anyone. So beware...

Q: What's the best thing about being a writer?

A: You lovely readers. I read all my reviews, and answer all emails and social media comments. Hearing from readers absolutely makes my day, whether it's via email or through social media.

Q: Who are you and where are you from?

A: A born 'n' bred Yorkshire lass, hurtling towards the ripe old age of 50, with two grown up sons and a Sproodle called Molly. (Springer/Poodle!) My 40's have been the best: I've done an MA in Creative Writing, made writing my full time job, and found the happy-ever-after that doesn't exist in my writing - after marrying for the second time just before the pandemic.

Q: Do you have a newsletter I could join?

A: I certainly do. Go to www.mariafrankland.co.uk or <u>click here through your eBook</u> to join my awesome community of readers. When you do, I'll send you a free novella – 'The Brother in Law.'

f facebook.com/writermariafrank

⊙ instagram.com/writermaria_f

♪ tiktok.com/@mariafranklandauthor

ACKNOWLEDGMENTS

Thank you, as always, to my amazing husband, Michael. He's my first reader, and is vital with my editing process for each of my novels. His belief in me means more than I can say.

A special acknowledgement goes to my wonderful advance reader team, who took the time and trouble to read an advance copy of Last Orders and offer feedback. They are a vital part of my author business and I don't know what I would do without them.

I will always be grateful to Leeds Trinity University and my MA in Creative Writing Tutors there, Martyn, Amina and Oz. My Masters degree in 2015 was the springboard into being able to write as a profession.

And thanks especially, to you, the reader. Thank you for taking the time to read this story. I really hope you enjoyed it.